H E A R T 2 :
THE CHARGE OF THE SANDRIDERS

FREDERICK GORDON KENNEDY

About The Author

In 1969, Mr. Kennedy graduated from Berklee with a diploma in Arranging and Composition. More interested in a career as a trombonist, he joined a newly formed Swallow, billed as a blues-rock band, culminating in a recording contract with Warner Brothers Records. Mr. Kennedy concluded his instrumental career in 1973.

Joining the workforce, Mr. Kennedy has worked part-time at a drugstore soda fountain and full-time for an automobile parking company, rising to management. Following that, he worked as a 'flask rigger' at a grey iron casting foundry in Connecticut. Returning to the Boston area, he found work in an electronics factory as an assembler, encapsuler, test operator, shipper, and, finally, at that company's help desk.

In the years that followed and throughout his time in Connecticut, Mr. Kennedy answered an inner call to write, finishing several short stories, teleplays, a screenplay and several book length science fictions, one of those self-published.

Dedication

I want to thank all those who helped me move forward in the arts and this literary effort.

Table of Contents

We Can Help This Galaxy

The words written on the plaque, in the aged, unchanged script of Modallas, read, *We Can Help This Galaxy.* The Helmsman's rapt gaze settled grimly over the few words set to a plaque on the wall of the dimly lit chamber. It was the only room on Modallas he kept for himself. No one, no Targan, had ever entered other than those who had done the actual construction. They had never seen the finished product which he caused to be created by their labor.

Targan never entered The White City. Special teams sent there were usually destroyed following the completion of any mission. The Helmsman saw to that himself.

On Modallas, trouble was afoot, more than before. The best of his Targan - some, that is – were proving disloyal. They'd lost their old fear of The Sky God. They'd learned much from Modallas and him.

Those aboard were, now, a technical society subduing civilizations and star systems one would not believe they could understand. They did.

They had changed much from what they had been. He wanted only fighters and those he'd gotten. Now, he could put them up against any society, any civilization, as well as their armies.

He yearned again for the open void between galaxies. That vast ribbon of stars that had built Modallas and himself was a pinpoint of light far away, getting farther away all the time.

This galaxy barely met his purposes. *Barely serviceable* was the phrase he liked to use. He reread the hanging on the wall.

In the time he'd known consciousness, his purpose had never been so murky. They never seemed further from him, distant, if not almost forgotten. They seemed alien.

Indeed, as he viewed the slogan there in the dim chamber, it had never seemed more unknowable, more vacant of meaning. When this pilot, The Ghost Pilot, was his, he would ask him what it meant.

Their paths crisscrossed in a thousand ways none could make out. This menial freighter pilot was not the person of an awaited coming, but was there, as something more mundane, having appeared on Modallas' doorstep from nowhere. This was the answer he was most likely to hear. Its connection, no matter how loosely formed, was real. Lord Soal, whether dead or not, was secondary. The insufferable insectoid that was his journalist came next, a distant third. He'd reported battle after battle from Marcellus in the old campaigns.

Then, the blue man of Dillisome, as obscure as his planet. There was hardly a listing for it in the Galactic Atlas.

Next, Julia, Soal's daughter and only child, could still place herself in his way. Like the others, she was a friend of this Magnean pilot. More disturbing was the question of how much use he, himself, would be to these Targan?

Ganempsha was a frail place, his reports told him, obscure, a planet in the galaxy's backwater. It offered little, but it did offer something to one he must defeat, this Ghost Pilot. The dunes of that sad place hid him.

The steel fingers of his battle armor tapped idly on a small table beside him. He sat awkwardly relaxed. It was unusual to see him so. Whatever served his body was contained on the inside. The Helmsman, himself, was quite content to remain within. The hard covering never needed repair.

He allowed his mind to wander, a rare indulgence. The room was silent in every other way. Across the small space, a few steps from the place where he'd stood, the dim light showed the plaque and each of the words on it he knew so well.

Occasionally, there was the sound of his personal guard shuffling their feet outside the door.

The Snow Beggar's ion blade rested beside him leaning back, pointed scabbard on the floors, hilt laid back against the chair seat. Thoughts of the Marcellean battle T'Sog came to him vividly, not as if in a dream, but, as if real.

In reality, the beast had not found this small room or the Control Center. T'Sog's were as unstoppable as their masters. The beast was on him, yet.

The random killings among his Targan, while all the time searching for her, left them unsettled, the last thing he wanted. Targan behavior was mercurial, capable of great understanding one minute and great violence the next.

The more sophisticated the Targan, the more sophisticated the rebellion. Loyal operatives continued to work at the identities of those currently in league against him. The possibility of a Targan successfully replacing him never crossed his mind. The Helmsman had his own ways of dealing with problems.

These few moments away from the Con where needed. There was no other rest for him, no other diversion. Control of Modallas itself was second nature. It was merely a tool in the maelstrom of it all. The Modallians were gone, long dead before the conquest of Marcellus started. Now, Modallas was his, as was the conflict. What would befall them at Ganempsha, he didn't know.

He rose, turned in his tracks, and froze. There was nothing in the chamber except what had been there. Something strange, something odd, was going on, and he didn't know what it was. It bothered him; he should have known.

It was so familiar. The sensation of the T'Sog had come on him suddenly. There was no time. He rushed the door and smashed through.

As he bowled over his personal guard, the room, left behind, flashed brightly, and an ugly howl tore the air. 5D's body crowded the chamber. The Helmsman sprang to his feet, ready for battle. 5D's checkered jaws flashed at them.

The Targans aimed their weapons, sighting their massive target. The beast had scented him now. Modallas itself became its prey and now, himself. Life was becoming more of a challenge, he thought, staring there into those flashing teeth. The Targan, firing, did no good. As their fingers pressed with practiced ease on the triggers, 5D went from view in a second brilliant flash. Only a whisp of smoke rose from the chamber floor.

Scorched by Targan blasters and 5D's teleportation, the plaque hung, dangling from one corner, yet reading, We Can Help This Galaxy.

The Helmsman turned on his heel and strode down the corridor as if nothing had happened. He would never enter that chamber again; it would be too dangerous. The Targan guard snapped to attention and went with him toward the Command Center.

Already aware of the incident, they had preparations under way for new quarters. A young lieutenant stood easily at the Command Console, his own hand on the pilot's grip, waiting.

2

Sandriders

Hoofbeats sounded in Cross Anchor that morning, early. A detachment came to the city. The sighting itself was rare, a wonder.

They seemed a smudge, a smear of dirty brown on the sand. It appeared a dapple of brown, a thin line coming down, two by two, of ragged-looking brown drizzle. Riders came down the near side. They were silent, quiet, including their big mounts, dribbling in twos like brown syrup down a breakfast plate. Sandriders rode close in, to Cross Anchor.

They were a brown-dressed tribe more so than military. In age-soaked ruins worn in tatters, their dress sad by any estimate.

A worn Sergeant, on Sredir back, moved toward one of his troopers. He snarled something beyond translation, fused with a brown particular matter, spittle enhanced.

His already beleaguered tunic was quickly splattered by spittle as was the Sergeant's. No one on either side moved or seemed to understand what was said. No one cared.

Their small number formed a thin sackcloth, ragged line, there in the earliest the city, equally ragged and tattered, from their squalid shelters.

Sredirs' hooves shifted a little stirring the sand

3 Parnel

Parnel, landing on Ganempsha, was near.

Traffic control was minimal. Care would have to be exercised was manual. Borter and Helio could do it in their sleep, but others who might be around could not.

Borter looked on from his seat in the cockpit. Helio moved Soarer into the slot, the ariel path all flyers used coming into a spaceport. He gestured with one hand toward the controls, meaning Helio had been given the honor of landing the little freighter. He thumbed the pages, not stopping long on any.

Helio's hands crossed the controls easily, as skillful as Borter's own. The Dillisome had learned a considerable amount in their time together.

Soarer was waiting for clearance into the slot. Like them, other ships, larger, smaller, waited for clearance.

That day, Parnel was slow. Soarer powered down. The green glow from his Marcellean power dots dimmed to standby levels. Helio switched stabilization to automatic and leaned far back in his chair. Borter was similarly relaxed.

The lights went down, and only the instrument panel showed a muted brightness before them. In a couple of moments, Borter felt the need to speak.

Borter stopped, giving his partner a raised eyebrow. He gave favor and let him go on. "Alone? I hope you have a plan – something subtle."

"I was thinking of something completely underhanded and sneaky - to tell the truth," He smiled. Helio smiled back, knowing they were already on their way.

"We're freighter pilots, right?" Helio nodded. Borter was most entertaining at these moments. "Resupply, right?" Helio nodded once more.

'We just get ourselves in line. We find out where they're keeping her – in and out!" "Love it,' Helio bounced back, and I thought we weren't going to be direct!"

The planet's horizon filled the windshield. Electronics filled the computer screens with readings from ground stations. Borter sat back; Helio had made dozens of landings under all conditions without looking at the screens.

He consulted the Galactic Atlas, just turning pages something usually left for Helio, more to his interests. There was nothing much to say about Ganempsha, as he confirmed from the atlas. Borter could not say why he bothered to make note of the place at all. That is, nothing much except Sand Rock.

There were the obligatory paragraphs, paragraphs only, that described the major land masses, there were no large bodies of water at all, tourist spots – none.

There were vast deserts, the largest called The Ords and gigantic farms showing lush vegetation. The one city was neither impressive nor large. There was nothing remarkable about the planet at all. Borter shrugged and closed the atlas with a sharp snap. He failed to take advantage of the note at page bottom to see Sand Rock under the music heading. They would not be there long.

Everybody knew Sand Rock.

The landing itself was easy. Helio touched down with hardly a bump and taxied toward their assigned dock. As they touched down, the voice of a lazy-sounding robot traffic controller assigned them to an old and disused-looking hanger.

It would do, they supposed. There was no sense in alerting agents of The Helmsman to their whereabouts. Except for a narrow strip of fresh tarmac, the field was a rutted affair, hostile to any known type of aircraft. Still, Helio got them to the assigned dock.

Across the expanse of the field, scrub brush grew in tight bunches beneath the double suns of that world at that time of day, at their hottest. Borter turned on the air-conditioner from his side of the console meaning to remain aboard until the daytime heat had passed.

The lights went down, and only the instrument panel showed a muted brightness before them.

4

The Rescue of Julia – Yardus Vid

Thee Starr stared back at Borter with hopeful eyes. He smiled like the hopeful boy he was. He looked more innocent to Borter than he had in his holo-vids. The pilot looked first at Starr, then at Helio who came down the ramp, wiping his hands, he announced that the Centralizer did, indeed, need an overhaul. Thee Starr shook his hand as Parnak introduced him. Helio, at the same time, smiled his rarely seen smile at Starr, saying he'd been a fan for a long time. Parnak was pleased. Helio was never difficult.

Borter glared at him. He stormed up the ramp past Helio and Starr toward the Centralizer. Along the way, he opened a storage cabinet and searched in the dim light for the overhaul kit. Finding it, he shut off the light in the cabinet and left. An angry hour later, the repair was done. Helio inspected it carefully before he allowed Borter to power it up.

There were a lot of ships carrying freight in the galaxy, he explained. Soarer was just another one, just like all the others. If The Helmsman was suspicious of one, he had to be suspicious of them all. That would be a big job even for him. When

Parnak reminded him that he also had a lot of Targan working for him, Borter shrugged saying that Targan were only Targan. Parnak, however, was correct. If Borter's plan worked easily and there was some reason to believe that it might, they still had to find Julia, free her, and get out alive.

They were away from Parnel and Ganempsha within an hour. Sensors behind read no sign of Targan pursuit. Soarer joined a line of freighters heading toward Modallas. They would come back to Ganempsha. This run came first.

They were only a few hours out before they saw their first wing of Modallian fighters. They were Targan pilots. Borter was not close enough to see them, but he imagined that he could see their dark, scowling faces in the tiny cockpits. They'd all seen quite enough Targan on Marcellus.

Borter described Modallas to Starr, who'd only heard wild tales. He accepted the kilometers-long size of the thing but could not grasp the speed of it. Borter had to laugh at this and shook his head. That afternoon, Thee Starr heard of Targans and The Helmsman. The Pilot unfolded his accounts of the final battles for Marcellus itself, to him. He told of Soarer's escape from Modallas.

"You are the Ghost Pilot, aren't you?" Starr exclaimed with great enthusiasm. Borter winced, not knowing whether he could endure such innocence.

He replied calmly. "No. There is no such person. Your Ghost Pilot is a fiction. Something made up by some foolish journalist. One who's long past his prime!" He nodded in Parnak's direction, but Starr's eyes never followed it.

"What's this?" Starr pointed to an empty slot on the control console between the two pilots' seats. Borter shook his head, glad that any discussion of the Ghost Pilot was dropped. He didn't know. It did nothing, he said, and it was in none of the manuals. He'd forgotten it.

Helio returned from the freight container, and Starr left the cockpit. "You've made a friend, it appears!" Borter took his friend's dryness of speech for sarcasm and grunted.

"Yeah. Thanks to our friend, Parnak, the Ghost Pilot has a pal!"

"Thee Starr hasn't taken his eyes off you since you first saw you. He's polite to me, civil with Parnak, and sure of you. He's an intuitive, you know. One knows another!" Borter grunted another time and said nothing.

Soarer had barely settled onto the runway at Parnel before Borter asked clearance to leave an hour later. He looked at Thee Starr and said, "No passengers!"

He glared at Parnak for making the decision without him or Helio. Thee Starr smiled broadly beside them having already grown used to the word no in his career.

Borter shouted into the cargo tube to Helio. Helio was to check the gaps in the Sub-neutron Sequencer and stabilize the Centralizer, whichever. Helio had the misfortune to lose to Borter at cards getting the job. In fact, Dillisome were ferocious card players having little else to do on their frozen planet. Helio had lost purposely. Borter was a terrible mechanic.

Borter turned back to Parnak, very much the commander of Soarer. Parnak glared back at him very much, the client paid up or not — and ready to pull all the still drop us at the concert site, in The Ords. I am still your client, and that still means something in this galaxy! Parnak shrugged and stalked away. It's only an hour's jump from here." Borter was left looking at Thee Starr. Contractual strings at his disposal.

You can still drop us in The Ords, can't you?

I am still your client, and that still means something in this galaxy! Parnak shrugged and stalked away. It's only an hour's jump from here." Borter was left looking at Thee Starr. contractual strings at his disposal. "OK, but – we have another little stop-off before that."

"Stop – off?"

5

Parnel – Again, Heroes Need Not Apply

Borter sat in the command chair of Soarer with Helio as co-pilot. He looked tired. Helio did not, he never did. This fact was something that annoyed Borter, as he did all facts he found less than convenient. Soarer was nose down in orbit as they waited for landing clearance from Parnel Control.

There were freighters, like their own, lined up both ahead of them and behind, waiting for clearance into the slot. That day Parnel was slow.

Borter powered down. The green glow from his Marcellean power dots dimmed to standby levels. Helio switched stabilization to automatic and leaned far back in his chair. Borter similarly

relaxed.

The lights went down, and only the instrument panel showed a muted brightness before them. In a couple of moments, Borter felt the need to speak.

Borter held the thought of how to do it deep in the back of his mind but couldn't seem to get it out.

Helio said it for him. "We're the only non-Marcellean pilots ever to have evaded Medallas' guns, and we've dealt with her fighter cover. I suggest something subtle."

With Borter, in any plan, the word subtle was not regarded as any speck in any part of reality. "I was thinking of something completely underhanded and sneaky to tell the truth." He smiled. Helio smiled back, reassured, knowing they would go anyway.

The Helmsman was taking no pains to keep Modallas' whereabouts a secret. She would be easy to find.

Borter was sure he'd be remembered by The Helmsman. He'd been there at Lord Markham's killing, and Soarer had been Lord Soal's flagship during the Modallian invasion, which covered the evacuation of the planet. Yes, remembered, but not fondly, he was sure.

They'd broken that blockade to deliver Parnak. This bit of journalist's life had been a mystery to them, and so, by design.

The Marcellean web reached anciently and far into the galaxy. Their mark is not always seen but always there in many places, in many ways. The pilot's stay on Marcellus was both short and violent. The Helmsman, yet pushed his reign of terror across the Inner Galaxy, taking planet after planet.

6

Ganampsha

The planet's horizon filled the windshield. Electronics filled the computer screens with readings from ground stations. Borter sat back; Helio had made dozens of landings under all conditions without looking at the screens.

He consulted the Galactic Atlas, something usually left for Helio, more to his interests. Borter could not say why he bothered to make note of the place at all. There was nothing much to say about Ganempsha, as he confirmed from the atlas. That is nothing much except Sand Rock.

There were the obligatory paragraphs, paragraphs only, that described the major land masses. It seemed there were no large bodies of water at all.

There were vast deserts, the largest called The Ords and gigantic farms showing lush vegetation. The cities were neither impressive nor large. There was nothing remarkable about the planet at all. Borter shrugged and closed the atlas with a sharp snap. He failed to take advantage of the note at page bottom to see Sand Rock under the music heading. They would not be there long.

The landing itself was easy. Helio touched down with hardly a bump and taxied toward their assigned dock. As they touched down, the voice of a lazy-sounding robot traffic controller assigned them to an old and disused-looking hanger.

It would do, they supposed. There was no sense in alerting agents of The Helmsman to their whereabouts. Except for a narrow strip of fresh tarmac, the field was a rutted affair, hostile to any known type of aircraft. Still, Helio got them to the assigned dock.

Across the expanse of the field, scrub brush grew in tight bunches beneath the double suns of that world at that time of day, at their hottest. Borter turned on the air-conditioner from his side of the console meaning to remain aboard until the daytime heat had passed.

The lights went down, and only the instrument panel showed a muted brightness before them. In a couple of moments, Borter felt the need to speak.

Thee Starr smiled, motioning them outward down the ramp toward the streets of Parnel, uttering something about – cutting an erotic swath across the city – and would they help?

7

Yardus Vid

A few minutes came and went. Before Starr flicked down his eye shield, he pressed a few keys on the control console to start the vid. Everything was computer controlled.

The media could be anything. Huge quantities of video phones and tapes that played them were sold across the galaxy.

The festival on Yardus was classic. Borter had never been to a Sandrock festival, nor had Helio. He'd heard all about them. All the top groups from across the galaxy came. It had been the biggest and loudest ever. Borter would have hired out as a transport carrier to the site but had other work.

In the video, Borter walked on a broad plain, Yardus. Turning, he saw that the plane was filled with people and that he was moving toward them, walking.

In the far distance, in the center of everything, were the stage works. Borter's vid-phones kept him walking toward them. Holographic lighting and anti-gravity equipment are centered there. The pilot liked it. He'd been in space for a very long time without relief. Flyers, freighter pilots, tended to do that. That is, live on their freighters.

He knew those who hadn't set foot on a planet for years at a time. They simply flew between orbiting planetary slips, offloaded, unloaded, and left for another run. It was almost endless, first it became a habit, then a life.

Borter saw Helio in the distance, also walking. He waved to him, and the Dillisome waved back.

Parnak was there, too, farther back, though. His wave was more belated. In their video fantasies, they saw Borter as well. Each had the distinct sensation of walking far into the Yardian plain and sharing it with many other humanoids.

Borter continued his trek. It was easy, anything he wished came to be through the computer. He liked that. He looked around. There were lots of women around, young, beautiful women. He'd wished them there, so they were. One dangled on each of his arms, both young and attractive. They laughed at his jokes and smiled brightly as he told them.

Vid-crawlers, as they were called in the vernacular, sometimes played tricks on each other.

Borter wished something for Parnak. Beside him, from nowhere, the pilot's imagination appeared one of the pretty, young women. Parnak jerked back suddenly as she took his arm as the others had Borter's.

Then, the insectoid's manner changed, and he seemed to enjoy himself. That young woman on his arm was there to stay.

Parnak seemed to smile, though he did not have the physiology for it. Borter came to a stop, looking aside for a second, undecided whether or not he was the trickster or the tricked. Physiology did not matter in vids.

The pretty girls in his arms were much to his liking, but they served only to remind him of Julia. There was nothing he could do for her, nothing for Lord Soal, and nothing for Marcellus. He'd really wanted to help there despite his initial resistance. What he had been able to do had been worth next to nothing, so he thought.

He continued his journey toward the stage area. Nothing had begun yet. Things were still being moved on antigravs and being set up and were hardly of interest. The video-phone computer sensed his feelings and read his thoughts. It responded. There was a soft beeping in his ears.

He looked around for a source but could find none. His surroundings blanked out twice, completely white. Then, winked back. It had changed subtly, but a change anyway.

The pilot could feel it instantly. He looked to either side and discovered that both his new friends were gone. The vid-phone flashed dead again, exactly as it had before. A second later, on his arm was Julia as he'd wanted her.

She awed him as before. He ached that he could do nothing for her. Still, she was there in that dream. He thought about it for a second and then he did not. She was there as he had wanted her. It was growing late in the day.

The video image enhanced itself. Day became night. It was as he'd wished it. Julia stood looking into his eyes from a height just at his shoulder. She gazed at him as if there were no other man in the entire galaxy, and he gazed back.

At the same time, Helio settled with the imagined young woman that Borter wished on him. He did not mind; it was what his partner termed as better than look-ing down the barrel of a smoking blaster. This meant, in short, taking what you got.

The music from the backup group, second or third on the bill, an anonymous assemblage of musicians, began their set.

For a change, Helio relaxed. The stage hovered or, at least, hung in the air at the center crowd. The band's name or where it had come from interested him. Only among the great, the knowledgeable did identity matter. In fact, he might have already reviewed this event. The girl nestled closer in his arms as the music swept over them. He'd have to check his notes.

Ultra-guitars and holograms dominated the vid. For a short time, several moments, he forgot this was merely a vid-induced experience. He had no need to work at all. It would have been simplicity itself to relax, but not for him, *Parnak, The Great,* journalist of the galaxy. Work was more natural than relaxation. It seemed more natural than life to him.

Thee Starr felt it was more sad than curious. So, it be-gan. The video judged them ready. The crowd settled as one as the backup act struck its last distorted chords. Thee Starr was next.

A shudder of anticipation went through them as road-ies crossed the stage and, once across, crossed back. Then, having once recrossed, they crossed a thousand times more, it seemed.

Finally, it was ready. The stage darkened. The crowd silenced. Glowing ranks of anti-gravity disks blurred as they rushed upward another time. They formed themselves together and flew at high speed across the expanse of the festival grounds.

Everyone watched as they swept the night. Thee Starr and his band took the stage under cover of darkness. They were ready and silent as the crowd began to ooh and aaah the performance of the disks. They gathered again and rushed downward toward the stage. As they did, Starr's first chords rolled out like new thunder.

Starr oldies came first, those favorites from the early years. For Starr, there had been many early years.

Titles, names of songs, and album collections reached out into the night, a fistful of memories of youth and romance, of expectation and innocence that told their story of male and female life kind, the whole galaxy.

From his first album, a classic among Sand Rockers, Another Dawn, Another Day, Another Planet, and a second, Between Consenting Quarks, the title unexplained, dubbed an instant success across the galaxy.

Critically, it was pronounced a revolution in popular music, appealing, they said, the critics, because of the unconventional acoustics used by the recording studio, aimed at the inner mind directly, rather than the ear, they mused.

He could have retired from then on, living on continued royalties, but he did not. Starr's fortunes went on rising with his fame. It wasn't long before several small star systems were under his control, some rich, most though, middling in wealth.

As a landlord, there were no rebellions, no unrest. In fact, things on the poorer planets improved. Overall — most satisfactory.

It seemed to Borter he'd spent the entire three days of the festival with Julia, but he hadn't. The time spent from the first note to the last had been just a little less than four hours. His visions of her from first to last had been managed by the video. After the final explosions of color above the stadium, he, like the others, found himself facing a grinning Thee Starr in the hollow of Soarers tube.

The computer, having taken the insectoid's

measure, made the girl's image equally persistent, and each time he put her off, it simply made her appear more beautiful to him. Parnak fell without realizing it. Parnak thought himself incapable of such feelings.

Helio, all the while, was quite agreeable and enjoyed himself immensely. Starr's concert had been a terrific success. Now it passed, his head cleared, released from the control of the computer. His ears rang slightly from the roar of it all.

Borter was another story. He sat silently, his face grim, having been reminded of his love lost. Julia, if she was still alive, was a captive of The Helmsman aboard Medallas. There was little he could do.

The tube of Soarer became a stark place, a place of loneliness. Their respective lives as pilots, a journalist, and singers drew up in bleak contrast to the video they'd all, moments before, watched.

Borter was sure he'd felt it alone and, if asked for a comparison between himself and any of the others, he would have said just that.

No one said anything, strangely enough. It was a sort of withdrawal, said Starr, later on, affecting even the most experienced Vid – Crawler.

8

Quantum

A host of things dawdled through Borter's mind as the landing showed itself to be nothing more than routine. At the same time, refuse. He thought of his android, Quantum. What would he do with her? He couldn't just go away and leave her, but he could not at the same time refuse another crew member. He thought blankly of Julia. He had to do something for her.

Helio did not view it exactly that way. As Dillisome, things are different in a more equitable way than Borter did, perhaps not.

Reality was not a good description for his partnership with Borter.

His planetary origins were of no help either. To say he was from that Dillisome was simply a statement of fact. Borter argued with everything. Helio mostly went along. Nothing in their partnership made sense except going along.

He knew, at least, that, as always, when the time came, he would be there beside Borter.

Now, this pain in the neck seemed different. Parnak had said the right words. "Yes," Emmick confided at last, "I follow The Heart," in a changed voice that spoke through Parnak's translator. There was nothing more to be said between the two. "Those two?" Emmick asked, "They are special to The Heart?" Slide turned back toward Hammer, saying thanks. Quantum followed but in a less garrulous manner. Parnak stayed behind for a moment, confronting Emmick.

Parnak regarded the globe in which Emmick floated above the floor, regarded him as if he'd never seen him before. Beneath the journalist's penetrating gaze, he glowed a little less. His green faded just a little into the grey that floated him in the globe. Parnak smiled what little smile his own physiology would allow. At last, he knew about Emmick. Parnak's iron gaze won the truth from many during his long career across many worlds. He'd hidden his secret long enough, for quite some time, in fact.

"You follow The Heart, Emmick?" For a moment, his color paled. There was no word from him. All his senses focused on the journalist. He'd never thought much about Parnak. This insectoid was a whirring sort of know-it-all, just the type that made everyday life miserable, pompous, arrogant, and all the rest.

"Tulso Slide and Quantum?" Parnak smiled his little smile.

"Slide is The Ghost Pilot. There has been all that talk about?"

"No, Borter." Parnak came back, laughing as he could. "Ah. There is no other flyer in the galaxy like Borter, not even Tulso Slide."

The high giggle came another time. Emmick glowed within his container. "Well, Soarer delivers."

"The Heart chooses its champions well," the journalist mumbled.

9

Alien Night Life

New kid humanoids rushed to the dance floor, joining those already there. The place thundered to Sand Rock. More came into the room.

The place became jammed as Parnak finished his first drink and went to work on the second. From the dance floor to the bar, the place overflowed. No one left the club. Parnak supposed that they would be safe for a while.

It would give them time to rest and time to plan. He was content to sit, allowing the drink to muddle the signals coming from his antennae and to gaze at the lovely Quantum.

The hologram announced - a break and would be back with more in just a few minutes. The video seemed unctuous and a little over-solicitous. The audio stage disappeared, gone with a hiss. With nothing more to look at, the club patrons turned to each other. The floor cleared in favor of the bar and waiter and waitresses, all of them android, slipping between bar and tables.

Even Odds on Norvado

It showed ability, but that was not the plan. They would continue to rumble along. There have been six bad storms in six days in this place. A place said to be forsaken of The Heart. Rain brought flooding, then the big hail, then rain and floods again, snow, more rain, and again the freeze, this time worse than any, coming down from the legendary Black Cragg. The oldest of the rangers stuffed himself, like a child, down in his seat, glaring out the nearby window.

Tension in the others eased a bit. None would look at Tyad, all wishing to relax and forget his complaining. This plan, all along, that the transport be flightless, slower, that the trip to the freight depot is difficult, therefore, noted a delay. Targans watched one hundred of them by scanner count. The cities, even the towns on the planet, were obstacles that slowed the forest-bred fighters, though not much. One object, the box, slowed them not at all.

Tyad was the first to spring from the overturned wreck of the transport. The first and second Targan who greeted him were cut down. Behind them came the others. Targans stormed the road as a mass. Raising their blasters, The Marcelleans fired. The main thrust of the attack was blunted. Other Targans fired from cover, the effect of their blasters lost against Marcellean armor. Those who remained on their feet from the original charge renewed their effort against the thin line of fighters.

Dras Mul and Tyad met the first of them, with the others backing them close behind. Thus far no Marcellean had fallen, but Targan were difficult enemies. The blade of El Auth claimed the next closest. Buus Jadding had the second and third.

The blue light of the blades was nearly lost in the bright light of day. However, the effect of the ancient weapon was not. Targans crumbled away before them as they had on Marcellus since time began.

At last, the survivors ran. They would return. The box was not yet delivered. More Targan lined the route, to be sure. The six set their transport on its wheels and drove on.

Crop Dusters, Mad Moz the Wingman

Both men nodded. They didn't like working as crop dusters over the farm's vast acreage, but it was what Parnak had been able to arrange, like it or not. Mere planetary flying seemed dull to pilots of star ships, but it was done, agreed. They walked behind him as he turned away and left the dock. Parnak wore what all other journalists wore, that is, those who covered combat, a waist-length battle jacket, a beige one for around the ville as they, to a man, called cities and towns. A recorder on a sling, nothing at all in weight, it was a slender black box availing the journalist of a host of most needed functions. Kaki knickers to the tops of his unwanted boots were the next order of business. The knickers bagged in all the right places, and he was able to move easily in them. As for the boots, Parnak himself told them that he'd seen no worse tortures inflicted anywhere in all his assignments as a war correspondent. For this, his latest campaign, he'd found an astonishingly beaten-looking hat to cover his antennae. With a wide brim of clay, a felt, yet unnamed by some misfortune of fashion, curled toward its crown.

A wide hatband of animal skin was flung all the way around that crown if it could be called a crown as, indeed, the denuded beast that suffered a fate as damaging and unfortunate as had the one that had gifted the knot of the hat with bright feathers.

The entire outfit appeared to be random snatches taken by surprise from certain of the galaxy's beasts stupid enough to wander too close to any open conveyance in which Parnak had obtained a window seat. Walking behind a little, Borter and Helio talked quietly to each other. After so many days in space, it was reassuring to have a solid planet underfoot again.

Soon, again, they'd be aboard Suther Dann's little hoppers spraying crops. Borter sighed, walking along, thinking of it. It did not seem to bother Helio at all.

Moz is going to flip when she hears we brought Thee Starr home." Helio looked over at Borter. "Yeah," Borter smiled at the prospect, "let me tell her, okay?"

Dann's child had quickly attached herself to Borter. "What is it they call him, his fans? Believer, is that it?"

Helio nodded. By this time, Parnak had overheard.

The three walked a little farther without speaking.

Then, Parnak told them more. "You know, of course, Thee Starr is the leading exponent of the planet's youth. To see him is to see them all. I've decided to investigate something else. I'll be asking Dann for your services to fly me out into The Ords to meet with the leader of the Red Clones."

Dwellings cascaded like stacked cracker boxes beside the wide streets on both sides as they walked away from the spaceport. They trailed through the streets.

All sorts of businesses dotted the ground floor levels. Gradually, the streets narrowed, becoming more and more shabby, signaling they'd walked across the main part of the city to the outskirts, on the other side of town.

"You know, all these kids dress like Starr," commented Borter, "and like Moz!" He had not put it together that they dressed alike for a reason as had Parnak and Helio.

Parnak spoke to the Dillisome in a tone of exasperation, "Hello," he called, letting the fatigue of the day's walk enter his voice, "I think I'll ask Dann to let you fly me out into The Ords. Your conversation is so much better!"

Borter's head swiveled toward Parnak, bearing a look of hurt on his face. "Gee, Parnak! I was looking forward to another of those little talks with you."

"You wear your sarcasm well, Borter." Parnak kept his eyes straight ahead. Helio looked first at one, then the other, smiling a smile that was a statement of his own.

"I think you wear it better!" The pilot kept walking.

The three had nearly reached the outer area where surface vehicles were allowed. Mad Moz could be seen just ahead, waiting beside a sleek black sedan that would carry them to the Dann's farm.

She looked as rebellious as did all the other of the planet's children. That is, dressed in striped military fatigues of mottled vegetable green and the tans and reds of The Ords. Beneath the generous folds of duty fabric, nothing hid from the eye her woman's figure.

Moz waved enthusiastically to all three, or so it appeared. She saw them all, but really, only Borter. These attentions he studiously ignored. Parnak and Helio said nothing, one winking slyly at the other. Still smiling, she took her place behind the wheel of the sedan. Parnak entered the car through a rear door after Helio, leaving Borter in just the position he did not want, beside Moz in the front seat.

"Good day," Parnak smiled as best an insectoid could. "I'm glad you could meet us," he said, "it's a long walk from here."

"It's a long walk from anywhere!" Moz looked back at him. "No problem!"

The Way To Suther Dann's

Borter set his eyes forward, listening to the ever-present Sand Rock that played through the sedan's radio. They got underway.

The journey to Dann's farm was not short, a little more than an hour. Around them, the countryside sped by. Ganempsha sprawled lushly in all directions beyond Cross Anchor. Borter spent his time noticing the tall green trees growing in densely rank-and-filed orchards.

Beneath the trees themselves, the ground was covered by dusty grass. Here and there, access roads cut through the trees.

For some time, they'd been on Suther Dann's property. In a hopper, it took a single day to fly it end to end. Moz turned from her duty as a driver and smiled warmly at Borter. In the back seat, Helio roused to peer behind at the cloud of fine dust that billowed in their wake. Parnak directed his attention into the passing orchards, mulling idly his intended trip to the Ords, the desert home of the Sargon clones.

In the late afternoon, dusk was falling. In another hour, the system's second sun would be left to brighten the planet to full daylight and, then, as slowly, sink beyond the horizon. The sedan rushed toward its destination. Within, the passengers shifted, restless, in their seats. Music still played out its thumping beat, and no one spoke.

Helio glanced first at the preoccupied Parnak and then at Borter, who seemed lost in his own thoughts. Borter made such an effort to ignore Moz. Poor Borter, he thought! He wondered if some feeling was there.

Moz slowed the car and eased to a stop in the farmhouse driveway. Slowly, the passengers of the sedan pulled themselves erect from the opened doors. Helio glanced toward Borter and asked if he wanted to go down to the pads and check out his hopper for the next day's flight.

Shaking his head, no, Borter said he'd rather do it just before takeoff, that too much could happen to it at night. "I don't trust Kees," he said, extracting his flight bag from the trunk. "He's a Targan. you know?"

Helio hardly bothered to answer. He'd noticed Kees' jungle eyes as quickly as Borter.

"A couple of the others are too, I think, but I haven't got a close enough look at them," he said. "They're Kees' wingmen, that's close enough for me!"

Parnak agreed. Targans were not much abroad in the galaxy. Their savage nature made them trainable and useful, only in the cause of The Helmsman and Medallas.

Moz, who they'd forgotten in their conversation, drove on. She kept back her questions. She'd never hear the story of these three otherwise. In the weeks they'd stayed she'd learned nothing, never seen Soarer, and had nothing but evasions for answers to her questions.

The door to the farmhouse opened, spilling light out onto the flat, red desert stones of the front porch. Something blotted out the light. A big man stood for an instant in the yellow house light. He turned, working several switches on the inside beside the door. A post lamp went on in the bright yard, then off, then on again. Finally, a light went on above his head.

Moz recognized her father. Suther Dann came forward reaching the car in a few easy strides of his long legs. As he came, he loosened his blaster in the holster slung at his side. Drawing it, he checked the charge and setting, and then he stopped, even with Borter and Helio.

"Something in the fields," he said quietly, in a near whisper as if he were talking to himself, "Killed two of my help. Tore them apart. Kees' wingmen, I hear."

For an instant, his eyes met those of Helio and Borter, "Let's go," he said in a soft, low voice, "Take blasters from the house if you need them. I know you boys carry your own. Bring 'em if you want!" He walked on.

Moz bolted for the house quickly. "Moz!" The big man called back. "Go inside and stay there! This is liable to be tricky. I don't want to have to worry about you!"

Moz stopped in her tracks. Dann headed for the landing pads. Clenching fists at her sides, she hissed, and a deep anger gripped her. She stamped her foot, and without looking back, she headed for the small armory in the house.

Behind her, Parnak was hurrying to Dann's side. Borter and Helio were making their way toward their quarters and readiness, then on, to join the search.

In time, they arrived at the hopper pads, the only square piece of level ground jealously given up to the needed landing place for the tiny hoppers. As the two flyers arrived, a hopper was just taking off, kicking up a cloud of dust, obscuring partially its own red and blue maneuvering lights; a single great eye of light shone out in front, casting a harsh beam down into the orchard. Parnak had squeezed aboard a hopper with Suther Dann and was gone. Moz waited, then came to the pads.

"You can't come," Borter droned just loudly enough to make himself heard above the departing hopper. Helio said nothing, readying his flyer.

"I get paid to fly just like everybody else," Moz bawled at him.

"Your old man said to stay – and you get paid to follow orders, nothing else," Borter shouted back!

She made a face, sticking out her tongue, and slid behind the controls of her hopper. "You better hurry, Borter," she called to him as he stood there, still protesting where she'd left him, "You'll miss all the fun. We're wingmen, you know?" With the whine of her engine, she drowned out Borter's reply. Then, seeing no hope of changing her mind, he climbed into the single seat of his flyer and got ready for takeoff.

Finally, Borter eased his hopper into the air behind Moz and Helio. The little flyers could take quick turns and make good speed. Borter and Helio had seen them take much punishment and stay in the air. Above the pads, they lined up on each other's red and blue maneuvering lights. Together, they switched on their forward searchlights. The beams cut paths deeply into the Ganempshan night. As they moved forward in close formation, forward skids were retraced gently into the fuselages.

Released from their locked positions on either side of the hopper produced an even more striking comparison to an insect.

The trio sped across the rows of trees toward the beast's last known sighting. In touch by radio, the flyers kept tabs on each other. The attack had been on the farm's edge of the desert. Radios crackled with static but were otherwise quiet. In the darkness of night, they probed ahead. A hopper pilot watched his screen at night or when it was impossible to see. Often, big storms came in from the Ords, and, at times, they were filled with heavy dust and sand instead of rain.

They pulled into close formation, as was the standard practice. The three of them were so close they could see the dim lights of one another's instrument panels. At times, there would be a sweep of darkness in the cockpit as a moving hand or arm worked one control or another, guiding flight across the sky.

Ganempsha's single moon rose as they flew, making visibility a little better. To Helio, a great red eye, and it viewed all that happened below. At times, at night, when flying above the white clouds of some planet or other with a strange moon staring down at him, he'd thought of Dillisome, hanging far distant in space, its ice resembling clouds under its single pale moon and dying sun.

He missed his planet, wondering how things were for his family. Most often, he would say he didn't miss it and didn't want to go back, banishing any thought of home as it crossed his mind.

Reaching the halfway mark, Moz looked across at Borter's hopper, though she could not see him in the dark cockpit. Suther Dann would be angry went he found out she'd disobeyed his orders to stay home. That is, if he found out at all. Ganempsha in the darkness or the vast orchards of the farm at night had always intrigued her. The orchard had been her escape from a big house that lately seemed more prison than home.

They'd lived there forever, it seemed, since her mother died before she'd died.

Dann kept the place for her, trying to be mother, father, and orchard keeper all at once, with mixed results. To Moz, it seemed, turned out all right. Dann's attempts to be all seemed to her overprotective. There was still some question her growth had reached its full potential. She felt lucky to have learned to fly a hopper at all - the flyer that she taught had been fired.

Borter had come with Parnak, hadn't he? She mused to herself that possibility, smiling a wry smile to herself in the cockpit darkness. Her feelings had grown quickly for this pilot who'd come with another strange guest, this Parnak, and the Dillisome, that quiet blue man, Helio.

It was unusual that the two men they were going to hire had not stayed or eaten with the rest of the farm help. The four had dined with her father and herself. After, she'd been wished out of the room. The four had talked late into that first night in the house in low voices from which she learned nothing.

Borter could almost feel her eyes on him in the dimly lit cockpit. It was a talent of most Magneans, being able to tell when something was about to happen. It was what made them such good pilots, he'd decided long ago. It was true enough.

Magnus had produced more than enough good pilots. Their names read from any history of the galaxy like a roll call. The insectoid had written a huge history of Magnus and her flyers and a History of the Galaxy by Parnak. He'd forced both Borter and Helio to read it.

The work had achieved some fame and became a required study at, of all places, the redoubtable Fleet Academy where anybody who was anybody as a flyer was educated, self-satisfied, except the Magneans, of course. Moz was getting to be a problem for Borter. Loving her meant settling down, changing his life.

Magneans got old like everyone else. He just wasn't ready for that and especially not ready for Mad Moz. In a way, he was attracted to the prospect Moz held. As Suther Dann's son-in-law, he'd have it made. Plenty of Magneans were farmers, and it wasn't so bad. Where had she gotten that name?

13

Rand Sabbling – To Kithron Show Mercy

Other things were afoot on or near Gamempsha, a planet in the star system Laura Zed. Invisible in the first pre-twilight haze of Ganempsha's first sun, a small shuttle in a great deal of trouble had entered the atmosphere. Its lateral stabilizers were shot away, as were its radio and rear deflector. The craft's twin engines were near failure from other damage done. There was the briefest of contrails in the upper air as they finally winked out.

His hands moved across the control console of the Kithronese shuttle. The great deftness of the Marcellean armor he wore made his control almost easy. That, however, was not going to save him unless he did something fast. The shuttle, an ungainly aircraft, was beginning to show signs of wanting to break up.

Blasting away from the enemy flagship, he been set upon by a Stiletto which had inflicted damage to the craft.

In turn, Kithronese fighters set upon it. This was too late for the shuttle, in any case, except it preserved the pilot or, at least, forestalled his death for some length of time, the time needed to reach his destination and his fate, Ganempsha.

The Kithronese fighters, after destroying the Stiletto, sent word back to the fleet that one of their shuttles was damaged and its trajectory, but there was little else they could do. The fleet itself was too greatly damaged to aid its own in near space to go chasing off toward Ganempsha for this ship bearing an unknown person or perhaps no one at all.

Rand Sabbling angled his forward deflector and wrestled the controls for stability, hoping the fuel in the rocket thrusters would hold him until he could make a safe landing on the planet rushing toward him. There were seconds in which to pick a spot that was clear try.

The shuttle leveled a bit. Angling a single thruster forward, he slowed the ship with a sustained blast. He had waited until only a few thousand meters from the surface to break the dive. Rand Sabbling felt himself pulled forward by the breaking action. He set aside the fuel in that thruster for a second-breaking action when he wanted to kill his speed altogether on landing.

He swooped in on the Ord desert, a remote area near nothing.

The stabilizers shook. The deflector would hit first in front manual override so that it wouldn't switch off as it was supposed to. He fired the forward thruster and descended onto the red sand. He felt the deflector hit and vibrate the whole ship. The last thing he remembered as he crawled away from the smoking wreckage was the beat of many hooves coming nearer.

Near Laura Zed but more distant from Ganempsha than Rand Sabbling had been, Medallas moved through space within the turning cylindric shell. The Helmsman slowly paced behind the helm. The black starship, Soarer, was on his mind.

It had escaped him on Marcellus. Now, it bedeviled him at Laura Zed. Moments before, one of his captains brought news that the freighter had been tracked to Ganempsha. Then, there existed his only link with the Heart of Marcellus. The captain stood waiting a few moments for new orders as The Helmsman considered his options.

Such an undertaking would demand his personal attention if this gypsy freighter was his remaining link. His right hand, the hand that steered Medallas all the years since its creation, absently caressed the hilt of the Snow Beggar's ion blade sheathed at his side. He turned toward the waiting captain.

"Captain." The Targan stepped smartly forward and, sharply clicking his heels, halted coming to attention. "Take this message," The Helmsman spoke. "Reinforce all operative cells now on Ganempsha. Top priority is given to all requests for resupply until further notice!"

"Yes, Sir!" The Targan was ready to turn and carry out his orders, but before he could The Helmsman went on.

"And, Captain, I want AF6 in this action."

"Yes," The Targan looked at the creature in the black body armor whose face he, like all others who called themselves Targan, had never seen, made their forest blood run ice cold. The dark amusement in a voice as the words were spoken, "is for them. This is just their work."

The captain was quickly on his way. Even for a Targan, ones who prided themselves on their fear of nothing, he was glad to be away from The Helmsman's presence.

Never, even among the most brutal of those newly from the forest, did he experience the master of Medallas and the Inner Galaxy dread as he felt when near.

Early, on the outskirts of the farm, just before dawn, a small circle of hoppers was drawn up around a gruesome sight. Borter and Helio stood together with Parnak and Suther Dann, Moz wedged between them. Borter whispered to Helio suspiciously from the corner of his mouth, at the same time nodding toward the grisly remains,

"It must have gotten very crowded here," he said. He turned to leave, "In fact," he said, fighting a wave of nausea, "It's very crowded here now!" Not far on, he gave up his last meal to the soil of Gampaha. In a moment, Moz followed suit.

14

Chibba the Spy – The Battle in the Bar

The limousine bearing Chibba the Spy rounded the corner, taking up much of the narrow street in Cross Anchor. More of the general population already knew of Kithron's destruction. Chibba had known before it happened.

There was little he did not know. The big car came quickly to a halt. A thin man approached, who at once looked unlikely to have ever seen such a luxurious automobile much less have business with the bold-eyed denizen who sat in its back. An opaque window slid down with a muffled electronic whir to one quarter open.

Chibba's dark form leaned forward to hear. "They will be here sooner or later. Sooner, I think, these flyers like to drink." The thin man strained to see into the dark car but could only make out Chibba's forest eyes glaring from the darkness.

Chibba grunted. His wide limousine sat across from a dingy bar stuck halfway between street corners. Chibba stared at it, his normal scowl invisible to the thin man as he sized up the narrow door of the place. It had a back door, too, he supposed. The bright neon light in the window inviting females of any species to enter would have hurt his eyes had it not been for the opacity of the car's glass. The forests of distant Marcellus were Chibba's, and the night, even in the city, even one such as this. The window slid closed, and the thin man stepped back as the limousine moved away from the curb and back into the rough street. Much was left to be done. His orders had come directly from The Helmsman himself; the Ghost Pilot was to be destroyed at all costs before the invasion of Ganempsha.

They were to arrange it, to carry it out. The job agreed with Chibba, the long hours, the plotting, the occasional random violence. Enough to make it all worthwhile. He glanced briefly behind. The light dust and trash in the street caught up in the draft of a passing car.

The street was on the edge of the downtown area of Cross Anchor. Certainly less than splendid, it served because of its abandoned buildings and lack of light, good spots for ambush. At last, he would know who was The Ghost Pilot. This would please his master, too, he knew. For some unexplained reason, this pilot drew his ire.

Chibba knew of The Heart. This device could alter the very fabric of the galaxy itself. Its power was that of the old ones, too old to be named, the nameless, those most ancient of Marcellus, those who were no more.

This flyer must have something to do with it, he thought. Even knowing its location. This was speculation. Chibba could take his time, then act and know for himself. Mere speculation was less than efficient and, in his business, dangerous. The network of informants and killers he supported would therefore bear fruit, his efforts would not be wasted. Chibba was shrewd. He knew that the Ghost Pilot would come to him and all he had to do was wait.

15

Suther Dann's

Moz motioned him in. Borter crossed the threshold, shaking his head, unable to convince himself that he indeed wanted to enter the room with Moz there. Suther Dann, because he was a friend of the great Parnak, the Jillian, denied him no part of the house or any hospitality. Borter did not want to admit the inevitable; he was in love with Moz and resisted with all his waning strength of will in the matter.

She sat him down and smiled quickly, looking into his eyes. This was to be Borter's initiation into the world of vid-phones, singularly, a delight. It combined the senses into a recorded experience. Most of it was Sand Rock, some of it was merely outrageous, and some of it was truly lewd. Its main point was that it involved the user in the recorded event. Events, many, were available and could be cross-edited to one another, making the possibilities endless. Just what Moz was thinking. Borter said nothing.

He'd heard of phones long before. Everyone in the galaxy had. The patent holders had licensed them out universally. It was a mainstay industry; another business with such effect was farming.

49

"It's better than hallucinogens," she giggled as she helped Borter get the helmet on and took another for herself! He couldn't see and he couldn't hear. The helmet was no different from any crash helmet he'd ever worn. It was comfortable so he left it on.

Moz pushed the button, and the video began. Slowly at first, with the passage of countryside much like the ride out from Cross Anchor. Lush, manicured orchards like those Suther Dann owned, all vast, surrounded the viewer. Held midair by Sand Rock and imagination, Moz was there beside him. He reached out and took her hand, feeling it and the wind in his face.

Borter settled back and let the images come. At the Thee Starr concert everyone would have one. It was the greatest thing in mass-media since video came in many styles and could be customized to personal specifications. Moz's player was a small, but expensive, home model and she had many cartridges for it.

She pulled down her eyepiece, then Borter. There was an instant of total darkness then a flash of light and they found themselves in a they in a huge arena filled with people, people like themselves. There was music, loud, loud Sand Rock music, threatening to rip the very air from around their ears.

Borter turned to Moz and her toward him. They began to dance, at first slowly, eyes fixed, then more intensely, their eyes locked on each other.

They danced, oblivious to all else. First, the J^O-JSee-Z^O9s played their thumping mix of planetary music. Second came the Mit(^ t^eU^Ac^ f>f S^^luc Four Star

Band, whose performance was riddled with much-choking smoke and dancing lasers.

Last to appear was Thee Starr, the main attraction. Borter watched with some interest. It was nothing he'd expected Starr to be. A hologram of his own band subbed for them, LH<>£^ k^^J luc, was performing elsewhere that night.

Starr went to work. In fact, Starr enjoyed performing with the holograph. It avoided arguments. Most often employed in small bars and clubs, the practice replaced band members or whole bands whose cost outstripped their budget. Starr took it with him everywhere.

Starr floated from the stage over his dancing followers on a special effects system all his own. His music seemed to hold him in the air as it heaved out over the crowd. He cut a romantic figure from the bottoms of his boots to the top of his head.

His blond hair fluttered in the night breeze. His backdrop was a smokey dull light and seemed to go skyward behind him. The blast shield still covered his eyes as their opaque protectors looked straight out, intently at the audience. His words, lost in the roar of it all, but, always, he held center stage.

Moz was dancing in Borter's arms. For a moment he hadn't noticed it. In that instant, a chill went down his spine. Borter smiled and continued to dance. He felt happy she was there. His vid self said nothing, the crowd roared approval as Starr raced overhead to the deepest reaches of the stadium, appearing to ride nothing more than a beam of light.

The concert ended with Starr tearing off, straight up into the air leaving the crowd breathless and making even Borter gasp as the beam of light timed with the music bent back toward the ground changing color in time for the deep pulsating chant that had taken the music.

Growing in volume from a point almost inaudible to that which shook them all to the core of their beings as Starr thundered back down toward them in a spectacular storm of light to climax the show, a stunningly well-placed medley of his greatest hits from the beginning of his long and successful career to the present, all sung from the center of the great stadium, in midair, just at the level of the second deck.

As it all went black, Borter found himself sitting next to Moz as he had been when she placed the vid helmet on his head, there in her father's house.

16

The Battle In The Bar

A day later. "It was nice of my dad to give us the day off, wasn't it?" Borter didn't answer with words. Instead, he rose to his feet, gently pulling Moz with him and standing with her in his arms as they had in the playback of the concert, he pulled her against him, kissed her, his lips against hers for a time.

Once there, the thin man ran up to the limo. Inside the bar, the pilots found seats at a card game with a couple of the locals amid toiling dancers and loud music.

Before each was a drink, across from each was another card player. Both men were Ganempshan, and neither Borter nor Helio had seen them before. Helio dealt with and called the game as was the dealer's privilege. Dillisomian Death Deal, he announced, for keepers, he added, making it for money instead of a friendly game.

Dillisomian Death Deal was outlawed on as many planets as had heard of it. Ten cards went to each player except the dealer, who was allowed twelve. All the rest were placed in the center of the table as the draw.

In some places on Dillisome, Death Deal was still played only for the life of the loser, this was only in the most backward parts of that distant ice planet. An uncle of Helio's had died in such a game, a card hurled into his skull as he lay down a losing hand.

A rough looking man kept his eye on the game from the bar. No one there had seen him before. None of the regulars looked his way. His eyes seemed to glow in the half-light like those of a great jungle cat as he shifted to one side, then the other, glancing, now and again, at the card game across the room. Time passed.

Helio noticed him. Borter saw only the hand he'd been dealt. His partner knew better, hearing the snap open on Borter's holster, releasing the powerful blaster to an easy grasp.

The hair on the back of Borter's neck stood limply as he noticed the man. He gave it little thought. He had several draughts of something called Moon Bag, by then, a Ganempshan specialty, and was finding it difficult to raise excitement about anything. Helio had had a similar helping of the stuff and was enjoying himself immensely.

Burlesquing, Borter leaned over to him between hands, a serious manner, smiling, seeming to concentrate on raking in the pot from the last hand won. He affected an air, not difficult at the time, and informed Helio in an airily high – pitched, sing – song voice that aped disregard for his personal situation, "The man at the bar is a Targan."

Helio shifted, smiled affably, nodding, glancing toward the dark figure some ten meters away, absently arranging a new hand of cards as he did so in reply. "What do you say, we let this one get away?" He smiled wryly at Borter.

"Well, all right, if he leaves us alone." He heard the snap of Helio's holster guard as the blue man released it, "But, if he leaves us alone first!" He caught the savage glint of the Targan's eyes as the man stared at them. Helio tossed in a credit chip and dealt himself into the pot examining his cards, his best hand all night. Borter raised and called, throwing in three cards, and the other two players called. "Six Targans," muttered Helio, putting forward the hand. The faces all around the dingy table twisted curiously at the word Targans.

As they stared at him, Helio stared back and then said, "I mean, six pairs." They threw in their cards.

"Too good for me," said one. The other agreed heavily, sighing. "Big day tomorrow, fellas," he muttered, excusing himself from the table.

"I'm clean," They picked up their money and made for the door, scuffing their chairs back on the bare floor, making a loud scraping noise doing so. As soon as they were up, Borter felt a wet kiss on the side of his face that made him reach for the Reggian blaster already loosened in its holster.

"Moz! What are you doing here?"

"...*fuh*, it's getting a little crowded in here," Helio guffawed. The Dillisome spoke to Borter loudly enough to draw his attention before Moz could answer.

"What?" Borter looked at her, slightly annoyed, through the alcoholic mist drifting through his brain.

"Earning the mad part of my name," she said, pushing in as the warning hairs on Borter's neck forced themselves stiffly erect. "Dad really did it this time - ordering me not to come here!" It was then that Borter fully regarded what Helio had seen. Moz was leaning over, her arms around Borter's neck, her back to the bar and the door.

"Uh . . . Borter?"

He looked into her eyes, met her eyes with his, clearing his throat, "It's getting a little crowded in here!" She looked hurt, feeling her attentions were - unappreciated. Her gaze dropped away.

Borter gasped as six big Targans circled the table, making no effort at all to hide their blasters as they did. A self – appointed leader gaped, about to speak, and as he did, he placed his right hand coolly on the butt of his blaster, still holstered at his side. Helio viewed the blasters, all hung on their right sides. Targan were all right-handed, he noted.

The leader stared down, his eyes glaring in the low light, and rasped menacingly, "Tell me about the black starship?"

"Uh ... Moz? It's getting a little crowded in here – " He spoke the line again, looking every bit as hurt as when she'd said it that morning at dawn.

Borter spoke as the Targan edged up. Nonchalant to the end, he smiled, staring again into her eyes, and quipped, "Say, uh . . . kid. Did you come in here – alone?"

He turned his smile into a self-mocking, one-sided grin that said he wanted, hope against hope, this would be some big misunderstanding and these six impossible looking fellows around them were just having a joke on some likely strangers. And, they would all laugh at it the next morning.

Borter's attention went to the Targan's hand, which still rested on his well-used blaster. "How did you get in here?" He demanded an answer.

Two of the Targans stepped forward, stepping heavily, drawing their blasters from beneath the forest green cloaks they all wore. The leader held them back, reaching out his left arm against their movement.

"You'd better tell me," he grinned coldly, leaning forward against the table. Borter and Helio had not been so close to a Targan since the battle at Nine on Marcellus the year before. "Or, you can tell them," he said, squeezing all the terror he could from his words, looking around at his men!

"Well," Borter grinned, leaning back on his chair, trying to look at ease, "in answer to your query, my friend —
"

The Targan cocked his head like a big mastiff confronting a curious bug at its feet. "We arrived two months ago, passengers on a tramp freighter. We took down a couple of pieces of prime farmland out near the Ords! Fine land!" The pilot shrugged, smiling, brows raised. "Thinking of settling, yourself?"

The Targan growled.

"No? Well, we don't know anything about black starships. We're just — these guys." Borter shrugged as they moved forward, all at the same instant.

The charge halted abruptly, the Targans diving for cover. Their leader fell to the floor, a playing card deeply embedded in his forehead.

"Borter," Moz whispered vehemently between clenched teeth, "Assuming that we survive this, and my father finds out that I'm here, I don't want you to lie for me. Understand?" Both dived for the floor.

Borter nodded, "I understand!" Wood from the overturned table near Helio's head blew apart and burned in scattering shards.

Another followed that, and then another. Smoke filled the bar, and it became hard to breathe. Borter fired with his setting at full. Half a room away, a table exploded. He could see nothing and didn't know whether he'd hit anything or not. Targans did not give themselves away by crying out when wounded. The fighting continued.

It looked bad for them. There was nowhere to go, no other door other than the one through which they'd entered. Other Targans guarded that. And, there were five of the first six between them. They'd have to do something.

The Targan sitting at the bar called out, waving to his men to hold their fire, "Ghost Pilot? Ghost Pilot! Surrender yourself, and your friends leave unharmed!"

Borter and Helio exchanged nervous glances. "Damn, Parnak! He's got us into it this time," Borter moaned. The smoke cleared a bit, and then more fire, again from the direction of the voice.

Borter hunkered down on the floor with Moz as a fusillade of blaster fire went overhead. Helio was off to one side, safe, unseen for the moment amid the wreckage of overturned tables and chairs and spilled cards. His own blaster was in his hand. He waited for a clear shot.

In front of him, something moved on the ceiling. It kept to the shadows, in its right hand, a blaster. The Dillisome knew it was no friend. He'd seen Targans run straight down steep escarpments on Marcellus. The blaster rose to fire.

Hardly any motion and no sound came as it pointed toward Borter and Moz.

From among the spilled cards, Helio lifted a face card. Good enough, he said as he hurled it at that sinister figure. The next instant, a blaster clattered to the floor, and the Targan made for cover as Borter bolted up and fired a shot that sent him crashing to the floor, the playing card still piercing his wrist.

Borter glared at his partner across the wreckage. "How do you do that?" He demanded through clenched teeth.

Helio merely shook his head. He shrugged off Borter's glare as another blast exploded the wood of a roofing strut nearby.

"Geez!" Borter cried, getting off another shot at a coming Targan.

Helio risked a quick shot at another but missed. "How do we get out of here?"

Borter shouted back, firing. "Should I make you a new door?" He shrugged. "Why not? Just tell me where you want it!" Borter stopped, grasping the idea in his words.

"Right there! No. Right!" Helio gestured at the rear wall of the bar just behind, "I meant over – there," he shouted, pointing.

"You don't have to yell," Borter snapped at him.

He glanced back and forth between the Reggian blaster and the wall. He turned the power indicator up to *illegal*. He fired, and a second wall became an exit.

From the moment he wrestled it away from the Reggian pirate, to whom it belonged – originally, the blaster had never let him down.

The man had tried to kill him with it, and Borter had taken it away from him; as a precaution, he said, "There's nothing like – leaving a deadly weapon in the hands of – someone or something that wants to kill you."

Then, he'd used a line Parnak swore would haunt him the rest of his days. "Right, just because you're good to eat, it's no reason to invite yourself to dinner!"

Stone from the wall burst outward into the dark alley. The three quickly followed it, Borter and Helio had been thrown out of many of the galaxy's worst drinking establishments; this was the first time they'd made their own door out! As they ran, they covered their escape, each turning to fire back into the dark room, until another cloaked figure stood in their way, facing into the bar from the newest hole to the alley.

Borter stopped for an instant, half in wonder, half in dread. He'd seen this before and did not ever want to see it again. He knew that stance, the bearing of the figure, and the particular cut of the cowl and cloak. Borter, Helio, and Moz ran on into the alley, cutting a path through debris.

As he came even with Helio, he shouted breathlessly to the Dillisome, "Did you see that?"

Helio nodded. "That was quick thinking, Borter," he gasped, keeping his pace. "I guess that's why you're the Ghost Pilot." Borter was running too fast to make the correction.

Borter, Helio, and Moz ran through the shadows of Cross Anchor's deserted streets until they thought they were safe, and then they split up. Borter and Moz toward the spaceport and Helio toward the park. Their clothing stuck to them as they silently went their separate ways. It had been hot that day and humid and had rained shortly before that night.

Cross Anchor's streets echoed hollowly with their footsteps as they walked along hand in hand, feeling safe. Borter hazarded a glance behind. There was no pursuit. But he didn't know why not. His experience with Marcellus had taught him not to take safety for granted just because he saw nothing. He paid attention to the warning hairs standing on the back of his neck, especially where Targans are concerned.

At times, the dim lights of the street fell across Moz's face, and Borter took to looking at her, seeing her youthful beauty for the first time. She was tall for a female, almost as tall as himself, and the curves of her body were supple, and her limbs were strong. Her face held him, though. Her lips were a light red, and she smiled, showing straight white teeth, her eyes forcing him to stammer and say foolish things when he could get the words out. Her hair was dark and fully framed her face, which then glistened with settling moisture in the air of night offered by Cross Anchor.

It reached her shoulders in length and there spread on them like a soft mantle. She, like Borter, feared pursuit and saved her questions about what he had seen as they'd raced down the alley, for a later time.

Moments before the eruption of violence inside the bar, Chibba's limo slid from the curb across the street, hissing forward as it picked up speed on the rain-slick pavement. His troops from AF6 landed on schedule. They had gone in and were in charge of their own situation. He was no longer needed. As an important person, he left his further service to The Helmsman and Medallas. He chuckled to himself as he was driven away at hearing the news of Kithron's destruction. He'd like to have seen the maddeningly smug looks on the faces of those Kithronese as their end came.

Odd, The Targans within the bar, which were no strangers to visitors from far planets and so-called itself and even went so far as to say, on their cocktail napkins, 'A PLACE IN SPACE, stopped short, for a second, burning hot as they had only rarely, before. The figure that filled the newly created exit to the alley, standing draped in darkness, was no mystery to them. For this effort, no one needed a leader. This was purely biological. Whoever it was stood silent, the tiny red dots on his shoulder blinking into the murky depths of the bar. Language had never been a barrier in these times, since those times, on far Marcellus.

In the instant the Targans waited the armored figure had a single sign for them, a sign that identified him and let them know as well as they knew themselves, who and what they faced.

At his left hip, a blue light began to appear, a blue light that stretched to the length of a man's arm. Someone spoke out to all around. It said the word, the last word for them all, its own name with a reverberation that shook each to his boots! They faced "Rand Sabbling – Companion Blade," his shoulder falcon announced.

One of the Targan spoke, bewildered, disbelieving, "Isn't he dead?"

17

Borter and Moz in the Ords

The roar of Soarer's engines paled as she swept low over The Ords. Borter and Moz her down a little beyond the Dann farm. Sound trailed off and waned completely as Borter taxied under the trees; wings tucked back. There was just enough room.

Borter taxied far enough to bring himself cross-corner and leave Soarer ready to fly facing out into the dese. There was nothing on the little freighter to reflect light. The new shell put on by Old Face was friction free, it absorbed nearly all light, including after burn. They were safe from sensors day and night.

The two came down the loading ramp aft into the remainder of the Ganempshan night. Borter's arm was around Moz's waist as much to hold her close as to guide her in the dark. Usually independent, this time, she did not seem to mind at all. In another hour or two, Helio would be there to pick them up. Until then, they were alone beneath her father's trees.

Borter took her in his arms and kissed her. Moz stood on her toes to reach up to him, throwing her arms around his neck. A very little bit of moonlight filtered through the thick, leafy covering branches overhead. They held each other close and kissed again.

Borter felt her against him, a softness here and there; she held herself against him for a long time.

Within the orchard's night canopy they felt obscured, anonymous, and safe. The night hid them and the dense trees. Borter wished that the night would never end, that he would never again hear of the galaxy beyond Ganempsha, but images of the battle in the bar haunted him, told him of things to come.

He peered into Moz's face into the dark sockets where he knew her eyes should be, he could not see them. For an instant he stared into all of space and saw planets he'd never reached, all hanging out there, beckoning him to come. He thought of Parnak, Helio, The Helmsman, and of Lord Soal himself.

Life in space was no longer for him. He thought never – again. Moz came back before him, resting in his arms. The other things in his mind disappeared for a time.

In the cooler night air, he felt himself beginning to sweat. They found a wide tree trunk and settled back against it. Moz tucked neatly against Borter's side, his arm around her shoulder. It was not long before they dozed.

The loud crack of a fallen branch woke them, both staring at their feet. The Reggian blaster already in his hand.

He searched the night for whatever made the noise. Moz, beside him, had also drawn her weapon. She was at Borter's back, scanning the trees behind them. There was nothing in the branches. Something breathed just a few meters away, something bigger than a Targan.

Borter stood side by side, then with Moz, blasters drawn, ready to fire, then there was nothing. Borter's ears strained into the darkness for anything, even the slightest sound.

After several moments, he relaxed. Moz looked at him, not sure what they had heard or whether or not they had really heard anything.

Borter resolved to stay awake and watch. Again, the air was still, and the orchard silent. He let Moz lie back against the tree and told her to sleep, that he'd wake her for a watch very soon. He'd nearly convinced himself that there was nothing to worry about, self – assured, whatever it was, had been too small to worry about, and, anyway, was gone. Maybe he'd walk over to Soarer and lower the ramp. It had a dim light, one not bright enough to attract attention from outside the trees.

The ramp let itself down with the slightest electric whir. Borter slowly looked around as it quieted, one hand on his powerful blaster, holstered, ready at his side. Nearby, Moz slept, breathing evenly like a child. There was nothing out there. The hairs were not standing up on the back of his neck. It was funny; he thought, the whole thing. He reached to switch on the light. He remembered vacantly to himself they'd stood up when the branch cracked or when he'd heard the animal breathing. It must have been something.

The entire area bleached white for a second, then returned to complete darkness. The light that flooded the area left Borter blinded temporarily. He heard Moz cry out and call his name. He took the blaster from its holster and, though he could see nothing, tried to cover the area in front of himself. Borter's night vision would not return. All sorts of bright colors flashed before him.

He called for Moz to come to him. She could not. Then, something wide and very wet licked his whole face. Borter stepped back and fell over. Again, that something licked his face and, as it did, breathed heavy warm air into his face, a breath that reminded him of a swamp at dawn. This stirred his memory. He could hear Moz laughing as the gigantic tongue slurped his face another time.

"Geez," he cried, putting away the blaster with one hand and pushing the large jowls that held the tongue away! "Geez, Moz! It's 5D!"

Getting to his feet, Borter felt his vision clear, and he found the ramp light he had been going for in the first place. At last, he eyed 5D suspiciously. "Who's brought you, boy?" He took a step toward Moz, who took joy in assessing him of the obvious - saying with some pleasure that the beast liked him.

For a second, he stopped, turned, and gazed at the panting beast. There was no mistake. Could it have been another of the same kind, he asked himself? No, this was the one and only. How could any other have found him in so large a galaxy? Lord Soal was dead, left that day at his own orders, beneath a red flag on Medallas.

5D could have teleported his old master from the place. Had he? Damn! If not one Marcellean, then it would be another. Borter had not liked being used the way he, Helio, and Soarer, had been during the last days of Marcellus.

About doing so again. Borter resolved to leave Ganempsha that day. Trouble was coming, and that meant only one thing,   Modallas. There would be no other reason for such a presence. He looked at Moz, then back at 5D.

Borter smiled with gritted teeth as if working to suppress anger. He was more surprised than angry, however. "This old boy means trouble," he said, jerking a thumb over one shoulder at the beast!

The next day, Helio arrived as planned. They crowded into the tiny cockpit with him. Moz sat on Borter's lap with her arms tightly around his neck. Borter, for his own part, took it all very seriously, looking forward out of the cockpit. Helio smiled at them like a Dutch uncle.

Borter told him about 5D. The blue man did not seem surprised. He made his point that he did not wish to serve another stint for The Hea. Helio chuckled. "You've not bothered with the morning's news?"

He turned to his partner, smiling. Borter, confused, they had not. From Helio's manner, he judged that something was very wrong.

"Kithron's been destroyed," said Helio, solemnly looking around the cockpit. Both Borter and Moz were astounded. The power that was Kithron held the Inner Galaxy in awe.

Kithronese culture had been the light of the galaxy. To think of it as gone, destroyed forever, was not possible. Moz closed her arms around Borter's neck more tightly. Borter feared that there was more Helio had not told them - and he was right.

18

Parnak in the Desert

It was at the moment they emerged from the ruins that Kith Ree turned to him and smiled again, that wonderful smile that seemed – to say everything. His coal dark eyes looked up at him for an instant then into the daylight bright sky toward the place where Suther Dann's farm lay beyond sight. And, from where hoppers would come across The Wastes to them.

Kith Ree's eyes brightened as he turned his elder, fragile child's face toward the open sky, waiting for the sound all of them knew must come and then the sight of that which must.

He could surely hear what made the sound they heard and Parnak with the wonderful senses, fed by his antennae did not.

Parnak strained, but nothing came. Kith Ree murmured that the others had been standing as he saw them for the entire time they had walked the corridors of the old ruins.

After some minutes, Kith Ree turned back toward the waiting Parnak and said, "The great attack force has landed in our desert, and your friends and those of The Heart come for you in their machines." Parnak turned to stare at the clone and was caught in the darkness of the little man's eyes.

In his travels, Parnak had become familiar with the most elusive Kithronese philosophies, primitive to ultra-modern.

Of those planets knowing the Sargon Clones and of their beliefs, many said they were the ones to see for personal peace.

Kith Ree stood before him smiling his knowing smile as he had since the moment they'd met. It was the identical smile all the others wore, respectful, happy without mockery. Like the rest of Kith Ree's manner, it bespoke wisdom, patience, and virtue.

The drooping whisps of a moustache and beard on an aged but nearly wrinkle free red face with the round, smooth forehead that sloped backward, gently toward the thinned and receding hairline left an impression of youth and wisdom at once with age and a fatherly patience and experience.

In his daily appearance, in the way all knew him, he dressed humbly, wearing a long flowing outer robe of common material and long trousers loosely fitting, protection against the heat of the Ords.

The clones wore the same beard and mustache, as they did clothing. They were identical, the same, clones not imitations.

Parnak thought he did look small. All were mustached and bearded, hair length, a few centimeters long. Facing into the winds blew the hairs back onto their smooth, high cheeks. Of them all, Kith Ree was merely the first. "We are clones, not obstacles!" He began. "Won't you come in?"

They had spoken of The Hea in those days Parnak had spent in The Wastes. Kith Ree said precious little of value. In The Ords, he said, there was no past. The sands took care of that. Everything, he said, was reduced by that and the heat. This, to know the history of The Ords, said the little man, was to know nothing.

The thought of an attack force on the planet chilled him, even in the burning light of Ganempsha's dual suns. The Helmsman was near, Parnak knew.

Without planetary defenses, the work would be quick, even for the most inept of Targans. Those who came for The Helmsman were not inept. They would be the very soul of speed and dispatch.

They stood near the other clones who waited in the sun as they traveled the empty corridors of The Ords. They seemed lost in studying the sky.

It was a thing Parnak had not seen before in his days with the clones and he meant to ask Kith Ree about it, thinking it some kind of exotic meditation. The clones stood in a relaxed line beside the journalist seeming not to take ken of him at all. Others began gathering behind them swelling their ranks. Parnak had never seen all the clones together before. He knew their numbers to be several hundred. They surrounded him now, those within easy earshot numbering about twenty-five.

"Kith Ree?" Parnak turned to face the clone who was the leader. He was surprised to hear all those who heard him answer softly in unison," Yes?"

For a moment there was silence as Parnak looked from identical face to identical face for the one that belonged to Kith Ree. To the delight of the clones around him, he could not pick him out. They stared back at him gently, befitting in a manner a kindly old uncle viewing a beloved but confused child. Parnak felt the pa.

"There is no Kith Ree," said one.

"There may be no Kith Ree," another said.

"We are all Kith Ree," yet another clone added.

Parnak was staggered as he looked around. His wonderful antennae could not find a clone he thought was Kith Ree, the one he thought he knew so well.

Finally, one of them moved forward smiling, gently taking Parnak's arm and leading him to a spot a little ways from the others.

"We are, and we are not Kith Ree," said the clone, "we are not the Kith Ree you expected to find, I think."

Parnak shook his head at the sudden madness in his ears, "Are you the Kith Ree I met when I came here?"

The old clone chuckled playfully, his thin whiskers blowing in the wind, his thin lips still held together despite the laugh he gave. The wrinkled child's face turned upward to look at him and in another moment spoke more.

"When you came," he began slowly, trying to let Parnak understand little by little, "you picked him who you sensed was the single Kith Ree. We only wished to comply with your wishes, to make you happy."

The clone paused, "There is no one, Kith Ree," he added flatly. "There is only one – way. We are here to point the way only!"

That Kith Ree smiled another time trying to ease Parnak's mind. "Yours is a mind that craves facts. Here in the wastes, there are no facts that are not worn away by The Ord winds and their blowing sands. We cannot deny it. This will not change!"

He paused again. But only before adding more, "There was a Kith Ree. We are all from his mold, exactly as he was for all time!"

"If it is our history you desire, I can give that to you — it is worth little. It will take no time at all." The little man stepped backward as if needing more room to speak.

"In our beginning, there were none of us, except, of course, the first Kith Ree." Parnak found a flat stone nearby on which to sit. From there he watched and listened as the simple history, the facts of their existence, were placed before him, to grasp or not.

"It was the time of his passing, and there were none to carry — on. There had been a great war on the planet, and everything, or nearly everything, was dead. Kith Ree was the last of his kind. For a long time he lived alone, finally wandering into The Ords, expecting here, to find the end of his life. That was not far from what actually happened!"

At his side, Parnak's little recorder faithfully took in every word for — posterity as he sat. It had been his closest ally throughout his whole professional life; to forget it at this point would have — been unforgivable.

The little clone sighed wistfully as he went along, continuing that which, but for the insectoid's lack of understanding, he would have called a legend rather than a history. That did not matter. What would happen would happen as it was meant to happen, as they thought.

"It was at that time the Ancients were here." The sound of the word Ancients moved something in Parnak. He'd heard of them before, Ancient Ones. Old Ones, they were the same everywhere. He constantly walked in the footsteps of the old Marcelleans, and he listened with renewed interest to the clone's tale. Parnak began to have the same warning itch as had Borter.

"You are disturbed by this revelation? That you have mistaken many of us for only one, Kith Ree?" The clone gestured to the many others gathered not far off at that moment, waiting for something from the sky.

"Don't trust your mind. Don't trust anything! It is when we are drawn to someone, such as yourself, that it matters. And then, what does it matter?"

Parnak sat very still for a minute, expecting more. No more came.

He thought to himself, wondering, really, at this new being he had suddenly discovered. Kith Ree had a single mentality. He'd expected similarity, but not this.

The present Kith Ree went on. "It does not mean any-thing. We are all Sargon." *To this mystery, he added, Sargon was their designation from the Ancients, perplexing Parnak only a little more.*

"Then," Parnak asked," your mission here is to spread the message of your perfect peace, the peace for which you are known in this world?"

This set the little man laughing, again his expression a so of the mask, his thin lips stretched wide in a doting smile, etching the deep wrinkles of his face into crow's feet and sudden age around watery eyes. The clone, in laughter, seemed to Parnak a scolding for a well – liked, but poor student.

"No, my friend," Kith Ree went on, getting to his feet, "Our mission was defined long ago by the Ancient Ones. I'm afraid you've missed the point.

Peace, indeed, a mission - not to be wasted on those who will not listen? No, friend Parnak, our peace is not for them. It is for us."

Kith Ree went on, hardly looking at the journalist, pacing like some great professor, like any found at any of the universities that dotted the galaxy, avoiding his gaze in order to go on musing about some difficult problem.

"The clone struck on, "Our mission is not peace. It is to point the way. – nothing else. It is most important when we are drawn to someone, not someone to us!"

"We are what we are and nothing else. You took the others and me for one single Kith Ree, so we became what you wanted. We became your truth, but this truth is not our truth. Our purpose is to remain here as the old ones commanded – our own heredity demands it. Who would teach among the ungrateful?"

"We are all and none. We are that copy of a copy, replicas, images of the image. To learn, the grateful - must come here."

Kith Ree looked at him as if requiring an answer, and Parnak merely shrugged. Either he took this as the answer or, at least, he didn't let it bother him. Kith Ree went on.

Parnak nodded silently as Kith Ree chanced a second look.

"We reject that we are Sargon, and we reject that we are not."

He went on importantly, pacing, gesturing into the air making emphasis with an index finger. "We are what we are, we do not know this. We reject the notion that anything may be known. This we reject as we reject everything else. "Now," he said turning his attention to the horizon, "my other selves and I await the arrival of the dark starship."

"Why?" Parnak's question buzzed from the translator.

Kith Ree turned to him, leaning close, he whispered, "It is for us to point the way!"

Only a few more moments before three small shapes came into view, Parnak stood with the clones watching the sky. They were still very far away as he saw them first, mere specks growing larger as they came. Borter was recognizable in his center position as he led them on, Helio was to his right as always, and their new third was Moz. He did not know her as quickly. They came in at once, retro-ing, flaring back to lose speed nearing the sand.

Borter was the first to jump from his hopper. No longer protected by his shaded canopy, he was exposed to the strong daylight of The Wastes. He raised his hand to cover his eyes from the sudden intensity he found and the occasional sand-filled gust of desert wind. The now wisely worn blaster was again at his side, and those of Helio and Moz were also evident as they emerged from their small flyers.

Even among the normally silent clones, There was a noticeable hush in the desert as the blue man came into view. Parnak, sensing this, raised his recorder into position for any posterity that might be afforded. As a body, all the clones moved toward the blue man from Dillisome.

So intent was Parnak on recording the scene he did not miss the presence of the Kith Ree from his side. In the moments before the actual landing of the three hoppers, he'd become more used to the idea of having many Kith Ree's around him, but the sudden loss, even so temporary a loss, a new anchor on nothing to hold wouldn't hu. They had all gone at once to Helio.

Seeing there was nothing to fear whatever from the group of identical, old clones, Borter and Moz worked their way around the edge of the benign mob toward Parnak who out of habit, still, held his recorder high catching the scene for later galactic broadcast. Borter wore an amused smirk on his face as he approached Parnak.

Parnak said nothing, not even so much as to acknowledge their presence.

Moz spoke first, knowing there was no danger as the clones took Helio's hands and half bowed in turn as each presented himself to the Dillisome,

"What's this, Parnak? What have you done? I've never seen them so worked up!" A look of amazement and concern took her face as she questioned Parnak searching for a cause of this new wonder.

Helio smiled brightly as each of the clones came before him and bowed, clasping his hands as if he were some long-lost friend. Through all of it, he remained cordial, speaking a word or two to each one forgetting for the moment his friends of longer standing watched from the edges of the loose crowd, most amused.

Moz, continuing to wear a confused expression, remained with Borter and Parnak near the gathering around Helio.

Parnak, engrossed in the scene still unfolding - a short distance in front of him, said nothing. He'd not heard Moz's question, and she had not cared to repeat It. There would be time for questions and answers later.

Several of the clones now spoke to Helio at greater length. They seemed very happy to see him, even excited. Helio himself did not seem to mind, and he didn't glance toward his friends for direction.

The clones beamed up at the taller blue man and nodded heads forward and backward in wise, knowing manners, hardly noticing anything else existed around them.

Finally, Helio was led away toward every hospitality the ruins had to offer. It would be some minutes before one of the red clones would return to Parnak, Borter, or Moz to guide them to a place where they could find more comfort. In that time, Borter's smirking grin would fade, and Moz would still have her question unanswered.

Parnak stared down into the recorder's playback, engrossed in the repeating scene, and said nothing.

They awaited a guide, and they were unsure if anyone would return for them. The Ord ruins were lit as they had not been before in anyone's memory. And, they had been in The Ords a long, long time!

A festive air took the old place. Colored lights sprang up everywhere, their sources unseen by the eye. They were so subtly hidden that even the sensitive Parnak had not noticed them. Their guide came and ushered them inside.

The whole place had come alive, it seemed, because of Helio's arrival, soft music from mysterious flutes took the air, as dancers took the floor of the main hall. Borter observed that they were just the same old clones he'd seen before.

They were not as pleasing to the eye as other dancing clones he'd seen in other parts of the galaxy, but he once again observed dryly; you had to consider where you were and make allowances!

In that time, Borter's smirking grin would fade, and Parnak would, at length, turn his recorder off. Moz would still have no answer to her question put forth to Parnak.

He would speak to it, making what explanation he could, of the events just seen. It made better sense to have your face nowhere, remain anonymous, on camera and say nothing, until something did, make sense.

It was simple economics, he thought. You could starve long before anything in the galaxy had the chance of the most minute glimmer of making anything remotely sensible.

Parnak's work always had Parnak in it.

When he was ready, Borter circled the celebration with Moz at his side. In the middle of it all was Helio, looking very happy, his face smiling out in all directions at everyone. Parnak stood nearby with one of his Kith Rees. If Helio enjoyed himself, he decided, there was no harm.

The pay was not closed to others, but it was not his own, Borter preferred to remain a little distant.

The celebration was given in honor of Helio, something Parnak had quickly told them as they'd been invited in. The clones had been too thick around Helio to allow much else.

Borter did not think much about it. But, Parnak considered it significant the clones had known the men who flew the dark ship.

His present, Kith Ree, explained that it had come in a dream one night, not long before. All of them had the dream the dark starship of their most ancient legend was about to appear.

The legend had not made much sense to Parnak when he'd first heard it. That, of course, had been long before as he'd prepared to write his most definitive and exhaustive work of the mythology and legends of the stars, aptly titled The Mythology And Legends Of The Stars. Borter yawned when he heard the title.

The compendium had netted Parnak a tidy sum already on the tax-free planets — and he could touch none of it.

The poor verse, he recalled, having nearly excluded the scrap of paper it was written in from his work and that, a misfortune in the writing business, commonly labeled carelessness, led to its eventual inclusion.

So short was it, the original paper on which it was written escaped his usual editorial purge of the larger manuscript and was delivered en mass with everything else to his publisher and was in print before he could do anything about it.

Had its inclusion been a mere accident? Parnak did not know for sure. It sometimes crossed his mind nothing that happened to him had ever been by accident.

His years on Marcellus, his many years there, showed much in his life, controlled by The Hea. Now, as then, a familiar pattern began to emerge, a plan, a purpose to the things he did.

It was a big galaxy to suppose the things that connected events in far – flung places and things he'd seen in them were coincidence, and he was too sophisticated to believe in fate.

This he learned in his many years on Marcellus, his many years, he often thought to himself, growing old, viewing himself in a mirror, somewhere, in some third-class planetary hotel which, then, served him as a base had become known to him.

Yes, Parnak was old, very, very old. The actual truth of that would astound his closest friends Helio and even the often-smug Borter.

As the strange celebration went on, far into the dese night, a drone hung its mechanical eye at about shoulder height, taking in everything. It moved silently following the night's action, sliding smoothly from place to place just outside the lights.

For a while, it followed Borter and Moz as they casually edged their way around, listening as best it could in the din to all they said to each other and faithfully transmitting that and their images back to the Targan commander of AF6, Commander Judd, and from there to Chibba the Spy.

19

Kees

Borter and Moz awoke shivering in the early morning of the Ords. One of Ganempsha's suns had just risen above the horizon. Borter rose, loosening himself from Moz's embrace despite its warmth, shaking himself out as a sudden chill took him. They'd slept in an isolated part of the ruins, having wandered there in the late hours of the dese night, tired after a long flight and a longer night to get there. They'd seen nothing more of Parnak and Helio since the beginning of the celebration.

Moz rose stiffly and stretched herself, her arms skyward, trying to capture the meager warmth generated by the yet lone, risen sun. Her small hands curled into fists that tensed, and seemed to shake at the sky as she yawned drowsiness away.

The horizon was an early morning blue in which he saw nothing except its color. Above that, the sky clouded, first in a so of dull haze, then brighter, into billowing fair-weather clouds that reminded him of Spring on Magnus and good flying. Borter stared out far into the great desert around them.

Moz looked at him and smiled weakly, the early morning showing a little in her young face. She'd never loved anyone as she did Borter. He was independent, with nothing to hold him. She loved that.

Borter smiled as he returned her look. There was the smell of food in the air, and it flooded their senses; both turned toward it as if the odor had triggered some automatic reflex. It could only have been breakfast.

"Food," Borter exclaimed. He said it proudly as if there could be found no more valuable thing in the galaxy. It was as if he discovered a whole mountain of trillenite, that singular substance that rendered anything it coated friction-free. In fact, it was that selfsame substance with which Old Face had coated Soarer. However, it was so rare that Borter wouldn't have recognized it had he stepped on it, and he often did.

"We'll have to leave the planet today," Borter said with authority. "Ganempsha is no longer safe for any of us."

Moz looked at her feet as they began moving toward the smell of breakfast. "You aren't even going to stay for food?"

"No," he said, "It will be too late then!"

Moz looked at him curiously as if a Thee Starr concert in this, the Ords, would solve everything. She looked up innocently at Borter, her eyes wide. The smile had left her face for the moment.

"Not even Thee Starr can stop this. Everyone will die," he said sternly, "I want you to come with me." Finally, he added. "We can find another planet, begin another life together!"

20

Judd and Chibba

Chibba turned from the sensor screen and smiled coldly at the commander of AF6.

"I have an operative at Suther Dann's farm capable of dealing with our problem." Judd nodded toward the screen, eyeing Chibba for his reaction.

"Aren't these the same ones who shot their way out of that miserable establishment in Cross Anchor?" Judd placed it even more coldly as Chibba looked down at him at his command console at the very center of his attack force position. They were, yet, kilometers distant from the Ord ruins from which their spy, a drone remote, reported on the Sargon clones and their guests. A trace of disbelief crossed his face.

"The troops for that operation, come directly from Medallas, had help in escaping the Marcellean." The hint of sarcasm became more marked on the commander's face as he watched Chibba squirm. However, he hadn't gained the position he enjoyed by squirming at the questions of others. He caught himself and went on.

The agent I have in mind is well suited to this purpose, even for a Targan." A leering smile came to his face to counter that of the commander. "Call in your remote,"

Chibba told him quietly, showing displeasure as he did so, "we will have no more need for it. My operative is already on the trail of this Ghost Pilot!"

The commander shook his head from side to side in disbelief at the same time chuckling "So - the troopers from Medallas are no longer good enough for you?" His face wore a smirk as he looked at Chibba.

"They prefer the metal corridors of Medallas, now, to the forests of home," said Chibba. "And, as you know, my friend, we must have this Ghost Pilot before The Helmsman."

The glances between the two became more knowing, more conspiratorial as they went on. Both Targans swept the room for casual eavesdroppers, but the place was empty to their cat-like forest senses. Speak as they just had, would bring a swift and sure death if overheard. The mood between the two became more careful.

"The Helmsman borders madness in this questing after the pilot," claimed Judd, "He's no more than a freighter pilot, a carrier of merchandise around the galaxy!"

"However, The Helmsman wants him - or them," Chibba corrected casually closing his eyes, making a dainty affair of getting it right. "And, if The Helmsman wants it. So do we! He's the connection to the Marcellean Hea. Their starship. Finding out is a risk, but a risk worth taking if it leads us to The Hea!"

"Maybe," Judd did not accept reasoning, "but I don't think so. This is a blind chase," he spoke solemnly. "The Helmsman must be mad to search after such an insignificant victory."

Judd paused and looked at Chibba, who stood before him, "These thousand years of struggle have been too long for him. The inevitable has come to pass!" He shook his head again, not wanting to believe what he believed. "We will not take The Hea here, nor shall our master! This foul little planet will yield us nothing unless it is our own deaths." Kees grunted and smiled broadly. Life is not so much that I would live it out beneath a madman. You are too good a leader yourself to be any different! Judd smiled to himself, staring at the floor. "The Helmsman is mad. For that reason, I have Medallas for us. Put our loyal troops on moment's notice. Judd rose to his feet, facing his partner! "Then, the pilot will be asked quickly," taking Judd's hand, "to accept the new deal."

"Yes," he answered, "there will be no interference from my agents."

Chibba turned quickly and said nothing else as he walked toward the bunker door.

"We have to be ready. And, when we strike, it will be quick!"

"They are ready, Chibba."

21

Breakfast with The Clones

Borter sat near Helio among the gathered clones. Moz was near him and Parnak, a bit distant, with another of the kindly Kith Rees. Low chatter abounded during the early morning breakfast as the clones talked among themselves excitedly and nodded or looked in Helio's direction. It had been a late night and Borter was feeling it.

Disinterested, he could not understand the sustained excitement of the clones. They were older than him, shouldn't they be more tired?

Breakfast, such as it was, was served from a common pot brought 'round behind everyone and served to each in turn from the left side as was considered proper among the Sargons.

The Pilot recognized in the mixture several vegetables, cruelly mashed into a kind of mush, to be ladled out to each from the left as was deemed proper by the clones, onto a flat, hard bread given out with the gruel, but from the right by another clone. Like it or not, he took a helping, saying thanks to the Kith Ree of that moment, who was, of course, the one with the pot - on his left.

Later, Parnak would explain to him what he'd been told by one of the clones, that all realities are the same.

And, having said that, would explain why all the clones were identical, meaning, all Kith Ree's were the same, or nil.

It didn't matter which one you talked to; they all knew the same things and, given the same set of circumstances and the same conversation, would all say the identical thing in return. Mostly, they were glad for any company because talking to someone who already knew what you knew, the total knowledge of the Sargon Clones was boring to the point of madness.

In fact, so hungry were they for outside contact that most had already taken a turn at conversation with Parnak, before he realized the difference.

In the end, his then-present, Kith Ree, had felt obliged to set him straight. That had been just as Borter, Helio, and Moz had been landing their hoppers at the ruins.

Helio looked straight at Borter and told him directly to head off any argument with a Kith Ree. He spoke without emotion, expecting a negative response, but Borter seemed all right with his co-pilot's decision.

"Borter, I'm going to be staying on here for a while!"

Helio smiled tipping his head playfully, boyish, his head going side to side. He said to the pilot, "You go if you want. I'll be here when you decide to come back. I've much to learn of this place!"

That was all he said before he turned and walked back to the delegation of clones, all of them exactly the same Kith Ree in every movement.

Borter was about to say something but didn't, knowing he would not understand the answer. He was stunned, to say the least. This was the first time Helio said anything about going out on his own, ever. He shrugged, disbelieving.

He'd spent time trying to talk Moz into leaving the planet, too, and found her unmoved.

He'd explained that Soarer was capable of breaking the blockade with ease. He told her how well-armed the ship was and that the weapons themselves came from the Techno-Dwarves of Marcellus.

"Marcellus, you know - the Old Ones?" There was no answer. Borter croaked out, "No?" His throat had gone dry.

Moz seemed to look at him differently after that. Her smile seemed to radiate more deeply from within as she looked at him. Borter tensed, not knowing what exactly he should do.

Moz was putting the pieces of the old planetary legend together. She sold out the pieces of it. Most she'd not heard since childhood. For a while, at least, his fate was cast with theirs, the Children of the Planet of The Hea.

Parnak also stayed on, surprised as any by the turn of events in the desert.

22

Ganampshan Skies – Heroes Need Not Apply

Kees was the last of them, and when he was gone, there'd be no more. He watched that day as they had taken to the air. Borter and his daughter had only just returned from The Wastes when they were, again, off to work. Wanting Moz to rest before she went up with Borter, he'd offered him the day off or, at least, time to rest.

That was not the norm on any of the farms during the growing season; a flyer did not expect nor did he receive any favor because of a late night out or, case at hand all night, even if the Magnean had said okay. Moz refused and returned to her hopper with Borter. Her father's one consolation was that she flew with him. He'd never seen a few better pilots.

A second bit of fortune crossed his mind as he watched them leave - Kees hid as far from the young pair as the boundaries of the farm would allow.

Kees landed his hopper alone in a remote section of the farm. The area had been dusted the day before and there was no one around to see him. Above, the sky was a clear, pale blue. Beyond, still a little way, stretched the formidable Ord Dese.

His cold thoughts ran to all four adventurers from the farm if you included Moz as a partner with Borter. Helio and Parnak. Kees did.

As he went about the task at hand, he mulled over the failed attempt on the flyers at the bar in Cross Anchor. His points had slipped with Chibba because of that. It was bad for Chibba with The Helmsman, too. This time, in the sky, there would be no Marcellean intervention. Targan was not accustomed to setbacks. They were a breed apart, different from the rest. Generations of their ancestors had thrived and honed their skills aboard Modallas. Their hunger was no longer tied to the ancestral roots of Marcellus' forests. Theirs was Modallas.

In the forests, they'd hungered for the destruction of everything Marcellean. That was a biological heritage born of the planet. That born of Modallas is the conquest of the galaxy.

To the left strut of the little hopper, he attached a long straight tube of grey metal. At the forward end there was a cone of about six centimeters from base to point. The base itself was about four centimeters wider than the grey tube. Which had a diameter of about two centimeters. At the rear edge of the tube was attached a six by six by four, box of identical color connected to the fuselage by a thick, flexible black cable. He would do the same for the right side after finishing the strut.

Kees looked old as he went about his labors, older than either Borter or Helio and certainly more so than the eternally youthful Parnak. His physical condition could be described as hard, his face leathery. His manner was all business moving around the little flyer with a fluid grace that would have awed a dancer.

His hands were powerful, but quick, and fingers showed exacting practice as he fixed the tubes. The arms were long enough, not too long. Thick hair fell in a single lock across his grim forehead as he bent to his work. It appeared slightly like a pelt, long, piled on top a bit and cut neatly around his ears.

Modallian instrumentation installed that morning mottled the light in the now crowded cockpit. Information flooded a tiny computer that presided over it. Kees' targets had been detected and put under surveillance earlier. There would be no repeat of the battle in the bar. Their time in life grew short.

The beast was once again on Modallas itself. The dead were found everywhere. Rumors and stories were rampant. It was impossible to tell one from the other. Panic flooded the air. The Helmsman raged at Chibba. He had in turn blamed Kees, raging at him, though none of it was his fault.

The Targan knew fear well enough when he smelled it, and this was secondhand fear, The Helmsman's. Here was something he was afraid of, terrified by, this. His wingmen had died searching for it in the orchards the night before. He'd known what had killed them but said nothing. There was little he could have done.

His first task on Suther Dann's farm was the destruction of the Ghost Pilot. Doing anything would have given him away.

Finally, Kees drew himself up straight and stepped back to view his work. There were no armed hoppers on the farm. None were allowed. His plan counted on that. This is one hopper, and he would not return to Suther Dann.

He would never take the Ghost Pilot that he knew on his black ship. In a slower, unarmed crop duster, it would be different.

Modallas' vast intelligence network had been all his that morning. Borter and Helio had been pinpointed in the desert, along with Dann's daughter in the ruins.

The grey rods and cones beam of the new pulsars stared back at him as he gauged the precision with which he'd aligned them. These twins would be terrible enough to sweep Ghost Pilot from the skies once and for all.

They would make quick work of all three hoppers over the desert. The two pilots, the journalist from Jillian and Suther Dann's girl. He would have to destroy them all in one feld swoop to be sure he got the one who was truly the Pilot. He regretted only the necessity of her death.

Targan had wanted her for himself. She would have been formidable even against the women of the Targan forests, he thought. Her ways might have seemed mad to those of her planet but not to him. It was too bad she'd not live out the day.

Kees climbed aboard, settling himself in the single seat. A screen came to life on the control console, and the computer's crisp, dry voice sounded in his ears, speaking pure Modallian, a language now dear to Kees and the other Targans calling Modallas home, more so than the guttural, grunting Knruul that was the tongue of the forest.

The savagery that existed there seemed distant, even to those who could claim no more than a few generations aboard the artificial, cylindrical world. Except for Kees' leathery appearance and his stoic manner, one seeing him in the orchard preparing for takeoff, in this newly weaponized hopper would have found him quite civilized. That is, excepting knowledge of his mission.

The hopper's turbine whined, and it left the ground quickly above the trees of Suther Dann's orchard. The computer began to track two hoppers flying abreast, coming toward the farm from deep in The Wastes. Information from Modallas confirmed the track, but there could be no others. Kees' hopper went for all the altitude it could gain. He would swoop in from behind them without mercy. It would be swift!

It was midmorning before Borter and Moz lifted off their tiny flyers from the desert floor. The third hopper remained there in the ruins. If Parnak and Helio decided to return to the farm, they would be able to do so at any time. However, from the look in Helio's eyes, he does not seem to be back soon.

The sky was clear. Any clouds that had been there had long since burned off. Borter liked the clouds because they gave the sky a fairy tale effect. An open sky held no secrets or surprises for a good flyer. As a child, Borter enjoyed all the tales of sky-borne castles and lands of giants hiding treasure he could. In the sky, there were many such adventures.

Moz flew as before on his left, banking with him as if they flew only one hopper. Borter pulled back on his stick and pushed his throttle to maximum, climbing to the limit of the little craft's ability. Ganempsha stretched beneath them, a pale red.

They chatted ship to ship, thinking they were alone with their shared thoughts. Borter thought of settling down. The life of a flyer was difficult at best, and in the company he lived, it went from marginal to short in terms of quality. Moz had not spoken it, but she thought of him as running her father's farm someday.

They talked of things, avoiding the present unpleasantness surrounding the planet. Modallas and The Helmsman were far away for a few moments and did not figure at all in the plans they made with each other. They flew toward a sun as red as the desert itself. A good portion of the horizon was available to their eyes. The planet stretched out the entire width of a cockpit. They still had far to go.

Borter would finish his contract with Parnak. If Helio, his friend, could stay on the planet, so could he. And there was Moz.

Ganempsha's sun lowered in the sky, twin orbs forever, each in the other's grasp. The way it should be, Borter thought.

They returned from the Ord Ruins. He was willing to chance it that one of the returnees was the Ghost Pilot. Two flyers would be one-third fewer problems than three. The armed hopper descended slowly, waiting for the proper angle to take the two close-flying hoppers under fire.

The pulsars could track and destroy targets through the onboard computer. Kees could sit back and watch a turkey shoot. If one flyer should happen to survive, he could kick in his afterburner and deal with it personally. The added boost was also a compliment to Modallas. With it, he could far outrun his targets, even if he had to reach sub – orbit for rescue.

The two flyers were quickly in the target window, and the twin pulsars opened fire with telling accuracy. One of the hoppers exploded into flames instantly, trailing thick black smoke and debris down to the desert floor. The second limped away, trailing smoke and flame from its own exploded fuel pod, one side ravaged by the explosion of the other ship, and a pulsar hit from above. It veered sharply back into the open desert. Its attitude controls shot up and useless, letting its list to the right, heavily.

The hopper spun down toward the desert sands. Kees followed at a more respectful distance, waiting for the helpless flyer to ram into the ground and finish itself.

It would not last much longer. The little flyer was in its death throes. Kees wondered what was on the pilot's mind at that point. He would never know.

It clipped the top of a sand dune, cutting a crescent-shaped gap and sending a plume of sand high into the air on each side before it continued to the next and the next after. Kees shot overhead, amazed at the strength built into the cockpit of the crop duster as its skids, engines, and everything else on its exterior sprayed outward, leaving only the ball – shaped pod itself.

As Kees overflew, the hopper came to a rolling stop near the forced plain of The Ords itself. Planning to come back and destroy the downed craft, he turned back. Sweeping into the turn, he saw a figure stumble onto the sand from the pod. It lay on the sand, unmoving, waiting for him.

Hardly fifty meters above the plain, Kees began his strafing run, which meant to kill that survivor. Nearing his victim, he pressed the fire button rigged to his control stick. The pulsars fired, smashing powerful energy into the sand and driving on toward the pilot.

There was a quick motion on the sand. Kees was not sure that he'd seen anything until the first round of blaster fire smacked into the windshield, throwing a spray of glass into the cockpit.

He covered his eyes and veered away, overshooting his target.

Shoving the throttle forward roughly, trying to attack altitude, then getting it, he dived toward the ground at a steeper angle than before.

The pilot was running lamely toward the dunes the hopper grazed as it had crashed. The figure turned quickly, bracing a blaster on the raised crook of one arm, firing at the oncoming hopper.

The half-chance, half-skill, pot–shot sheared Kees' lateral controls. Before he knew it, the helpless craft shot spaceward, its pilot grappling with shattered controls.

Borter looked on with amazement as Kees' ship rocketed away, trailing the faintest wisps of smoke behind it. He lowered the blaster that had served him so well at that moment and in times before. It dangled loosely in one hand at his side, his fingers numb to it, and he let it stay there. He felt more tired than he'd been his whole life, heavy beyond sleep, battered and bruised, but alive. Borter agreed with the little voice in his head that he was hard to kill. No voice said the same for Moz!

Borter sank to his knees and then lay on the ground. His injuries, great and small, gathered on him, forcing him down. He lost consciousness with a roar in his ears, a roar that turned into the sound of hoof beats. Bearing down on him hard.

23

Quantum Rejected

Quantum choked back tears, the first ever in her brief life. The receiving borgs had made it plain, though gently so, that she would not be used among the chosen. Her implanted knowledge told her only that she should return to space. A fact that would take a few minutes as she returned to both would suddenly overjoy her.

As she winded her way through the narrow streets of Cross Anchor, more of her implanted knowledge awakened, but no more than it was time for, as her makers had intended. It was true, she enjoyed the full flower of young womanhood, her firm, roundly curved form swung attractively though the busy streets like the child she yet was.

She wiped her face with the back of her hand and sniffed loudly, walking on. There was little in her mind save a sorrow that her primary purpose had been scrubbed. Targans were unknown, Modallas, or the turmoil that swept the galaxy. Many watched her appreciatively. So did the following Targans.

Were they not Targans of the planet Marcellus? They were the best of that race in the vast forests, and were, in some cases, many, in fact, well educated.

They did not think of it for too long. There was the mission.

The female android was leading them to the Ghost Pilot, the one who had eluded their master for so long. It would be worth it for them to go into trouble by either capturing or killing that one.

The Targan's first impression of androids had been one of amazement. One could say astonishment at the perfection of those androids who worked the city. Aboard Modallas, it was they who did that kind of work, but in the streets of Parnel, they saw these perfect beings conducting ordinary tasks instead of themselves. There, a sort of chord sounded in their mind as they realized they, to The Helmsman, were the same as the race of androids to the masters of Parnel.

However, they were still Targan, forest creatures, forest men, if only half – savage or half – civilized.

It would be worth it to them to go to the trouble of either capturing or killing that one. They did not think of it for too long. There was the mission. This female android led them to the Ghost Pilot, the one who had eluded The Helmsman for so long.

The streets were choked with off-worlders and working androids; Targans did not stand out particularly. They wore loose trousers of faded khaki; loose shirts were black, and night cloaks were kept elsewhere, safe. At their side, each wore a powerful blaster of Modallian design. There were two. Quantum did not notice.

Parnak rarely stayed behind on any voyage of Soarer. Today was different.

As Quantum turned the corner toward the Odeon, a door slid open, and a slender arm reached out, whisking her sideways. Within, it was near dark as Parnak put a finger to his lips, demanding silence as she was about to scream. The door slid shut, quiet, unnoticed, seconds before the Targans turned the corner onto their street.

Inside, it was dark within as Parnak put a finger to his lips, demanding silence as she was about to scream, before the Targans turned the corner onto the street.

So skilled were they at tracking, they did not waste time, at a glance, the knowledge already between them. She was gone!

The street was a grey, short, with high sides. The area was not one of the better cities and the Odeon was sided by a multiple dwelling from which lines of laundry were hung to the top floors. It was difficult even to see the sky. They moved like forest cats.

Parnak watched as the first one faced, then the other came to the windows, and then left each with that silent, hunting animal grace possessed only by the savage humanoids of the Targan Forests. Quantum had calmed as she recognized him. And, he released his tight grip. She trembled silently until her fear passed.

There was a hoarse scream and commotion in the building across the alley. Parnak knew what had happened and wasted no time in seeing them both to the deep, safer recesses of the old theater. The Targan crawled through the open windows only to face enraged tenants instead of Quantum.

City police were on their way.

"I have two seats for us in the *orchestra*!"

24

Sandriders Rescue Borter

He rose awkwardly to his feet some distance from the wreckage of his hopper. It lay crushed, its windscreen broken, electronics torn and burned.

He staggered a few more steps from it and fell to the ground, dazed and sick in the pit of his stomach. As he did, he saw them coming across The Ords' sands toward him. Sandriders. His ears rang as badly as his head.

Everyone perceived them as miserable. Their mounts were large for the desert. No one knew their origin; they were just there.

The large Sredirs hooves were broad, ideal for the sands of The Wastes. The riders themselves looked terrible, dirty, sweaty from the desert, worn uniforms so long in disrepair that they were barely recognizable as such. Each carried a long lance. Their points are glinting brightly in the dual suns of the planet.

The column rode double file, two by two, as they reached him, calvary style. A forward trooper held an unreadable pennant on the post, though they hardly put in a regular military appearance. It was quite plain to him that it was the only appearance they were able to present. They dismounted as he got to his feet. Had he needed it, his blaster was still on the ground. They were a part of a planetary legend, Suther Dann told him.

25

Suther Dan talks to Borter

"Sandriders are a myth among the people of this world. In days past, they were especially endeared to our young as protectors. In recent years, our children seem dissatisfied.

They believe they have been forgotten; they have fallen into disfavor. I can't say that thought has not crossed my mind. The Children of The Heart, the children of this legend, want more.

They were taught that the Sandriders would someday defend them and rescue them from great evil. These desert men and their Sredirs are all that have come, all that has ever been, a ragged lot hanging on the outskirts of town or in other abandoned districts.

In the old days, they were a force to be reckoned with, but I don't see it now. If so, no more.

It has been too long, too many years in The Ords. Our children ridicule them, shout insults, and throw stones at them.

That Sandriders would appear one day, a day of ultimate doom riding against some great evil — an unknown force to come, is only a myth, a story, only a legend.

They live on handouts. They go into The Ords. They come back. They are not what they were, if anything."

The crusty, disheveled NCO, a sergeant in ragged stripes. All the others waited beside their mounts. The man looked grubbier than the others by far and walked as if he hadn't been off his Sredirs in a week. His walk was that of an old man. Their single officer dismounted and came after him.

Borter thought he smelled bad, too, worse than any of the others and most certainly worse than the animals they rode. He growled as he looked into Borter's eyes.

"I've seen worse falls from the backs of Sredirs! Don't be such a baby. Stand up straight!" The sergeant growled.

Borter sneered back. He hated blowhards. He hated military blowhards even more, even one as ragged and comical as this one appeared to be, making money bringing downed flyers back to the farms.

"What are you supposed to be?" He spat back. "Somebody's mother?"

The sergeant's face reddened beneath weeks of stubble. He smiled through ugly green teeth, the butt of a really cheap and misused cigar shoved unceremoniously between his uppers and lowers.

"Well, we got us a smart one," his breath flooded Borter's face disagreeably. Borter had no question in his mind what the man had eaten for lunch that day and that it was exactly the same thing eaten by his mount. Smoke from the cigar followed, not a relief.

Borter mounted behind the corporal, or the man he took to be a corporal, from his chevrons. The rider, too, smelled bad and looked worse. The column countermarched itself, one hundred – eighty degrees in the sand.

Borter held on for dear life though his head and stomach reeled with effort.

It struck him suddenly that Moz's flyer was nowhere to be seen. Then, he remembered what had happened to it and her. Kees' hopper had lurched away under his fire, but, he thought, it stayed airborne.

At least it didn't crash right away. He looked to his side and saw his blaster was there, replaced and securely holstered. The Sandriders moved out into the desert. Suther Dann's farm was left farther behind.

The desert mounts rode smoothly. Borter had expected worse. They were covered with long, shaggy hair that was matted in tendrils as long as his forearm from head to hoof and front to back. Borter had seen nothing like them, ever.

The ragged column moved along slowly by two, farther into the desert. Travel by Sredirs was far more tedious than by hopper, especially in this desolate place. Borter protested, at first, pointing out that Suther Dann's farm was in the other direction.

The old sergeant laughed roughly and was even joined in doing so by others. It was a totally disgusting performance as the sergeant ended the exchange by propelling an angry stream of brown spittle into a nearby patch of scrub brush. They continued into The Ords. It was as if the desert meant to open up and swallow them. The scrub brush said nothing.

There were not more than twenty of the little band, which seemed smaller the farther they went into the desert. The Ords were vast, but not vast like space, Borter thought. His back and legs hurt miserably. He longed for his pilot's chair aboard Soarer, even for the cramped, hard seat of a hopper. As for the desert itself, he'd rather the closeness of buildings, if only those of the grittier space ports he knew across the galaxy.

Space was not so imposing as these salt flats they crossed. The sergeant spat more of his brown juice, staining the stubble of his chin. His uniform also bore less recent evidence of the practice.

This was a strangely disciplined little band as it lurched across the dry plains toward the camp. The camp, the way, the Sandriders themselves called it.

They held together in the heat, the result of long practice. The sergeant never turned to his men. They would be there, he knew.

Borter grew more miserable. After the first hour there was a halt and the sergeant grumbled ordering him to dismount and had water poured over him.

"Nothing's too good for one of our guests," the man laughed at his own joke! He spat. Borter turned away and became very ill. He wretched into a scrub of brush. The sergeant, pretending delicacy, commented, "For somebody who complains about my treatment of the ecology, you're not treating that poor thing very well!"

All laughed at this except Borter. The Sergeant gathered his mount, the pilot; the rest followed suit. They rode on.

It was the dusk of Ganempsha's second sun before their camp came into sight. Long before that, the Sredirs had quickened their pace, smelling home. Shortly, Borter was jerked and jolted down the narrow path to the valley floor where the Sandriders made their camp. The barren character of the place reminded Borter of Helio's home planet. Dillisome, of course, was an ice planet, but it felt the same.

Things were spare, sometimes rudely built, for service only in a hostile, barren climate. There was a main street made of zip–domes, a surprisingly modern innovation for such a primitive setting. Outward from the gate, the domes became smaller, reaching the outskirts of the camp. In any direction, between each row of domes, was cut a sharp military street. On the rest of that valley grew grasses, miraculously grown, for Sredirs.

The little troop stopped in front of the largest dome, the most central of the domes on the main street. There flew SandRidge's banner. It was the only bit of ornamentation to be seen anywhere in the dusty valley. It was multicolored, bright blue, red – green, white, and a particular yellow found only on that planet, called Ganempshan Yellow. Borter never found out the significance of the individual colors. Helio was the sub-culture specialist.

The place, indeed, reminded Borter of Dillisome. For like Dillisome's main concentration of population, this place served – without name.

The sergeant smiled his brown smile at him as he held the door. Inside, though, the sergeant said he'd get him from the Captain. Borter entered.

The Captain, on the other hand, greeted Borter like a long-lost friend, shaking his hand vigorously and clapping him on the shoulder.

"So, this is the flyer we've heard so much about," the sergeant heard him say on his way out, "from our good friend, Suther Dann." Borter smiled, though his head ached as he remembered Moz's death at Kees' hands. Praise always embarrassed him.

It was true. Suther Dann had been asking for him. Borter hadn't wanted to be the one to tell him of her death, but if it was for him to do, he'd do it.

Search parties had been dispatched, he was told, but one of their regular patrols had found him first, immediately after his crash, in fact. The rest was a matter of communication.

Yes, Suther Dann had been told of her death, and her body had been returned to him. Another Sand Rider patrol had taken care of that. Her hopper's wreckage had come down several kilometers beyond Borter's. Kees had not been found. They suspected him to have made a safe landing beyond their reach. Sorrow had not yet settled on Borter; he was still too numb from his own close call to feel sadness.

Had he heard about the Ancient One? The Captain asked with great animation.

There had been a crash the week before, a Kithronese shuttle. Aboard, they'd found an Ancient One in full battle armor, alive.

The man babbled on with great excitement.

Borter forgot the pain in his head and shuddered. Marcelleans, he thought, *damn*! The man babbled on – the Marcellean and the big, checkered thing, gone in a flash of light.

The legend was almost complete, he, the Captain said, and the Sandriders were ready. Borter had almost asked for what the Sandriders patrolled, but he didn't want to know. The man leaned over the dead radio, and he babbled.

"Our main duty has been to endure! We wait for orders here on this device." He pointed to a frosted globe mounted on a wooden box.

Borter wondered why he was being told this but said nothing, letting the captain finish. He wondered – how long they had been waiting. It had that familiar Marcellean flavor to it, which sounded good but made no sense whatsoever. He crumpled to the floor, at last, unable to endure the pain further.

As the Magnean reached the floor. The globe on the radio unit glowed brightly. The captain rushed to it, nearly brought to tears.

It was two full days before Borter awoke. When he did, there was no thunder in his ears and no ache in his head. Putting his feet over the side of the narrow bed, he sat up weakly. His clothes were hung across the room, and he was alone in Suther Dann's house.

Ganempsha's twin suns crept into the sky. Most of the clones went into the ruin for the shade. Helio and his Kith Ree followed suit. Much that the clone had said to him made no sense.

It was not him, the one the truly favored of the clones or the Heart of Marcellus. It was Borter. Borter was oblivious.

26

Helio in The Desert

Parnak was somewhere else, below ground. One of the clones was showing him around. Helio didn't think much about it. Just then, The Ords were most peaceful. The sky was clear, like spring on any of a dozen planets he knew. The morning had a coolness about it that made it special. There was no reason to think or to suspect the disaster that had overtaken Borter and Moz.

The red clones stayed nearby. They liked him. Their ruins in this desert stretched to the horizon. They were old, older than ancient. Broken columns reached up like uneven, stone fingers. Beside them, the building blocks of a great civilization all tumbled down long ago.

He'd seen nothing like it anywhere. The double suns took the white of the stones and made it so bright it was painful to the eye. In the desert was the sound of thunder. There were no clouds in the sky.

All the clones were called Kith Ree.

He'd been there the day before finding out, not only did they all look exactly the same. It did not matter who or, rather, which of them was beside him. Parnak had not caught on to that.

"Sandriders?" Helio asked with a growing interest.

"Sand Rock." The clone offered. He raised a curious eyebrow. Strangers did not easily understand the truths of the ancient planet, specifically the reason for Parnak's tour beneath the surface in the cavernous ruins there.

An amused expression played on his face. It made Helio wonder. How could Parnak have no understanding of the ruins below ground? His people were from the deep tunnels, had been and were still there.

"It happened quite a long time ago, friend Helio. "

The Dillisome was not discouraged. In his world, children were brought up in stories because there was not much else to do. He let his Kith Ree go on.

"It happened a long time ago."

"You already said that." It was, also, a habit among the children of Dillisome not to let the storyteller become boring or repeat himself. The clone did not seem put off.

"Tell me," said Helio.

"It is most difficult," said the clone. "It is the knowledge of the off-worlder. That is, non-clones, those who are not of us, have great difficulty with it. With it, not beyond it or before it, all else is exclusion!"

The clone, Kith Ree, eyed him closely as they moved farther away from the other clones, an unusual act in itself.

"The knowledge of Ror," said Kith Ree, "begins, I think therefore I am nothing!" He paused and, seeing nothing in Helio's eyes, went on. There was more.

There is nothing to know. All that is known — is forgotten. We are here to point the way! It is the fate of the few —"

"Yes," Helio said solemnly, "I understand that I do not understand. Tell me about the Sandriders!" Helio nodded, urging the clone forward, sensing the loneliness of those in this place.

Helio stopped, said nothing as he looked into the strange old face, the only face of all survivors of the old race.

"We shall not see the things about to happen in our own world."

"The Sandriders were pledged to prevent such a thing, to defend against any harm to the children of this planet. This is their moment."

"The old power is theirs," he nodded toward the thunder in the far desert. His brow wrinkled with concern more than with his age. His eyes met Helio's, "They will not fail! Nor will the Ghost Pilot!"

27

Delivery - The Black Box

One peeled-away hit, not done to death. It sought to escape, taking altitude and space. The other looped over in an attempt to get behind the freighter and deliver a killing blow. This was not to be. Slide's Hammer disappeared without a trace.

Except for the rolling sands of the desert, there was nothing beneath. He circled one way, then the other. He zigzagged a course as crazy as his evade had been on the chase down. It was just as he was about to give up the search altogether that Slide popped up behind, got off a quick, telling burst, and sent the fighter plummeting straight into its end.

Quantum was impressed. Slide sending a damaged fighter back home, forgoing death. Then, the odds more even, he slowed, pulled up behind a second, damaging it so badly it fell into the desert and exploded.

Seemingly bored with combat, Slide, moments later, put the Hammer down in the desert – easily – then lowered the cargo ramp and delivered cargo, the black box, into the desert. Quantum looked on.

"Well, isn't this the address on it?" He gestured at the box.

Quantum nodded.

They'd met only two nights before.

28

Emmick – The Black Box

Emmick was not much to look at, not much as things go. He floated in stasis on the center floor, enclosed in a clear globe, a thick gelatinous mass, and no limbs at all. His round shape, even, within moving, shifting grey-green, in spheroid flux.

Emmick controlled the vast floor at Parnel Space Port. Those he worked for said he was the best floor man they'd ever had. Masses of material goods and equipment come across the floor every day. It was all scheduled down to the last scrap, finding the right dock and the best shipment method, all overseen and arranged by Emmick, the only manager of any kind in the spaceport. Above the planet, a long, carefully orchestrated line of space freighters waited in orbit. This he controlled, too. There was nothing that did not come under his care.

The day itself was fairly ordinary. Shipments on schedule were made ready and checked. A big consignment for Canus was late and jammed the floor. Emmick's foremen hurried their workers after it until it was finally put in place. Scanners showed what was happening throughout the operation.

"Tulso Slide. Welcome. I see you have been joined by Mr. Starr!"

Emmick went out to meet them.

Slide smiled at him as did Thee Starr."

His globe shined brightly.

"I have work for you – "

Slide continued to smile. "Sign me up! "I'm free tomorrow."

"Thee Starr needs a lift to The Ords tonight."

"I am Mr. Starr's roadie, you know?" Slide said, "It works for me."

The orb lifted up a little, nearly face–to–face. "Freight coming in tomorrow – also, for the Ords – and it pays a bonus!"

So, it was. Time was set and space arranged. The equivalent of a handshake closed the deal.

Thee Starr boarded the Hammer with Slide. Moments later, they were gone.

The next day, after a delivery for Canus was done and carried away by robot-driven, grav jacks toward its chosen dock for shipment, he noticed the six tired-looking miners unload, from their land transport, a large, long black box. From the look of the transport and the haggard look of the miners, Emmick judged it time to beef up security around the terminal. Security was placed on alert, and the black box came his way.

In orbit, the next freighter got into the slot. Shipping techs quickly made the box ready as consigners looked on, themselves on guard. The murky globe moved smoothly to a place above the box. Emmick again supervised the operation. His people supposed it to be no more than a routine check of their skills. He read the destination carefully from the label as it was placed proudly, squarely, on the box. It read an address deep in the Ord Wastes on Ganempsha – it was correct.

The Hammer just came back from The Ords, its tube empty, and glided easily toward the ground.

Tulso Slide had no more than slotted themselves for landing, asking for instructions when a voice broke in on their radio. "Mr. Slide? Is that you?"

Emmick had no real voice, of course. His words were translated and spoken for him by computer. Aboard the Hammer, Slide recognized him instantly, electronic voice or not. "Yes, It's me." Slide feigned enthusiasm. Quantum stood nearby.

"I could tell it was you before you even asked for landing instructions," Emmick's computer voice approximated a strange high – pitched giggle. His race of beings understood the concept of humor very well but knew nothing of laughter itself. Laughter, it seemed, was a singular trait of most of the galaxy's humanoid population. Emmick had learned it as best he could, simply as a social grace, now, used it quite freely to acknowledge the spoken humor of others.

He took over from the regular air controllers and rolled out the red carpet for The Hammer. The freighter glided down through a hail of other ships to land.

Emmick waited at their loading dock as they taxied up. In the center of an otherwise bare floor was the long black box that the six Marcelleans had struggled so hard to bring. The shipper looked it over from the corner of one eye as she walked towards Emmick's globe.

Green shone brightly within the thick grey of the globe. Among humanoids, he favored the Tulso Slide and could not help but show it. Greener among his kind was always a sign of favoritism in the presence of that – whatever being. It could not be helped.

"What's in the box?" Slide stood, hands – on hips, leaning his head in the box's direction. A high–pitched giggle, once more, reached their ears.

"Don't know, Tulso. "But, the greenish–grey ovoid went on, "it's not dangerous, and it has cleared Customs. It's to go right away, aboard The Hammer. The necessary documentation has been placed on your ship's computer. You're going to The Ords." There was a friendly, second, high – pitched giggle in Slide's ears.

Quantum helped Slide load the box and secure it in the tube. It was an average tube, the standard size for any interstellar freighter, not large. Still, the box did not take much room away from the sound equipment stored there. The Hammer attached, on occasion, container cargo and large affairs by bolts to the outer hull of the ship. If they were attached to the launch planet, they would make a vertical takeoff like a rocket. If they were attached in space, they could power away from the docks as they pleased.

Several modular configurations were possible for freighter delivery. Most interesting was the landing gear module that was attached to the lower cargo container, permitting a horizontal landing. They were serviceable on some occasions and dependable when Hammer's own gear was restricted by cargo. Slide always rented them.

He was not one to turn down an easy run, but he was always suspicious.

"Now, this is a rush order, and it pays well."

Slide smiled evenly. "The bill of lading says electronics. Nobody uses electronics anymore – "

Had Emmick been able to smile, he would have. The giggle came instead.

Tulso fared in those times no better than any other freighter pilots. Everything was chaos. Work was unsteady, and money was becoming scarce. Shippers, people were making deliveries for which they were not paid. Emmick could be trusted, at least as trustworthy as any other. To take the job was greater than his need to know what was in the box – nearly.

The Marcelleans stood by watching, glad to be done with the box and planet Norvado. Without ceremony, one of Emmick's men slapped duplicates of the lading bill into Slide's hand. The pilot stood dumbly, stuffing them into his pocket.

"You had better go now."

Slide turned back toward The Hammer, muttering thanks. Quantum followed.

Tulso Slide shook his head, smiling, shrugging. He didn't know. He could not imagine doing it again or for anyone else.

Emmick had no real voice, of course. His words were translated and spoken for him by computer. Tulso Slide recognized him instantly. Electronic voice or not. It was a day later. The hammer and crew returned as promised.

"I could tell it was you before you even asked for land-ing instructions, "Emmick's computer voice approxi-mated a strange, high-pitched giggle. His race of beings understood the concept of humor very well but knew nothing of laughter itself. Laughter, it seemed, was a sin-gular trait of the galaxy's humanoid population. Emmick had learned it as best he could, simply as a social grace, but now, he used it quite naturally to acknowledge the spoken humor of others.

He took over from the regular air controllers and rolled out the red carpet for the Hammer. The freighter glided down through a hail of other ships to land.

Emmick waited at their loading dock as they taxied up. In the center of an otherwise bare floor was the long black box that the six Marcelleans had struggled so hard to bring.

Green shone brightly from the thick grey of the globe Among humanoids, he favored Tulso Slide and could not help showing it. To glow a little greener among his kind was always a sign of favoritism in the presence of a selected being. It could not be helped.

Emmick would not have it otherwise had he been able to.

"What's in the box?" Slide; stood, hands on hips, nod-ding his head in the box's direction, the high – pitched giggle reached their ears again.

Emmick's men helped Slide load the box and secure it in the tube. It was an average tube, the standard size for any interstellar freighter, not small. Still, the box did not take much room away from the sound equipment stored there already.

The Hammer attached, on occasion, container cargo and large affairs by bolts to the outer hull of the ship. Attached on the launch planet they would make a vertical takeoff like a rocket. If attached in space, they could power away from the docks as they pleased.

Several modular configurations were possible for freighter delivery. Most interesting was the landing gear module that was attached to the lower cargo container, permitting a horizontal landing. These were serviceable on occasion when Hammer's own gear was restricted by cargo. He always rented.

Parnak strolled onto the dock as Slide eyed Emmick. "What else have you got for us, Emmick?"

"Nothing, Tulso, my friend. This is all!"

Slide was not one to turn down an easy run, but, of them, he was always suspicious. "What's in it?"

Tulso fared in those times no better than any other freighter pilots. Everything was in chaos. Work was unsteady, and money was becoming scarce. People were making deliveries for which they were not paid. Emmick could be trusted. To take the job was greater than his need to know what was in the box – nearly.

Parnak was poking around, as was his habit. His passive curiosity did not disturb Emmick, who had known the journalist almost as long as he'd known the flyer he traveled with. He knew, like himself, Parnak was cut off from his home by the unhappiness brought upon the galaxy by The Helmsman and his Modallian slaves. He shared the journalist's sorrow.

Without ceremony, one of Emmick's men slapped duplicates of the lading bill into Slide's hand. Tulso stood there dumbly, stuffing them into his pocket.

"You had better go now."

"Don't know, Tulso. But, "Emmick went on, "it's not dangerous, and Customs has cleared it. It's to go right away, aboard The Hammer. The necessary documentation has been placed on your ship's computer. You're going to The Ords. This goes with it." There was another friendly, high-pitched giggle in Slide's ears.

Parnak strolled onto the dock as Slide eyed the floating globe. "What else have you got for me, Emmick?"

"Nothing, Tulso, my friend. This is all!"

Tulso fared in those times no better than any other freighter pilots. Everything was in chaos; work was unsteady, and money was becoming scarce. People were making deliveries for which they were not paid. Emmick could be trusted. To take the job was greater than his need to know what was in the box - nearly.

Parnak was poking around, as was his habit. His passive curiosity did not disturb Emmick, who had known the journalist almost as long as he'd known the flyer he traveled with. He knew, like himself, Parnak was cut off from his home by the unhappiness brought upon the galaxy by The Helmsman and his Modallian slaves. He shared the journalist's sorrow.

Slide turned toward The Hammer, muttering, "Thanks."

29

Techno Dwarves

Soarer slowed to a stop. Borter shut own the freighter's systems and made his way toward the loading ramp and the baking heat of the desert. Helio came out to meet him. Behind him was Parnak, and farther back, all the clones.

Helio was about to ask whether or not Borter thought he had evaded Modallian sensor detection, but Parnak broke in with more direct language than the Dillisome would ever have used. "Are you crazy?" Parnak blustered. "Have you slipped off your rocker?" He was about to shout, "What's the matter with you? When Borter said it himself.

He glared into the Insectoid's eyes. "What's the matter with you?" The Magnean stood there, the image of impatience. Borter was defiant, leaning forward as if he towered over Parnak and not the opposite.

Helio led him away from the arriving clones and Parnak. He was calmer, more in control of himself, and ready for Borter. "What's wrong?"

He turned back to Helio, who waited and walked a few more paces away. "Things have happened. We've got to go."

Helio eyed him for a moment. Borter glanced at Parnak, who was pointing out something on Soarer to his then-present Kith Ree." Look at him," he nodded toward Parnak irritably, "he's giving guided tours of the ship. What next, us – a little show-and-tell, maybe?"

"Why do we have to go?" Helio brought him back to their conversation because this whole place was going to be an inferno.

"Everybody is going to die. Why us?"

"The Targan Attack Force that set up housekeeping in The Ords? Yes, and not far away!" he added, agreeing. "They could be a problem. The very worst thing is Modallas, though. Don't worry. They will never take this planet. This place is special, very special, as we have learned!"

The clones milled around Soarer. Returning, Borter shooed two or three from the cargo ramp and raised it.

This place – the pilot looked around himself at everything, wondering if he should take Helio by the shoulders and shake him like some naughty child. That would not help.

"Ganempsha is just another piece of - rock?"

His last words attracted Parnak's attention. He looked over sharply, making it an admonition.

Helio spoke. "I'm sorry about Moz. Nothing can bring her back.

Yes, in a way, it is just a piece of rock floating in space, and we could easily find another, but not like this place because of what has happened here!"

Borter heard Helio's words but did not want to hear about special things. He wanted to leave, to be gone from this place and all its special problems.

"This place is about to be destroyed – and you know it. The Helmsman will do with it what he did to Kithron and any other planet that gets in his way," Borter growled.

"This place doesn't have a military; it has Sand Rock concerts. It has red clones who philosophize that they know everything and can't prove it.

It has ragged beggars in its desert wastes who play at being, some – dismal calvary at best. And they all talk about some ancient power – that will save them. Helio, they have a commander out there who sits in the dark, at a broken radio set, waiting for the lights to come on! Yuh!"

I don't think so. Uh - uh," he shook his head from side to side, "Sorry! I'm taking care of Mister Borter this time." He jabbed a thumb at his own chest for emphasis!

"Borter, there are some things you ought to know!" Parnak walked up just as he had gotten the words out of his mouth. He was still angry from their encounter moments before. Borter nearly walked away. However, he chose to stand facing Parnak, looking him dead in the eye.

"Borter, for my part, if you want to go, you are released from our contract," he also turned to Helio," you are released, too, Helio. You need not stay. This surprised the pilots. They didn't know what to say. There was silence for a moment longer. Borter wondered. Either of them were free to end the contract. For the better part of that year, they'd taken Parnak's I.O.U.'s. This client hadn't paid them in a long time. Then, he wondered – why hadn't they kicked him out before? Why hadn't they let him off somewhere?

Well, they thought, at once, that's Parnak. To Parnak's chagrin, they broke out in laughter. The insectoid was about to make one of his famous Soarer's 'in tube' lectures complete with nodding head, pacing back and forth, and shaking that index finger when he stopped thinking at last that, as always, the two were incorrigible.

"This is the place of The Heart!"

If nothing else, Borter could say he'd not seen Parnak more intense. He believed what he said. Next to him, he could see Helio, again serious, backing him up. "Borter," said his friend, "this is where the Heart itself was forged, born, if you like. This is the place of creation."

He looked around at the ruins, trying to see something in them that would make it easy to believe. There were the ruins, sand, and the impossible red clones. There was no answer. It was merely The Ords, nothing different.

"Borter, " Parnak said. "I have been to that very chamber, the exact spot." He motioned to the red clones,

"They have convinced me, finally."

The story was incredible. Borter thought it impossible.

The place was thousands of years old. Parnak estimated the oldest civilization in the explored galaxy. It was not the place of Marcellus, it was a place older, even, than them.

It had been revealed to Parnak, at length, that they had come upon the place already in ruin in their early times and were themselves astounded by its antiquity. There was only the single original Kith Ree.

Everyone else was dead, killed off, fighting in the global wars that spread like a disease.

They were ragged then as they were that day. They had been a splendid body of fighters who had made themselves the protectors of peace, the protectors of the children of the planet. It became their punishment to roam The Ords, some said, until they were needed again. That was their punishment as it was the punishment of the clones, that of Kith Rees, to remain in the ruins, singularly and solitary, an example for others who would know everything, that they knew nothing.

He was halfway up the ramp when he saw Helio was not moving. He stopped and looked at his friend. It could be the last time the two would see each other. He said nothing, nodded, turning. He made is way up the ramp and into the tube, then into the cockpit.

30

Jibba And Chibba

There was a definite, succinct silence in the room. Judd watched as Chibba paced. The entire complement of Attack Force Six had been ferried down to The Ords from orbiting Modallas. Now, word had come that rebellion had broken out aboard the cylinder world.

Judd was silent, measuring the options left him. Chibba the Spy, also, was silent, but for other reasons. There was little else he could do aside from wait.

"You are nervous, Chibba. Do you worry for our great leader? The Helmsman can look after himself," the Commander seemed to chide.

Reports were coming in. They were sketchy at best and vague at worst. Judd, as any good commander did, bid his time and waited to make his patience a weapon. He did not trust Chibba. He never had.

Their orders – into The Ords – were too convenient. The attack force comprised most of The Helmsman's personal guard. They were considered an elite among the other Targan. Their present situation served the purposes of others besides The Helmsman. He was most curious about Chibba's involvement.

The camp had buttoned up as the Ord winds coursed their broad paths. This was the main base of operations on Ganempsha in the total military sense. Judd's sentries trod their posts. All was well. All was silent. Save the ever-present howl of the wind across the sand flats. It was like a presence, and sometimes it was not. To Judd, it felt exactly like the time they'd waited on parade for The Helmsman to arrive and review them. They'd waited hours that day.

Ganempsha darkened, her dual suns passing finally behind the horizon.

31

Borter Kills Kees

Kees made for the door. Once out, he went directly to his armed hopper. The hopper lifted swiftly into the air and was gone, The Ords not far off or Suther Dann's farm. Neither would do. Everything on Ganempsha, living or not, was his enemy.

It was at that moment when Judd had shouted "Find him" into his ears and that Kees had finally submitted to himself that something else happened, something that was to be added to a lengthy chain of events that would surprise them all. The Helmsman, Judd, and Chibba. Only the Ghost Pilot's lifeless form would save him.

Something big, black and wide, swept up on his tail. His sensors showed nothing, and now that nothing had pulled up, just above his head, its wingspan blocked out the two suns.

Suddenly, as suddenly as it had come up, it lowered itself toward him. There was a loud crunch of plastics and metal connecting. The controls nearly leaped from his hands, and he lost twenty or thirty meters at the altitude. It pushed him down and then went back, off to one side where he could get a good look at it.

Borter swept off just far enough and tilted his near wing down low enough for the Targan to get a look at who manned the cockpit. Kees was visibly impressed.

"Sir," Kees spoke into his headset, 'I think I've found him!"

Borter used Soarer's greater bulk to bash Kees' hopper lower in the sky and then back away again. He'd decided to play it out as long as he could. He would tease Kees for a while until it became boring. The Targan couldn't escape, even if he landed in the vast orchards.

Borter made up his mind to follow him anywhere, hunt him down, if necessary, in his own forests. Moz Killer would pay.

Armament lowered from wing pods. He took his time and took greater pleasure in shooting away the hopper's sensor gear. Next, the landing gear went. Borter laughed.

Like any good Magnean, he was flying him right out of the sky. Kees squirmed.

Drawing up on him again, he banged the top of the forlorn little flyer several more times before his computer alerted him to more serious competition, fighters, coming from behind.

He nudged Kees once more; the hopper buzzed down toward the desert floor, a better chance than he'd offered Moz. He gave Moz no chance at all and meant to give the Ghost Pilot none as well.

Borter took the time to watch as Kees impacted. His fuel pod exploded in a display that was impressive even in the light of Ganempsha's suns. As that happened, he hit

Soarer's throttle and flashed off into the sky. The computer images on his screen followed. There were four altogether.

He had never done this without Helio, but it made little difference. They came for him. He wheeled Soarer first one way, then another. He wove and dodged like a mad butterfly. He leapt forward and then fell back until he'd gotten behind one. A few bursts of gunfire later, and that one spiraled in easily. Targan were fierce fighters but didn't fly as well as they thought.

Two more went in then, the fourth. It did not seem at all difficult. Nothing to it. Borter felt satisfied. Moz had been avenged. He laughed at the notion that the Ghost Pilot had been the one to do it. He imagined the thoughts going through the dense little minds that had sent them in the first place.

32

Sandriders

In the course of things, another part of the legend stepped up to take its place on the stage of things waiting. In the hours that the Sand Rock concert began in the desert. Clusters of the city's children gathered, in twos and threes, taunting Sandriders, a fair grubby representation of whom could be found wandering Cross Anchor any time of day or night in sad-looking groups. The greyed and stooped old men were a late night, early morning weekend event.

The old Sargent, his jacket sprayed with the familiar brown spittle, walked in one such group. He was unshaven and ill-dressed, as were they all.

Thrown stones reached them. These were young people, children, brought up on planetary legend, part of which said they would always be protected by the Sandriders.

With the attack force in The Ords, they were afraid and needed to take it out on someone, someone more desperate, who could not strike back. Fear hung in the air, a real thing.

He pretended anger and charged a few steps forward at them. The children cowed and buckled backward but came back jeering with more stones. One caught him in the temple bringing him to his knees, causing even the stub of his unlit cigar to drop from his mouth. Help rushed to him. For the moment, it was over. Revenge against the children was unthinkable.

33

The Battle of Titans

It was Kithron's battle, with the entire Inner Galaxy at stake. Her fleet of dreadnoughts, her heavy battle platforms, with accompanying cruisers, gunships and carriers held space, near the star system Laura Zed. They were arrayed throughout the system in a million-mile formation.

For many days, agents of Kithron's intelligence service heard scattered rumors and received scraps of information on enemy movement, but in the area, a single, precious fact came from it all: they were by themselves. Their enemy was near.

Space did not seem big enough for those who manned the ships of the fleet. They had heard much of this strange, new enemy. Nerves worked thin as plans were made and remade. Gun crews drilled their firing regimen and fighter-scouts patrolled far outside the fleet. Commanders maneuvered their ships in mock battles and rang klaxons in practice as boredom set in.

Of the enemy, nothing had been seen. The Helmsman's agents, from time to time, had been discovered. Not much had been learned because they refused to be taken alive. They proved fighters, taking more than one captor with them to their oblivion. All of these things, fact, and rumor, traveled to battle with the fleet of Kithron.

The Kithronese heavy battle platform Giantro was the flagship of the fleet. Around its bulk, half a dozen protective destroyers hovered. Both to and from it, a constant stream of shuttles came and went. A crew of twenty thousand serviced its six-kilometer hull.

Giantro was the most ancient ship in the fleet. Its history of service to Kithron read like a history of the Inner Galaxy. She had risen from defeat so many times that one only had to mention the name Giantro, and stories would pour out all night.

Modallas took a nominally close orbit to Kithron. There, The Helmsman released the control grip of the gigantic artificial world to an automatic pilot. He turned from the command console at which he'd stood continuously since leaving the scene of battle days before, on the edge of system Laura Zed.

His control center was silent. Except for the occasional, going to and from, padding feet of his Targans at their stations around him. Sensor screens bathed everything with their dull lights and brought out the already deep lines and hardship worn in the already hard-looking faces of the forest men he'd brought to his cause.

Beneath them, rolling peacefully, lay Kithron, the crown of the inner galaxy. That world below them was not at peace as one might have supposed from the slow clouds that crossed its surface both night and day or from the vast seas that lapped against its shorelines. Not the defeated people one might have expected. Kithron, instead, was a blur of planetary defense.

True enough, The Helmsman had not destroyed the fleet at Laura Zed. They, instead, had been too disorganized to mount a counterattack and moved away.

Targans manned their huge battle guns, part of Modallas' defense. Ready to launch was an air corps to rival that of any planet in the galaxy, except for that one small and very special freighter.

The Helmsman stalked back to his quarters to wait. The days at his station had not tired him. He'd steered Modallas across the void between galaxies himself. That had been infinitely longer.

In that vastness, he had been there for Modallas and his masters, of whose realm this was.

The White City on The Third Plain, his thoughts turned back toward those first days of his service. Those, blurred and run together, so distant he could no longer make head or tail.

Overall, he had a dull feeling about it as of his years at helm and all the death his duties had brought.

Duty, that's all it ever was, and he supposed, all there would be, ever.

From every far corner of that cylinder world, created by beings so complex and diverse, Modallas, truly called, was a world unto itself. Clouds, a fact when first observed by Helio, astounded him. Borter had been too busy at the time avoiding Modallian fighters to look impressed.

Having clouds, Parnak later explained, hanging weightless in the zero-grav middle of the cylinder, from there, could be compelled a rain, as desired, onto the three large tracts of land clinging to the inner surface of Modallas. It had been within this place on the land mass known as The Third Plain that their adventure with Lord Soal played out, the leader standing his ground with the singular 5D as his own forces withdrew, under orders, to the waiting invasion fleet and escape.

From the big window at Control, one could see the Third Plain and the distant White City that rested there. At equal distances on either side of The Third Plain, two other land masses appeared to the eye, one descending from the clouds and one ascending to them in the curious rotation of Modallas.

These resembled gardens only a little less than did The Third Plain, but these also were not the home of Modallians, but The Helmsman's Targans, those gleaned from the forests of Marcellus as the best for The Helmsman's and Modallian purposes. These contained the fields and training bases in which The Helmsman's forces were readied for battle across the galaxy.

Beyond, far down the tube was a gigantic airlock that served Modallas as star port. The size of it dwarfed all but the largest Kithronese battle platforms.

Beside this, were several large, staging platforms on the outer hull for Stilettoes, the main fighter of Modallas' space and air forces.

Turning, greater, in sync with the cylinder of Modallas were the extended farming pods that fed all life on the artificial world, at places along the external surface, nestled between the constantly opening and closing shutters protecting the interior from direct sunlight or other harmful radiations plunging inward from space. This sky swung open and shut, with absolute precision, like ranks of saluting soldiers revealing space while allowing illumination to pass onto the land masses inside.

34

The Finian Run

He wished for once that Borter was nearby. Noisome as the man could be, he was a fair hand with a blaster as well as with Soarer. That purple field piece he holstered on his hip had more than once seen them safely out of trouble.

Once, forced to fight a particularly drunken Reggian pirate, Borter had taken the man's blaster for his trouble and the added peace of mind, knowing it would not be behind him as he left.

If he could make it to the spaceport, they could meet Borter and Helio. This planet was no longer safe. At worst, they would have to hole up in one of Parnak's islands of safe passage out, his magic carpet, and wait.

A trusted friend was to deliver a warning to the pilots if he could not reach them himself. The four of them could rendezvous later when things were safe. The galactic squeeze for money had sent Soarer off into orbital space on a long delivery route, a mission that Parnak envied in just these moments.

Otherwise, few off-worlders were privileged to see the city's more restricted areas, but there apparently had been some emergency, and, this once, excepting a particular ship, the ban had been eased.

The Targan stepped down from the Con, and The Helmsman retook his place. He turned Modallas toward Ganempsha, and the one thing yet standing between him and The Heart of Marcellus, Soarer and her pilot.

Days before, he'd reinforced his agents in his search for the small freighter he knew must be there. His blockade of warships, already in orbit, had all but stopped freighter traffic. Now, Modallas would join the hunt.

This small freighter, this Ghost Pilot, would not escape him another time. Its propulsion system heated, Modallas left that part of space for a reckoning with Ganempsha. The cylinder world would arrive before its support ships, those press-ganged from conquered worlds of the Inner Galaxy.

Finian it would be.

35

The Princess Odeon – Days Before

They sat, Borter, Helio, and Parnak backstage at The Princess Odeon. Staring blankly at each other, bored they sat at a round table of some artificially made substance, heat formed to suit this need - antique, something less than a meter across, a level plane, objects placed on it, of weight, and, therefore, sharing a reasonable degree of security. Before each was some remnant of breakfast.

During the meal, they spoke little. The night before had been a long one, preparing for and making planetfall at Parnel. The day that faced them began early. They signed on for a freight run from the planet.

Parnak's money had been shut off by the turbulence brought to the galaxy by Modallas. Soarer was forced into work other than chauffeuring the journalist from place to place. For Parnel itself, or for it, there was no story. That is, non-newsworthy.

Though it deserved the obscurity it had, it was not what might be called unknown. The Galactic Atlas listed it, told where it was, and listed its major exports. It also listed its mass, orbit, and other physical qualities. There was little said about its people. In fact, few of them had ever been known to leave the planet. They were considered the odd lot by the rest of the galaxy, and in fact, it was a bit crusty about that sort of thing.

That's exactly what the Atlas said about them in bold print and reason not to expect much there, the only space-port in the whole galaxy where off-worlders were expected, even required, to stay within assigned boundaries. They dealt with the outside through androids of foreign design. The android population was also responsible for all the heavy work on the planet, all the work, for that matter.

Many thought, those who thought about such things, that the Finians did make use of those who came to their planet directly, though it had never been proved, other than their androids.

It was explained in the galaxy manuals, the androids were of foreign design and that they are made to look and act like natives. Finian could mix among the androids, and no one would know the difference. Finian was a great laboratory for the study of all galactic life forms. Others suggested that if the first part were so, the second was merely entertainment.

Some coupled a mixture of Finian with the off-world recipe of the two with a need for anonymity – on someone's part.

Still, it remained. Everyone came to Finian to take something. The Finians were rich. They did not need it.

All wore blasters. All of them, including Parnak. It was early in the morning, still. There all night, waiting, playing cards as was their habit, that of most galactic travelers when stopped. Blasters were a telling factor.

The android who delivered breakfast dismounted his truck and knocked at the stage door.

Borter and Helio drew their blasters at that first sound. Parnak had been selected by elimination, but really by the tense nods of the others, to answer the door. It was as simple as it should have seemed. Parnak took money from the pilots, paid, and took the food. The android went away.

A feast for them, after so long of eating reconstituted food, got on their star travels. Parnak thought Borter, such an insensitive boor, the quality of food did not matter. Really, he was amazed that Helio, who he thought sensitive to the point of genius, found it possible to bear Borter at all.

36

To Kithron, Show Mercy

For one hour, there was silence behind the closed door of the chamber. The four guards watched. Behind it was The Helmsman. For the better part of the next hour, they would also hear nothing until he emerged. In the pitch dark of the chamber, none of them had even the slightest glimpse of what lay within before the door hissed shut. The master of Modallas, simply, was swallowed by the darkness.

In the narrow corridor that led to their master's quarters, there was a wide portal extending several meters long in. It was covered by a thick cover of transparent glass. Kept spotless, it afforded the walker, idle in the corridor, a superb view of Modallas, the best, in fact, that there was.

The Helmsman's chamber was on the trailing end of Modallas great, tubular bulk, above everything making the vast complex work, drove the Galaxy Engine that Modallas powered.

Vast in itself, above that, the complex supervising the creation of power and the management of energy rested but never stopped. Beyond that, reaching into the free space of the turning cylinder was Modallas' control, where The Helmsman commanded and coordinated everything that came in from every far corner of that entity created by beings complex and truly diverse enough to be called a world.

It astounded him. Modallas had clouds, a fact that Helio first observed, and it astounded him.

Borter, at the time, pursued Modallians – he seemed very impressed. Parnak, with them, later explained the clouds hung weightless in the zero-gee center of the cylinder and that from there, they could be compelled to give up their moisture, when desired, onto the three large tracts of land clinging to the inner surface of the cylinder.

It had been within this place, on the land mass known as The Third Plain, that their adventure with Lord Soal had, if ended, the valiant leader or standing his ground as his forces withdrew, under orders, to the invasion fleet and escape.

From the big window, one could look up at that time and see the Third Plain and the distant White City that rested there.

At equal distances on either side of The Third Plain, two other land masses appeared to the eye, one descending from the clouds, one ascending to them in the curious revolution of Modallas.

37

The Princess Odeon – Continues

For an hour, at breakfast, they sat facing each other or, if not, just at the table without speaking. The cards lay un-played and   unshuffled before them as night began to wear off and the day to wear on.

Each, at that particular, quiet and strange moment, was lost in traffic his own thoughts brought on in turn by boredom and fatigue. The theatre, as big as it was, had become a prison for them for several days. Outside, there were those who searched for them. It was at least a place to hole up.

In other days and now, sometimes, the Princess Odeon was a popular theater entertaining off-worlders exclusively on their layovers at Parnel. Its most recent days were those of disuse. Friends of Parnak had opened it for them. Friends of Parnak were everywhere and seemed to be a ga-lactic charitable institution.

Everywhere Borter and Helio shuttled him, there was always somebody there, waiting, on hand who knew The Great Parnak.

Right now, The-Great-Parnak sat with the not-so-greats, waiting for things to cool off. It had begun days before. Soarer had gotten work through Freighters Amalgamated Alliance. A cargo of androids was assigned from Finian in the Fourth Galactic Quadrant. Borter had a course there. There was little else to be done; they needed the money, and Parnak could no longer pay.

It was two days across and back. At the end of the second day going, they'd reached Finian orbit. There, large freight containers had been attached to Sower's tube. There were three, all large enough for a man to walk inside and down a narrow. Pathway left between the androids.

Soarer's outer hull bore hatches to each. This was the standard method of transporting freight in the galaxy. Soarer's tube was left to her crew. The containerized sealed and pressurized against the ravages of space.

Freighters were docked in orbit and delivered at the point of destination the same way. It was an easy run for good money. They'd seen no reason to turn it down. Finian and Sinobia were outside the Modallean influence sphere, at least for the present.

Out toward Finian, one of the androids escaped from its closed container, opened the hatch to Soarer's tube, and let itself in. Parnak, Borter, and Helio watched with great curiosity as they stumbled over things, even the most simple things that were common surroundings of Soarer's tube. Parnak cautioned them. Androids fresh from their packing cylinders needed time to become fully operational. Also, they could be dangerous during the process.

The android was unaware of its own name and answered to everyone else's. Parnak suggested silence as the best medicine. Helio, meantime, went into the cargo container and checked the parts list from the shipping cylinder. The name given on it was Quantum. He returned through the crate to the ship's more spacious tube, to the cockpit where Borter lounged in the captain's chair.

He'd turned around from the controls to watch the droid in the tube. Parnak sat patiently in the same spot he'd had before Helio left for the cargo container. The blue man from Dillisome jerked a thumb toward the confused figure in the and said her name softly to Soarer's passenger and pilot at once, "Quantum".

Quantum's head jerked around to the sound of her name and repeated it as if having heard it again after so long a time that it was nearly forgotten.

Consciousness for an artificial being seemed to be an indistinguishable shape at the end of a long, grey tunnel without light at the end. In another few seconds, she seemed oriented.

The flyers noticed the femineity of the form and the new grace that took its movements. The performance in the tube was no longer funny to Borter. It was commanding. The two pilots glanced at each other as if confirming in some known only to themselves, masculine secret, the evidence in their eyes.

Quantum noticed the attention and moved toward a darker part of the tube but, noticing Parnak was already there, shied away.

Parnak motioned for them to turn around in the cockpit, which they did. The tube of the small freighter in space was no place to get on someone else's nerves. Parnak smiled in a way that was, for his physiology, friendly. Quantum did not respond immediately. Instead, she stared at the floor and looked for something to do with her hands.

At last, she sat and looked toward Parnak as he spoke quietly to her. As he would explain later, androids were a lot like natural humanoids except that they were built fully grown and matured emotionally to what they were in a brief time.

Quantum looked toward the cockpit and found Borter looking back. Between them, there seemed to be a moment of electricity, at least for the android. Helio had busied himself with the ship and had not turned away from that task in some time.

However, Parnak observed, as was his habit. Quantum smiled at Borter and then seemed to blush.

Parnak smiled to himself. He was utterly bemused by what he'd seen. Borter looked at him, startled and confused, having felt something stir within himself. Quantum sat smiling calmly quietly without a word or making any move, her gaze settled on Borter. She seemed content.

Parnak rose, nodded politely in her direction, and walked to the cockpit and Borter.

"What's with the android, Parnak?"

Parnak snickered. "That she is an android, Borter!"

"She," he said grandly as if introducing the belle of the ball, bowing toward Borter formally and making a sweeping gesture toward Quantum at the same time with his arm outstretched his hand flat as it gracefully stopped at that area of the tube in which Quantum sat. "She is an android. And" he came to the part he'd been waiting for — "you've just been imprinted!"

Borter knew something was up. He didn't know what, but from Parnak's barely restrained manner, he knew it was something the insectoid journalist would like much better than he.

"Imprinted?"

"Uh – huh," Parnak's words, unlike his stiffy expressions, were faithful, but the Language Translator translated into the Universal language that both Helio and Borter spoke his own buzzing speech as impossible for them as Universal was to him. Universal was the official language of the galaxy. That which passed for a broad smile was on Parnak's face.

"It's a form of loyalty known galaxy-wide. At times, it's extreme. Most often, we know it as motherhood. In short, you've got a friend."

"What?"

"You're – a mommy!"

Helio laughed, glancing at the uncomfortable Borter, who peered past Parnak at his beaming ward.

38

Delivery –The Black Box –

Emmick

One peeled-away hit, not done to death. It sought to escape, taking altitude and space. The other looped over in an attempt to get behind the freighter and deliver a killing blow. This was not to be. Slide's Hammer disappeared without a trace.

Except for the rolling sands of the desert, there was nothing beneath. He circled one way, then the other. He zigzagged a course as crazy as his evade had been on the chase down. It was just as he was about to give up the search altogether that Slide popped up behind, got off a quick, telling burst, and sent the fighter plummeting straight to its end.

Quantum was impressed. Slide sending a damaged fighter back home, forgoing death. Then, the odds more even, he slowed, pulled up behind a second, damaging it so badly it, too, fell into the desert and exploded.

Seemingly bored with combat, Slide, moments later, put the Hammer down in the desert – easily – then lowered the cargo ramp and delivered cargo, the black box, into the desert. Quantum looked on.

"Well, isn't this the address on it?" He gestured at the box.

Quantum nodded.

They'd met only two nights before.

39

A Tale of Two Freighters – Black Box – The Journey To Ganempsha

The following days on the planet were unexpectedly pleasant as Quantum became more and more animated. Helio had relinquished his seat in the cockpit, and she had learned the controls of Soarer. Borter, of course, was her tutor. Parnak was a little less amused by this turn of events. Borter was surprising sometimes in the most curious ways. Julia's loss had left him hurt, especially the manner of her loss. Parnak had arrived just following the battle in the courtyard. Lord Soal and his guards were there only a few seconds themselves.

Across the stones of the vast square lay the bodies of Julia's bodyguard amid the smoking remains of Lord Markham's raiding party. Markham with one or two survivors of the party had escaped into the teleportation tube projected for them from Modallas. Julia had been there.

There was nothing he could have done personally to gain even her freedom. That day the Heart had claimed Lord Soal it had spoken, also, to Helio who covered the recall of Marcellean forces from the deadly Third Plain and laying down a hail of fire on The Helmsman's fighters.

Parnak covered all the main events of the day as Lord Soal's official chronicler.

The main thrust had been to cover the evacuation of the planet. The planet, once a place of greatness, was decimated and weary of fighting. Only a few days following Modallas first arrival and orbit twelve hundred years before, fighting began.

Lord Soal, young then, had battled from that time on. Parnak had been his chronicler since that time despite his other duties.

The Helmsman, himself, had made the briefest of appearances on that fateful day as he teleported himself into the pyramid where he killed Markham, who finally had collapsed mentally after having both failed to kill Borter and having discovered the reason that the White City had been secluded and the Third Plain itself reserved exclusively for Modallians. They were all long dead.

As far as any of them knew, Julia was still a prisoner on Modallas. Modallas itself had scourged the Inner, the most prosperous of the galaxy's star systems. The Helmsman's Targan, honed as a force aboard Modallas, from mere savagery, generations before, Lord Soal had battled their still savage brothers on the planet for many years.

The raiding party, the invasion force, fought the latest generation aboard Modallas. Borter took on Quantum's tutelage with some misgivings at first but soon was enjoying himself. His android smiled at him as he taught her the controls of his flyer. She was. He was different from the others but smiled only for him. Despite Parnak's information about age and the vast life spans of those called the Old Marcelleans, he had been unable to convince

Borter of the futility of his attentions toward her, which had greatly hurt his feelings.

Though Parnak said she would progress quickly, Quantum was really a child by any standard. She was beautiful to look at and would have done anything Borter asked, such was the reality of imprinting. It would, of course, modify as she went on, but this was the intended first step and very important in her development though not intended for the pilot who made delivery.

By the time Soarer reached Parnel, Quantum progressed far, perhaps, even, in Parnak's expectation. She and Borter had become very friendly. Helio looked on, but said nothing.

Borter perceived Quantum now as a young woman, a bit young, maybe, but interesting, nonetheless. Androids were born, so to speak, with fully mature bodies. It took some time, after they were psychologically awakened from the packing cylinders, they began to mature as Quantum had, Borter thought she had, the most perfect humanoid form he'd ever seen.

Her short, straight blond hair waved in the gentle Finian breezes. Her blue eyes shone brightly in the planet's sunlight. Her face always smiled, it seemed, always at him. True enough. Quantum had imprinted Borter, and it would be sometime before she would, of her own accord, even consider leaving him along. Thus, she belonged to him.

In a few short hours, she would be sent back to him from the android receiving center in Sinobia because she had imprinted Borter. At the center, new androids were carefully unpacked and sent directly into process, the specifications of which were particularly Finian. Most often, they were imprinted to a senior android, that is, if the new android was a socialized model. Others of lower caliber were imprinted.

Quantum was not such an android. Her intelligence matched her physical rating. When Parnak stirred once to the cargo container late one night aboard Soarer, he was quite surprised to note her designation as - agricultural equipment.

He wondered how much of her development had been included in her pre-awakening package and how much was influenced by transit, or Borter and her accidental awakening in the tube. They were still in orbit at the cargo docks when she was returned.

Quantum did not seem unhappy. She'd been more than happy to explain how she'd come to awaken midflight. The process androids in the center at Sinobia had been very understanding and just sent her back to the pilot.

Damaged goods, as long as they were androids, were not returned to a manufacturer for repair or reconditioning. Androids were considered a life form. In early models, more robots than androids, even in the stages when they qualified more as androids, that is, artificial humanoids, were sent back for repair. Now, if one misprinted as Quantum had, they were allowed to make their own way in the galaxy.

Quantum held back tears, the first ever in her brief life. The receiving androids had made it plain, though gently so, that she would not be used with the others. Her implanted knowledge told her only that she returns to Soarer and Borter, a fact that would take a few minutes to feel. A return would please her.

40

Quantum – Rejected – The Odeon

The streets were choked with off-worlders and working androids. The Targans did not stand out particularly. They wore loose trousers of faded khaki and loose shirts. Their black night cloaks were kept elsewhere, safe. At their side, each wore a powerful blaster of Modallian design. There were two. Quantum did not notice.

As she winded her way through the narrower streets, her implanted knowledge awakened, but no more than her maker intended. It was true, she enjoyed the full flower of young womanhood, her firm, roundly curved form swung attractively through the busy streets like the young girl she was.

The way back to the spaceport was instinctive. She wiped her face with the back of her hand and sniffled loudly, walking on. There was little in her mind save a sorrow that her primary purpose had been scrubbed.

There wasn't knowledge of Targans, Modallas, or the turmoil that swept the galaxy. Many watched her progress in her journey to Soarer with appreciation.

They did not think of it too long. There was the mission, this female led them to the Ghost Pilot, the one who had eluded their master for so long. It would be worth it for them to go into trouble by either capturing or killing that one.

Parnak rarely stayed behind on any Soarer voyage. Today was different. As Quantum turned the corner toward the Odeon, a thin arm reached out, whisking her sideways.

Inside, it was dark as Parnak put a finger to his lips demanding silence as she was about to scream. The door slid shut without notice, seconds before the Targans turned the corner onto their street.

So skilled were they at tracking that they did not waste time glancing between themselves acknowledging the event. The street was a grey, short, dead-end with high sides. The area was not one of the City's best, and the Odeon was sided by multiple worn dwellings from which lines of laundry were hung from bottom to top. It was difficult even to see the sky. They leaped to the walls on either side and climbed swiftly, without noise, like forest cats.

The doors of the Odeon were shut, and the theater was dark inside. To their forest eyes, looking in, there was no sign of movement.

Parnak watched carefully as, first, one face, then the other, came to the windows and then left; each with that silent, hunting animal grace, possessed only by the humanoids of the Targan Forests.

Quantum had stilled as she recognized him and released his powerful grip on her. She trembled silently against him until the danger passed.

There was a scream and commotion in the building across the alley as they were getting to their feet. Parnak knew what had happened and wasted no time in seeing them both in the deeper recesses of the old theater. The Targan had crawled through open windows only to face the fearful or enraged tenants they found there instead of Quantum.

Police were soon on their way.

41

Quantum – Alien Nightlife

After dark, the two fled the old theater for a safer place. Parnak knew Targans gave up only when dead, even those possessed of Modallian education and manners.

One of Parnak's friends, one who owed him a favor, was to meet them later on. The journalist's connections abroad on the planet and the galaxy itself were vast. The shadows took them willingly. The night was their new realm, silence, and secrecy, as well.

Quantum took to the dark with great ease. The Insectoid steered her through the streets with equal stealth. A dismal rain had fallen, leaving a dingy vapor across the night itself. The streetlights showed a pale, drenched yellow, coming down from above, and the lights, from the places they passed, glowing out into the slippery street, hollow beacons in the mist.

They kept the silence of the night between them, letting others make their noise instead. They'd picked up no Targan hunters. Of this, Parnak was quite certain. His powerful antennae told him no one followed. The city was big. Even Parnak, with his long legs, could not walk all the way across it in a single night.

Dim lights from places of nightlife dewed the city from any elevation. They would be hard to find within them. Parnak knew it, and he also knew that safety was not within one but within many.

There were those, of course, who would be inhospitable because they catered to those of worlds whose atmospheres were dangerous or merely unbreathable for both.

Parnak meant to cut a path through them, toward the spaceport, or until their contact met them. He did not further consider the possibility of running into un-friendlies along the way.

His shod feet began to ache, and he hated wearing shoes, but it reduced his attention to his mechanically jointed feet. Otherwise, his flexible exoshell made a very smooth, dark appearance. No one looked at him as if he were anything out of the ordinary. In fact, Parnak's home planet, Jinzikan, was very far from the Inner Galaxy, and he was a very rare individual.

He carried a small blaster in his pocket. Usually, he did not usually carry any weapons. However, his experience with Targans was long, and he did not survive it by taking chances with them. The weapon would be of use at close range only if he could get it into his hands in time. Better to use his powerful hands and shielded body. His insect's strength was great, and he'd learned many ways to kill using only his hands years after he had been a war correspondent.

Cars raced in all directions. The hiss of tires on the slick asphalt and the dying fading whines of their turbine engines droned into the night. An hour later, I saw them at the door of a nightclub. This time, the manager was waiting for The-Great-Parnak. The streets, too, had come more alive.

There was a succession of places, a club catering to inhabitants of water planets, for instance, where they were allowed to walk through a glass corridor as patrons viewed them. Interest was great in Parnak, and his lovely companion was everywhere. The water bar's DJs floated around them. Some merely dangled long tentacles. Some, Parnak thought, looked predatory, if not downright hungry.

In spite of himself, Parnak was becoming a little drunk from the free drinks his reputation earned him. However, his great physical strength and force of will held him in good stead.

Parnak was glad to leave, as was Quantum, though neither said so. They were more than halfway and doing well. Parnak's plan was working, coming together, better than hoped for. Ready for a fight, he thought, if one came his way.

This was all quite brave of him. Secretly, he was just as glad none did. There was enough fighting in the galaxy, and he'd rather not add to it.

The hand drifted slowly out of the mist or seemed to. He stopped short, so quickly, Quantum ran into his back. The vapors of the club's doorway were different from others. Quantum could not be sure that it was because they were made red by dim lights, or because they actually were red. Maybe, both.

The hand receded. Money and a business card were shoved into it by Parnak.

A few seconds later the hand reappeared and waved them in. With one arm carefully around Quantum, he went in. Dim light in the hall was nothing special, showing signs of both age and frequent use.

The hand's owner was a humanoid something, ascertained by Parnak when it came out of the mist and stopped them at the door. This humanoid, this man, was thick-set but moved gracefully, though his legs, too, were shorter than the average. Parnak followed with curiosity. His head was completely hairless and almost square-looking. The clothing was light and simple: beige, baggy trousers and a large, roomy shirt, both made of coarse material that covered him from waist to ankles and neck to wrists.

The man turned and motioned for them to wait where they were with the same gesture he made at the door. Parnak and Quantum stopped.

This time, Parnak caught a better glimpse of the man's face before he turned and walked farther down the corridor.

There was a familiar tattooed marking above the eyes and between them as well, it denoted a particular society, a warrior sect, from the planet Omega.

To meet one in this part of the galaxy was certainly a rarity, and to find him working as a doorman at a Finian night spot was nothing short of amazing. The warrior cult of Omega was one of Parnak's pet interests, second after the warriors of the distant planet Marcellus. The tattoo extended itself between the eyes to the bridge of the small, soft-looking nose and to the flat of the broad forehead just above the eyebrows or where the eyebrows should have been.

The color was a deep indigo. It flashed when caught just so in the light. The mark itself ended in dual prongs. The upper widened on the forehead to the edges of the eyes, and the lower, smaller, just draping itself over the nose's bridge to either side.

The Omegan returned, motioning leisurely, unconcerned with any need to hurry. Behind him came another humanoid, this one more squat-looking, rounder, less blank, and clothed for the evening.

As they reached Parnak and Quantum, the doorman stepped aside and the second man came forward quickly his hand outreached, offering to take Parnak's in a gesture of friendship.

The two exchanged greetings. Quantum and the Omegan watched quietly. The friendly hand reached out for Quantum's hand, which she gave happily enough, after Parnak's example. Without a word the Omegan returned to his post at the door.

The round man smiled broadly and gazed up into Parnak's face with twinkling eyes. He motioned them forward – a word spoken in Universal, coming to their ears through Parnak's translator.

The red mist permeated the place. They'd moved down the corridor to the main room. There, the music they'd heard since entering boomed in their ears. It was Sand Rock, a variety that saturated the airwaves of the galaxy, Parnak thought, all too frequently. Sand Rock originated on Ganempsha. The current, single, greatest exponent of that form was known as Thee Starr, a holograph of him and his band played at one end of the room.

Too, that end of the room was alive with writhing dancers, mostly humanoid, all young. The air was hung quite heavily with other things that were in the red mists, some of them illegal if Parnak's sensitive antennae were not wrong. The stout little man smiled broadly all the time they crossed the dance floor toward secluded tables near an exit. It was time for a rest.

Parnak thought. They had come far, and it was late. An android took their order, which it did with a minimum of warmth and a marked indifference to Quantum. Well, one android knows another, decided Parnak. It was sometimes difficult to get one android to serve another. Prejudices were everywhere.

However, as thick as prejudices could be at times, there were easily as many friends of Parnak in the galaxy. In the past five places there had always been someone who knew him if only by reputation or one friend had *halloed* another and called in a favor. At any rate, the Finian islands of light had been theirs to walk across as far as the spaceport.

Starr fronted his own band whose aggregate name escaped him for the dozenth time.

Parnak didn't dance but found he had no choice with Quantum. She almost dragged him onto the floor.

More Sand Rockers shuffled into the club. All seemed unfazed by their passage under the gaze of the Omegan at the door. Parnak breathed a little easier as he saw no Targan among them. They were tall, good-looking, male and female humanoids, off-worlders without doubt.

Quantum moved easily before him. He thought she danced as well as anyone he'd seen, ever. She looked very attractive to him, in fact, so much so that he almost forgot that they were on the run.

He wondered for what purpose she had originally been designed. At length, they sat. They found drinks waiting, compliments of the management.

Parnak nodded thanks to the short, broad man, the owner, who'd brought them in after the Omegan doorman.

The insectoid downed his drink quickly. A waiter appeared, "Another drink, sir?"

"Yes." Parnak answered with a wry nod, "And – no Targans, please!"

"Hold the Targans – yes, sir!" The waiter was gone quickly.

The place thundered to Sand Rock. New humanoids rushed the dance floor and joined those already there. Still, more came into the room. The others arrived early, before this, the main crowd. The nightclub became overrun just as Parnak finished his first drink and went to work on the, just arrived, second. Quantum touched neither drink before her.

From the dance floor to the bar, the place overflowed. No one left. Parnak supposed that they would be safe in the crowd for a while. It would give them time to rest and time to plan. He was content to sit, allowing the drinks to muddle the signals coming from his antennae and gaze more at Quantum. Some time went by.

The hologram announced it was taking a break and would be back from more -- in just a few minutes. Thee Starr, the hologram, seemed a little unctuous, too solicitous of his audience. The audio stage went off with an electronic hiss. With nothing more to look at, the club patrons turned to each other. The floor cleared in favor of the bar, and waiters and waitresses, all of them androids, were talking about their work.

Many watched her progress in her journey to Soarer, with appreciation.

The Targan first impression had been one of amazement, one could say astonishment, at the perfection of the androids who worked the city. Aboard Modallas, it was they who did that kind of work, but in the streets, they saw these perfect beings carrying out mundane tasks, instead of themselves.

A sort of chord sounded in their minds as they realized, they, to The Helmsman, were the same as the race of androids, to the masters of Parnel. They were the best of that race which battled the Marcellean warriors, they, from the vast forests covering the planet but, highly trained. However, they were still Targan, forest creatures, forest men, only half – savage or half – civilized.

They did not think of it too long. There was the mission, this female android led them closer to the Ghost Pilot, the one who had eluded their master for so long. It would be worth it for them to go into trouble by either capturing or killing that one.

42

Thee Starr – Coming Home – The Yardus Vid

Helio was never difficult. He stormed up the ramp past Helio and Starr toward the Centralizer cabinet. Along the way, he opened a storage cabinet, searching in the dim light for the overhaul kit.

Starr smiled, "So when do we go?"

He stalked Borter.

"In a few minutes," Helio answers politely. I just have to look over the repairs." He gestured toward the centralizer cabinet. "You have a VID for us, I hear?"

"Sure do. Have you heard of the concert I did at Yardus?"

"I think I've heard of that, but –" Helio shrugged.

"So – not?"

Parnak sat on the other side of the tube with his recorder.

Parnak did not like the idea of going to Modallas to rescue Julia as Helio explained. He liked it less as Borter joined the discussion.

Soarer's tube was dimly lit as it was most of the time. They talked there for a few minutes. The conversation went on in quiet earnest, and Borter did the most talking.

He'd shouted, shouted red-faced, "No passengers!"

The insectoid reached into his travel bag. From it came his service contract with Soarer – "See this little bit here." He held it for The Pilot to see. Borter refused to look.

"No passengers – and don't shake that thing in my face! I've read it more times than you! "

"Then, you know my rights. We're – Thee Starr and I are coming along!"

Borter stalked away. An angry hour later, The Pilot was back, "The centralizer is done, do you wanna take a look?"

Parnak very dimly answered, "No, thanks."

Helio rose and went to the centralizer. He shouted to the tube, "OK. Start it up."

Minutes later, Parnel Control authorized take-off.

There were a lot of ships carrying freight in the galaxy,

he'd explained. Soarer was just another one, just like all the others. If The Helmsman was suspicious of one, he had to be suspicious of them all. That would be a big job even for him.

When Parnak reminded him that he also had a lot of Targans working for him, Borter shrugged, saying that Targans were only Targans. Parnak, however, was correct. If Borter's plan worked easily, and there was some reason to believe that it might, they still had to find Julia, free her, and get out alive.

Parnak agreed in principle to rescue Julia. She was Lord Soal's daughter. It was the least he could do for his old boss.

Sensors behind read only Tulso Slide's Silver Hammer following them. From the spaceport, there was no sign of

Targan's pursuit. Parnak explained what had happened to them the day and night before. Borter said he would be ready. Orbit was clear.

Borter picked up his freight containers, big boxes that were longer than wide and attached to the ship's hull. Helio made sure the hatches from Soarer to them worked properly. He replaced the bolts that attached them to the hull with explosive bolts in case they were forced to dump them quickly. The system was in place, and dim warning lights glowed in the darkness of the tube.

Starr sat quietly, talking to Parnak with much animation. Every minute or so, he would look toward the cockpit at Borter's shape as he worked the controls. He'd sent Slide along to Ganempsha with the band and equipment. Starr, however, was more interested in Soarer, Borter, and Helio. He refused to go to the planet.

Soarer joined a long line of freighters heading toward Modallas. They were only a few hours out of Parnel before they saw their first wing of Modallian fighters. They were Targan piloted. Borter was not close enough to see them, but he imagined that he could see their dark, scowling faces in the tiny cockpits. They'd all seen quite enough Targans on Marcellus.

As the hours whiled away. He wandered the entire tube of Soarer and finally he came toward the cockpit. Helio was checking the cargo manifest in one of the containers and Starr asked permission to enter the cockpit itself. Borter looked around not smiling and not scowling, he decided Starr meant no harm and gave his permission.

Starr seemed curious about the controls of the ship and asked questions about the main computer running them.

Borter was happy to show him around the control panel, even Old Face's weapons panel, as it turned out. He ran the system test just so Starr could hear the maddening array of arcade buzzers, bells, and whistles the Techno Dwarf's technicians installed when they rebuilt the ship. Starr laughed.

Borter described Modallas to Starr, who'd only heard wild tales. He accepted the kilometers-long size of the thing but could not grasp its speed. Borter had to laugh at this and shook his head.

That afternoon Thee Starr heard of Targans and The Helmsman. Borter unfolded his account of the final battles for Marcellus itself. He told of Soarer's narrow escapes.

"The Heart?" Starr gasped the words out. "I follow the Heart, do you?"

Borter looked at him as if he'd just spit out a lizard. "No," he answered calmly, trying not to make much of it. Starr produced the palm-sized, round, crimson medal, which identified the Children of The Heart. It was uniquely Ganempshan, as was Sand Rock and the Children of the Heart. Borter knew little about the cult The Heart or the children of Ganempsha who made it up.

"You are The Ghost Pilot, aren't you?" Starr exclaimed at last.

Borter winced, not knowing whether he could endure such innocence.

He replied calmly. "No. There is no such person. Your Ghost Pilot is a fiction. Something made up by some fool journalist. One who's long past his prime!" He nodded in Parnak's direction, but Starr's eyes never left him. Nor did Parnak look back.

"What's this?" Starr pointed to an empty slot on the control console between the seats of the two pilots. Borter shook his head glad that any discussion of the Ghost Pilot was dropped, he didn't know. It did nothing, he said, it was in none of the manuals, so he'd forgotten it.

Helio returned from the freight container, and Starr left the cockpit. "You've made a friend, it appears!" Borter took his friend's dryness of speech for sarcasm and grunted.

"Yeah. Thanks to our friend, Parnak, the Ghost Pilot has a pal!"

"He hasn't taken his eyes off you since he came on board. He's polite to me, civil with Parnak, and sure of you. He's an intuitive. One knows another!"

"Go ahead, put them on. I'll start them up when you are ready." Starr kept smiling.

Everything was computer-controlled. It could be any-thing at all. Huge quantities of them, both the vid – phones and the cartridges that stored the videos. Vid–phones looked like masks with eyes and ears covered. They were sold across the galaxy. Before Starr flicked down his eye shield, he pressed a few keys on his control panel start-ing the vid – Yardus.

Borter had never been to a Sandrock festival, nor had Helio. They'd certainly heard of them. The festival on Yardus had been a classic. All the top groups were there, and people from all across the galaxy had. It had been the biggest ever. Borter would have hired out as a transport carrier to the site but was committed elsewhere and couldn't get out of it.

Borter walked on a broad platform. Turning, he saw it was filled with people and that he was moving toward them, walking. In the far distance, in the center of everything, was the stage. Borter's vid-phones kept him walking toward it.

Holographic lighting and anti-grav equipment were centered there. Borter liked it. He'd been in space for a very long time without relief. Flyers, freighter pilots, tended to do that. Borter knew flyers who hadn't set foot on a planet for years. They simply flew between the orbiting planetary slips, offloaded, unloaded, and left on another run. It was almost endless. First, it became a habit, then they feared leaving their ships at all.

He waved. Borter saw Helio in the distance, also walking. He waved to him, and the Dillisome waved back. Parnak was there, somewhat, farther back, though. His wave was more belated. In their vid-phone fantasies, they saw Borter as well as each other and had the distinct sensation of walking far into the Yardian concert and sharing it with many humanoids from that planet and from many others across the galaxy. Borter continued his trek into the crowd.

It was easy. Anything he wished came to be through the computer. He liked that. He looked around. There were lots of women around, young, beautiful women. He'd wished them there, so they were.

One dangled on each arm, both young and attractive. They laughed at his jokes and smiled brightly as he told them. Sometimes, *vid-crawlers*, as they were called in the vernacular, sometimes, played tricks on one another. Borter wished something for Parnak.

The insectoid jerked back suddenly as she took his arm as the others had Borter's. Beside him, from nowhere, appeared one of those young women.

Then, the insectoid's manner changed, he seemed to be enjoying himself. The insectoid seemed to smile though he did not have the physiology for it. The young woman on his arm was there to stay. Borter, looking on for a second, undecided whether or not, he was the trickster or the tricked. He raised an eyebrow at the journalist.

Borter was downcast no matter the surroundings. The pretty girls in his arms served to remind him of Julia only. There was nothing he could do for her, nothing for Lord Soal, and nothing for Marcellus. He'd really wanted to help there, despite his initial resistance. What he had been able to do had been worth nothing, so he thought.

He continued his journey toward the stage area. Nothing of the show had begun. Things were still being moved on antigravs and being set up, and things were hardly of interest.

The vid-phone computer sensed his feelings, read his thoughts. It responded. There was a soft beeping in his ears.

He looked for its source but could find none. His surroundings blanked out twice, once completely blank, then back. It had changed subtly, but it had changed. Borter could feel it. Looking to either side, he discovered both his new friends were gone. The vid-phone flashed dead again, exactly as before. A moment later, he was back, Julia in his arms. Parnak made his best effort at giggling.

Julia awed him as before. He ached that he could do nothing for her. Still, she was there, that dream. He thought about it for a second, but then he did not. In the computer dream, she was there because he wanted her.

It was growing late in the afternoon. In the blink of an eye, the computer-enhanced the image.

Julia stood looking at him. She gazed at him as if there were no other man in the entire galaxy, and he gazed back just the same way. He could influence the images as they came to him.

At the same time, Helio settled back with the young woman that Borter had wished on him. He did not mind; it was what Borter termed as better than looking down the barrel of a blaster, liking what you got. The music from the backup group, an anonymous assemblage of musicians, was beginning to play.

Helio felt relaxed for a change. The girl nestled closer against him, in his arms, as the music began to sweep over them.

The stage hovered, at least hung in the air about center crowd. The band's name or where it had come from did not interest him in the slightest. Only among the greats did identity matter. Could the true expert tell who it was? That would be Parnak, also lost in the crowd, that young lovely cradled in his arms.

Lights flashed skyward as if a dozen starships lifted off at once. He would report his criticism of the concert as he would have any other. There was no harm in mixing work with pleasure.

Ultra guitars and holograms pervaded his mind. He lost touch with the reality it was a vid-phone experience, induced. He had no need to work at all. It would have been simplicity itself to totally relax, but not for him, Parnak, the great journalist.

Work was more natural than relaxation. It seemed more natural than life itself to his race. Their host, Thee Starr, felt this more sad than curious.

It went on. At last, the vid-phone computer judged them ready. The crowd settled as one as the backup band struck its last crashing chords. Starr was next.

A wave of anticipation went through the vast assemblage as roadies crossed the staging and, once across, crossed back again. Then, having once recrossed, they crossed a thousand times more, it seemed.

All was ready. Finally. The stage darkened. The crowd was silent. Glowing anti-grav disks whisked away from the stage, blurring as they rose above the crowd. They swept at high speed across the expanse of the festival. Everyone watched.

As they did, Starr and his band took the stage under the cover of darkness. They were ready and silent as the crowd began to *oooh* and *ah* the performance of the anti-gravs. They seemed to gather once again and rush down toward the stage. Starr's first chords rolled out like thunder in the night.

First songs were Starr oldies, those favorites from the early years. There had been many early years for him.

Titles, names of songs, and album collectibles reached out into the night, a fistful of memories from youth and romance, of expectation and innocence that told the story of male and female life-kind, the whole galaxy.

From his first album, a classic among rockers, Another Dawn, Another Day, Another Planet, then Between Consenting Quarks, that title, unexplained, had instant success across the galaxy.

So appealing, they said because of the acoustics used in the recording studio, heard in the inner mind, directly, rather than the ear.

He could have retired from then on, living on continued royalties, but he did not. Starr's fortunes rose with his fame. It wasn't long before several systems of middling stature in wealth were under his control. Under his ownership, there were no rebellions and no unrest.

In fact, things on the poorer planets improved. On the whole, things became - satisfactory.

It seemed to Borter he'd spent the entire three days at the festival with Julia, but he had not. The time spent from the first note to the last was just a little less than four hours. His visions, from first to last, had been managed by vid. After the final explosions above the stadium, he, like the other two, found himself facing a grinning Thee Starr in the hollow of Soarer's tube.

Parnak, until the image of the young woman was supplied to him, thought himself incapable of such feelings. The vid, having taken his measure, made the girl's image equally persistent, thus, each time he put her off, it simply made her more beautiful to him.

Helio, all the while, was quite agreeable and enjoyed himself immensely. Starr's Yardus concert had been a terrific success. Now, it passed, his head cleared, released from the vid. His ears rang a little from the volume. Otherwise, he was fine. Borter was another story.

He sat, quiet, grim-faced, having been reminded of his love lost. Julia, if she was still alive, a captive of The Helmsman aboard Modallas. There was little he could do.

The tube of Soarer became a stark place, a place of loneliness. In the end, they all felt it. Their respective lives as pilots and journalists drew them up in bleak contrast to the screens they'd all, moments before, quite happily experienced.

Borter was sure he'd felt it alone, and if asked for a comparison between himself and any of the others, he would have said so. No one spoke, strangely enough. It was a sort of withdrawal, said Starr, affecting even the most experienced vid-crawlers.

It merely required the patience to outlast the temporary effect. Borter grumbled and made his way toward the cockpit as the others looked after him. There were things to be done, Ganempsha was near.

Traffic control was minimal there. Care would have to be exercised, landing on such planets were to a great extent manual.

43

Thee Starr

There were things to be done. Spaceport Parnel, at Ganempsha, was near. Traffic control was minimal. Care would have to be exercised. Landing on such planets was, to a great extent, manual. Borter and Helio could do it in their sleep, but others who might be around could not.

Borter looked on from his seat in the cockpit, Helio moved Soarer into the Ganempshan slot, the ariel path all flyers used coming into a spaceport. He'd gestured with one hand toward the controls, meaning Helio had been given the honor of landing the little freighter.

Helio's hands crossed the controls easily, as skillful as Borter's own. The Dillisome had learned a considerable amount in their time together.

Soarer was nose down in orbit. They waited for landing clearance from Parnel Control. There were freighters, like their own, lined up both ahead of them and behind waiting for clearance into the slot.

That day, Parnel was slow. Soarer powered down. The green glow from his Marcellean power dots dimmed to standby levels. Helio switched stabilization to automatic and leaned far back in his chair. Borter was similarly relaxed.

Helio got them assigned to a dock. The lights went down, and only the instrument panel showed a muted brightness before them. In a couple of moments.

The planet's horizon filled the windshield. Electronics filled the computer screens with readings from ground stations. Borter sat back; Helio had made dozens of landings under all conditions without looking at the screens.

He consulted the Galactic Atlas, something usually left for Helio, more to his interests. Borter could not say why he bothered to make note of the place at all. There was nothing much to say about Ganempsha as he confirmed from the atlas. That is nothing much except Sand Rock.

There were the obligatory paragraphs, paragraphs only, that described the major land masses. It seemed there were no large bodies of water at all.

There were vast deserts, the largest called The Ords and its gigantic farms showing lush vegetation. The cities were neither impressive nor large. There was nothing remarkable about the planet at all. Borter shrugged and closed the atlas with a sharp snap. He failed to take advantage of the note at the bottom of the page to see Sand Rock under the music heading. They would not be there long.

The landing itself was easy. Helio touched down with hardly a bump and taxied toward their assigned dock. As they touched down, the voice of a lazy-sounding robot traffic controller assigned them to an old and disused-looking hanger.

It would do, they supposed. There was no sense in alerting agents of The Helmsman to their whereabouts. Except for a narrow strip of fresh tarmac, the field was a rutted affair, hostile to any known type of aircraft. Still, the lights went down and only the instrument panel showed a muted brightness before them. In a couple of moments, Borter felt the need to speak.

Across the expanse of the field, scrub brush grew in tight bunches beneath the double suns of that world, at their hottest. Borter turned on the air – conditioner from his side of the console, meaning to remain aboard until that daytime heat had passed.

The Con screens showed both technical data of all Modallas and its visual appearance. To the right, the long, hollow tube opened like a great maw. Dotted around that screen were more screens, smaller, showing each of Modallas' plains, two peopled by Targans and the third, which held the city of the dead, called the White City of the Third Plain. No one lived there.

On the left screen hull activity was monitored. There, the great louvered eyes of Modallas, many kilometers of them down the body of the vast cylinder opened and closed lighting the interior. Maintenance crafts were about their duty across the turning face, their maneuvering lights flashing solemnly in the dark of space.

An angry Helmsman strode the Con that day. A tense line of his Targan officers stood at attention as he spoke to them as frightened raw recruits before a tough drill instructor.

The Helmsman towered over them, leaving no doubt in their minds about his physical strength. The tone of his voice told them that he was, indeed, prepared to use it. Before them, in full battle armor, face mask in place as always, he leaned, a figure to whom their every loyalty was pledged at birth. He was one of the few things in the entire galaxy Targans feared.

Rebels among them and among the corps of junior officers would be found out. None would be spared, he thundered at them shaking his armored fist in their faces. He demanded results and warned that interrogations were in progress that would reveal the conspirators, soon.

He was aware, he told them, forcing unaccustomed terror down their throats, that he was the undisputed master of Modallas, and that would remain a fact of their lives.

He turned and dismissed them with a casual wave of his hand as one of his more trusted junior officers came into the Control Center and to him with an urgent report.

"Where?" The battle mask demanded of the young Targan. "Plain Two! The attacks are coming closer to the Marcellean woman's quarters!" The Targan lieutenant nodded as though his acknowledgment mattered to the Modallian master.

The Helmsman returned to the controls on the Con. There, among the series of screens with which he could see any part of the vast artificial world and the custom-made hand grip with which he steered. He chose a single button and pressed it.

Instantly, a screen at his elbow came to life, and he was in touch with the Targan at the scene.

". . . same as the others, sir," the Targan gave his report in a more relaxed manner than had existed in the Control Center moments before.

"They're dead, killed by some large animal! The monitors picked up nothing, sir!" The monitor in use at the time swung from the young officer down to a pair of torn bodies close by. The Helmsman studied the screen for a few moments, but cared to make no comment.

The killings were becoming more frequent. Always, there was that bestial howl just after. He was incapable of fear, or he would have been afraid as were all his Targans.

The beast was, in fact, a Marcellean Battle T'Sog, bred over eons for no other purpose than the killing of Targans. What made them so deadly was not the wide, slashing jaws or their size, but the ability they had to teleport themselves over great distances and pinpoint an enemy.

They were rare. Only one still existed, that one, however, belonged to Lord Soal himself and it now had Modallas located.

If Soal still lived, The Helmsman hoped to meet him face to face. He patted the ion blade strapped to his side, which had been taken from the murdered Snow Beggar, Soal's father.

44

The Rescue of Julia

"Move the Marcellean woman to new quarters. Replace my personal guard with androids. Make sure no one knows of her movement!" The lieutenant saluted and was gone.

The Helmsman returned to his previous worry of wolves among his sheep. For months, there had been rumblings, intelligence reports, and rumors of unrest among the Targans. A few political murders had occurred within his staff.

The entity, once known to their forest ancestors as the Sky God, could no longer control his servants. Much of his time was now devoted to this alone. His hand, the hand that never failed, was less and less on the Con's steering grip.

The toll among the Targan from the battle was minimal compared to this. If there was no control, there would be no Modallas.

His operatives culled from among the faithful those who would betray him, still there were more. The woman was his lure to all things Marcellean, for through them, he would find and come to possess The Heart itself.

In that there was power and hence the control he desired. Even Lord Soal would come. His body had not been among the others that day on the Third Plain pyramid where his red flag had been raised. That had been a battle.

Modallas lay just ahead. It was a first for all aboard Soarer that they had never before come near Modallas without someone shooting at them. A freighter landed and took off every thirty seconds. Modallas' spaceport was in full operation twenty-four hours every day.

It had changed, making it more difficult to fly directly into the open cylinder. There was more building in the way, made, to accommodate the vast intake of freight. The magnetic field that kept the place pressurized against open space, was up and even stronger. It would be very difficult to punch through it, if they had to.

The cargo containers hid them well. It was doubtful they actually needed the camouflage. Borter saw at least three other ships that looked like Soarer in port, all black hulled. The Marcellean weapons pods were built into the fuselage and wings and were invisible to the eye except when ready to fire. If it came to shooting their way out, they would be very convincing. Now, their presence was secret. They had an hour before takeoff.

"You didn't say you were bringing a Sand Rock star." Borter looked around at Helio who smiled back. "I have business. You demanded – transportation – not just you and transportation, it was just you and Thee Starr.

We're going to do this – bit of business – before we deliver you and Mr. Starr to The Ords, fulfilling the terms of our contract."

Helio was still smiling. Parnak turned and went back into the tube.

Julia sat in the garden of her new quarters. They were much like those she'd had before. From the hallway to the new apartment, she could tell she'd been moved closer to the Control Center and The Helmsman. She looked back, the other direction down the space of Modallas toward the spot, invisible because of the vast area encompassed.

In all the months she had been there, she had seen The Helmsman only once, that was on the first night, the night of her kidnap.

Had she an ion blade or a weapon of any sort, before attempting escape, she'd seek out The Helmsman's throat with it. Looking toward that far, flat end of Modallas' cylinder, she had a feeling that day might be the day, her final day aboard Modallas.

Her Targan guard outside the door had been replaced by one of androids. She never saw Targan's face, but she knew when they were gone. The androids could come as close as they wanted, but not the Targans.

Targans were enemies much older than even The Helmsman and Modallas, they were biological enemies. In turn, only The Helmsman kept them from killing her. Her Targan guards were not allowed to see her face-to-face on screen and were the best controlled of the generations of Targan brought to Modallas for training. They were the very cream of his forces despite the current troubles.

Julia would have waded through Targans up to her neck, if it would have gotten her out of Modallas. It would not help.

It would only get her killed. For that same reason, Borter and his friends would find it difficult to rescue her. She would attract Targans like magnets attract iron. There was also that small problem of finding her.

The Helmsman was on the Con, hand placed firmly on the steering grip. He watched the screens around him easily. All of Modallas was yet under his control, within easy reach through his console. His junior officer, the Targan lieutenant was at his side busily overseeing the control staff. Modallas hung peacefully for the moment some safe distance from a bright star from which the life within the cylinder absorbed light.

Targans were stationed everywhere guarding against the Marcellean beast that was among them. Others searched for the monster in transportation tubes and transport shafts and in Modallas' open fields. The Helmsman knew there was no hope at all in finding this T'Sog or keeping it from its victim.

Stories of the beast were already blown out of proportion. The sight of armed troopers settled his Targan and let them benefit from drawing closer together. Much would be needed from them in the coming campaigns.

Targans were forest-bred. Even better, they were forged in battle. They'd fought their way across the Inner Galaxy. It looked as if nothing could stop them. One of his sectors checked in. Two guards had been found, slain, and two more, just as before. Then, another sector checked in and another in rapid succession. They were second only to the Marcelleans.

More troops were dispatched, and others were drawn away from the spaceport at Modallas' far end.

The Helmsman was relieved he was not Targan. It did make his chances much, much better. Lord Soal's pet would, of course, try to find him, as well. Modallas was far too complex to make it an easy task. Something did bother him though. He removed his hand from the control grip.

Two more guards were found dead, "as before." More troops were dispatched, and still others were drawn away from the spaceport to give help.

"He's here, '' the voice rasped from the covered helmet. The lieutenant drew his blaster and stood ready, looking around. At his command, The Helmsman's guard surrounded both, weapons at the ready. The Lieutenant scanned the area, the entire Control Center. "We are ready, Helmsman!"

The Helmsman snapped back to reality having been taken away by the sensation. He looked around himself at the circle of troopers protecting him as if he had just seen them for the first time. "No!" His voice came again. "That Ghost Pilot. He's here."

Ordering the lieutenant to take the Con, he stepped down, breaking through the circle of guards coming to his defense. Half of their number followed him out of the center, the rest returned to their positions, and one remained near the helm and the young lieutenant. The place grew silent.

Borter squared away his loose gear and checked the power indicator on his own blaster. He took care of issuing one to Parnak.

They would need computer access if they were to find Julia. Parnak's expertise in that field would come in handy for any necessary deductions to be made.

Soarer would have to break through the magnetic field into the tube of Modallas when the time came. They would not be allowed through merely as freighter pilots and company.

The Helmsman was in contact with Control. His first move was to seal off the spaceport. Targan guards appeared everywhere.

An eagle had come to roost that day. An enemy who had escaped Modallas twice.

He mumbled, "Where flies the Ghost Pilot also comes . . . "

The Targan gave it no further thought as he obeyed a further order to seal the spaceport.

"So, The Helmsman believed the Ghost Pilot had come to Modallas? If that one believed it, it must be so."

Borter worked on ways forgotten into the main tube, all through the flight to Modallas. There seemed to be no casual way to enter. The cargo containers were searched as a matter of course. That left smashing their way in with Soarer. Even as the containers were removed, they did not drift far from Soarer. Parnak watched them carried away overhead.

There was, therefore, a way out, noted the journalist as he watched. They faced a moment of truth or would shortly.

There were Targans moving toward them. He could feel it. He turned to Helio. The Dillisome knew just why they hadn't blown the cargo bolts on the way in and gone ahead with what they were about to do.

Parnak shook his head. Helio just smiled. They had to get closer.

He rushed to the cockpit. The fine hairs on the back of his Magnean neck stood out straight. The Marcellean power dots brightened. The Ghost Pilot was not to be denied his mission.

Soarer roared away. Ground crews ran for cover. The Helmsman teleported himself and a security team onto the runway - too late.

Fighters scrambled. Soarer attempted to reach open space, they guessed, rushing after her. As weapons pods emerged beneath her wings, Soarer turned back, speeding toward the interior of Modallas.

Coming in low enough, on the turn, the pilot recognized The Helmsman on the tarmac. He'd have strafed The Helmsman, if there had been a chance. With all of Modallas alerted, there was no chance of finding Julia. the little freighter raised shields.

As Soarer cut the barrier and was into the interior of Modallas, those accompanying The Modallian leader opened fire.

A full wing of fighters joined the action. Just as they emerged from the space portal, fire and tracking with other pursuits found the freighter from within.

Borter was already in the zero-gee cloud bank that floated at Modallas' center. Helio had gotten the computer to release the shields to his control, and Soarer's armament went fully operational.

"Modallian fighters," closing in from behind, someone said.

Three blips appeared on one of his screens, the fighters always worked in threes. Parnak stood in the hatchway just behind the pilots, his recorder poised. The Modallian cylinder was long, but in less than one half minute, the freighter would reach the end of it.

Helio watched his *distant scan*, measuring distance in seconds. Even if Borter reduced speed, it would still be a narrow escape. They'd miss the end of the cylinder, but would have to contend with its sides as they attempted to race back through the fighters and the spaceport. Borter swore to himself, if The Helmsman was still nearby, he would go after him.

More fighters entered through the magnetic barrier.

Helio timed it and found escape possible. They could be out before anything could be done to stop them. Not even the Modallian computer-operated gun systems were that fast.

Julia looked out onto the land masses of Modallas. She looked up at the white clouds down Modallas' middle sky. There was nothing to see, no indication of the contest unfolding there.

By this time, she expected no rescue, believing it impossible. Had she seen Soarer, she would have known who was there and why.

Modallas ranged far across the galaxy, often. From the warmth of any star for days at a time.

In her new apartment, far above the street, she could see deep into the cylinder. She belonged to Modallas for as long as she lived. Rescuers could not have known where she was.

It was at that moment Soarer broke cloud in cover, engines roaring.

It was a dream she thought at first, a vision. She knew that ship. She saw the Targan piloted fighters chasing it, closing. "Borter," she whispered!

Helio angled the shields behind. Borter had not reduced speed at all. Parnak thought that quite typical and made the turn anyway.

Borter shouted back into the tube as if Parnak were there instead of in the hatch. He wanted to make sure Parnak was getting this, he didn't want him to miss one exciting instant in the life of his creation, The Ghost Pilot. Parnak was already queasy from the turn, much to Borter's satisfaction.

The fighters held back. Helio held his fire against them. The Helmsman was very happy to let them tire The Ghost Pilot in the sky while he was trapped within Modallas. Sooner or later, that Ghost Pilot would have to land. It would be too easy - on the ground.

But Soarer's pilot had other plans. Borter executed a turn that the pursuing fighters could not follow and left Soarer hanging like a stunned butterfly riding a summer's breeze. He turned upward, aiming for the vast shutters, louvered spaces between Modallas' land masses. It was then Helio allowed the Marcellean weapons to speak.

Julia watched as Soarer blasted through the Modallian cylinder's wall into space, leaving amid a hail of debris to be dealt with by those who followed.

Shattered louvers tumbled away as Borter kicked in more power and put distance between themselves and Modallas.

There was a bright flash behind her. She turned. Two faces she'd thought forever gone looked back at her. They belonged to 5D and to her husband, Rand Sabbling.

5D looked on, his twisting geometric squares waiting for orders. She ran to Sabbling's arms.

He announced. "We're here to rescue you." He grinned, laughing gently and, in another flash, they were gone from Modallas.

45

Thee Starr Coming Home – (Continues)

Beside him, as Borter looked on from his seat in the cockpit, Helio took control, taking his regular seat, moving Soarer into the Ganempshan slot, the ariel path, all used, coming into Parnel Spaceport.

The blue man's fingers crossed the control panel skillfully, almost as skillfully as Borter's own. The Dillisome had learned a considerable amount from him in their time together.

The planet's horizon filled the windshield. Soarer's sensors filled the computer's screens with readings taken from automatic beacons on the ground. Borter relaxed; Helio had made dozens of landings under all conditions. Without looking to the screens Borter surmised that the place alternated between arid and lush.

He consulted the Galactic Atlas once again. He reread the obligatory paragraphs, brief writings only, that described the land masses, no major bodies of water at all, just major deserts. Still, there was nothing much to say about the place, nothing much, except, Sand Rock.

46

Yardus Vid – Starr – Erotic

Those vast deserts, the largest called The Ord Deserts, or just The Ords, or The Wastes, awaited them. Lush plantations, gigantic, featured thick, well-cared for, vegetation.

Cities were neither impressive nor large. There was nothing remarkable about the planet at all. Borter shrugged and closed the atlas with a sharp snap.

The landing itself was easy, with hardly a bump. Down, the voice of a lazy sounding robot traffic controller assigned them to an old and disused looking hanger. It would do. There was no sense in alerting agents of The Helmsman to their whereabouts.

Except for a narrow strip of fresh tarmac, the field was a rutted affair, hostile to any known type of aircraft. Still, Helio, ever vigilant, guided them to the assigned dock.

Across the field, scrub brush grew in tight bunches beneath the double suns of that world, at that time of day, the hottest. Borter turned on the air conditioner from his side of the console, meaning to remain aboard until the heat of day passed.

Refuse lined the sides and corners of the hanger-dock, making it look even more decrepit. Dust was everywhere, choking them with every breath they took, as they opened the cargo ramp at Soarer's belly and stepped out. Borter, true to his word, remained on board with the air conditioner on, full, while all other systems were shut down.

He leaned back as if relaxed. Alone at last, he closed his eyes, at peace with the knowledge that he would sleep undisturbed for a respectable period of time. He was, therefore, safe to sleep for that period of time or for any time exceeding it. He desired sleep, needed it, and had to have it. He was not to be denied. Soon, he slept soundly and would, without The Helmsman or Modallas in his mind.

He thought that a place like this was what he really wanted. Perhaps this was home, that place he'd long desired and imagined to be, that place where he could be free of the rest of the galaxy and its trouble. That place, since the Marcellean involvement, dogged both himself and Helio.

A place like this, he thought, would have some sort of milk-run business that would leave them plenty of time for other things.

"Borter's sleeping?"

"Right." The Dillisome nodded. They stepped off the ramp. Helio turned his translator back and pushed a button. The ramp lifted, closing the tube to Parnel.

Starr already attracted attention. "I like him, but I'm not sure how much," Helio moaned. They watched.

Starr, only a little ahead walked toward the street, looking back toward the two, he called. "Hey, guys! Wanna help cut – an erotic swath through the ville?"

Parnak quipped. "A matter of civic pride – I guess." Pausing, the insectoid went on, "Want a beer? I know a place nearby. "They laughed.

Then. "He's gone" gasped Helio, " – already," unable to spot the singer in the just gathered crowd! Helio stood helpless; his mouth hung open.

They got a beer.

47

Even Odds on Norvado

It wasn't cold enough on Norvado to classify it as an ice planet, it had life on it, life of a sort. That is, it was not a giant ice ball of frozen gases like those that hung out on the most distant edges of the poor solar systems. Norvado's sun had simply become a red dwarf. Any experienced traveler of space knew the kind.

The purposes of such a place were mostly industrial and scientific. Some planets, soon to suffer a similar fate, would send out their best research teams to find answers, to find cures.

Miners came to draw away such materials as they could before the planet vaporized when the sun went nova, sending whatever was valuable into space.

There were strings of freighters to such places and regular routes to run.

Norvado had not very much time left before its good weather, a few weeks of numbing cold before the seasonal big thaw, as it was put by those known among themselves as regulars.

All the comforts of home were brought to these places, temporarily, to be moved away when they were gone or when the sun was about to go nova. Suns did not explode overnight. Sometimes it took many years. Mining civiliza-tions, then, could last a long, long time.

Six of them struggled forward toward a small transport vehicle man-handling a large, black box. It, the box, was almost two meters in length and measured twenty centi-meters high and the same number wide. Its finish was black, neat labels carried a specific address for a far planet, halfway across the galaxy.

48

Dusters Mad Moz The Wingman

The space port was not safe. They were to return to work at the big farm owned by Suther Dann, an old friend of the journalist. Both nodded, they didn't like working as crop dusters over the farm's vast acreage, but it was what Parnak had been able to arrange, like it or not. They'd been on planet a whole week.

They turned and left the spaceport. Parnak wore what all other journalists wore, that is, those who covered combat, a waist length battle jacket, a beige one for around the ville as they, to a man, called cities and towns on an assignment.

"I think we let Starr off one stop too early," Borter said. Helio smirked.

Helio glanced at Borter. "Moz flipped when she heard we'd brought Starr home!"

"Yeah," Borter smiled at the prospect.

When they'd met, Suther Dann's daughter immediately attached herself to him. "What is it they call, his believers? Fans - is that it?"

"No. Sandrockers!" Helio nodded assurance.

By this time, Parnak had overheard and, becoming interested, had dropped back with them. "They're also called The Children Of The Heart," he added, because they believe in the legend, the dominant myth of this planet."

The three walked a little farther without speaking. Then, Parnak told them more. "You know, of course, that Thee Starr is the leading proponent of the planet's youth. To see him is to see them all.

"He's made me decide to investigate further. I'll be asking Dann for your services to fly me out into the Ords to meet with the leader of the Sargon Clones – the Red Clones."

They trailed through the streets of Parnel toward Cross Anchor. Dwellings cascaded like stacked boxes beside the wide streets as they walked farther away from the spaceport. All sorts of shops dotted the ground floor levels. Gradually, the streets narrowed becoming more and more shabby, a note they'd walked across the main part of the city to its outskirts on the poorer side of town.

"You know – all these kids dress like Starr," commented the pilot! He had not put together that they dressed alike for a reason, as had Parnak and Helio.

Parnak spoke to the Magnean in a tone of exasperation, "I know, I know! It's a social statement, a protest from the semi psychotic adolescent segment of the planetary population to the semi psychotic adult segment – of that same population!"

Helio can fly me into the Ords to meet the clones. Your conversation is – well, I don't know!"

Borter's head swiveled toward Parnak bearing a look of hurt on his face. "Gee, Parnak! I was looking forward to another of those – you know, little talks we have!"

"You wear your sarcasm well, Borter."

"Your clothing says the same for you," The Pilot quipped.

Parnak kept his eyes straight ahead, but Helio looked first at one, then the other, smiling a smile that was his own.

His pilots smiled broadly, nodding. Parnak did the best he could. The three had nearly reached the main area where surface vehicles were allowed.

Moz, *Mad Moz*, daughter of Suther Dann could be seen just ahead beside the elegant black sedan that would carry them to her father's lands.

She looked as rebellious as did all the others – Sand Rockers. That is, in striped military fatigues of mottled vegetation, greens, earthy tans, and reds. However, beneath the generous folds of duty fabric nothing hid from the eye, her woman's figure.

Moz waved enthusiastically to them all, or so it appeared. She did see all. Really, she looked only at Borter. Parnak and Helio said nothing, one winking slyly at the other.

Still smiling, she took her place behind the wheel of the sedan. Parnak entered the car through a rear door after Helio, leaving Borter in just the position he did not want.

"Good day." Parnak smiled as best an insectoid could manage. I'm glad you could meet us," he said, "it's a long walk from here."

"No problem," Moz glanced back at him, "it's a long walk from anywhere!"

Borter set his eyes forward, listening to the ever-present Sand Rock that played through the sedan's radio. They got under way.

The journey to Suther Dann's farmhouse was just under two hours. Ganempsha sprawled lushly in all directions. Around them, the countryside rushed by. Borter spent his time noticing the tall green trees that grew in densely ranked and filed orchards.

Beneath the trees themselves, the ground was covered by dusty grass. Here and there an odd, narrow access road cut through the trees.

For some time, they'd been on Suther Dann's property. In a hopper, it took a single day to fly it from end to end. Moz turned from her duty as a driver and smiled warmly at Borter, who ignored her all the more intensely. In back, Helio roused to peer behind at the cloud of fine dust that billowed in their wake.

Parnak also directed his attention to the passing orchards, mulling idly his intended trip to The Ord Ruins, the home of the Sargon clones.

In the late afternoon, first dusk was falling. In another hour, the system's second sun would brighten the planet to full daylight and, then. as slowly sink beyond the horizon. The sedan rushed along. Within, its passengers grew restless and shifted in their seats. The music still played its thumping beat, no one spoke.

Helio glanced first at the preoccupied Parnak and then at the pilot who was lost in his own thoughts. Borter made such a thing of ignoring Moz. Poor Borter, he thought, he wondered if some feeling still rested there.

The pilot did feel something.

The car eased to a stop in the driveway of the farmhouse. Slowly, the passengers of the long sedan pulled themselves erect from the opened doors. Helio glanced toward Borter and asked if he wanted to go down to the pads and check his hopper out for the next day's flight.

Just before takeoff, Borter said. He'd rather do it later – that too much could happen at night. "I don't trust Kees," he said extracting his flight bag from the trunk. "He's a Targan, you know?"

Helio hardly bothered to answer. He'd noticed Kees' savage eyes as quickly as Borter. "A couple of the others are too, I think," he muttered.

"They're Kees' wingmen, that's close enough for me," Borter replied.

Parnak agreed, adding that they were agents of The Helmsman. Targans were much abroad in the galaxy, their murderous nature going ahead of them, trainable and useful only in the cause of The Helmsman and Modallas.

Moz, whom they'd forgotten in their conversation, looked on. She'd never heard the story of the three.

The door to the farmhouse opened spilling light out onto the flat, red desert stones of the porch, then something blotted out the light. A big man stood for an instant in the light. For a second, he turned, working several switches inside, to one side of the door. A post lamp went on in the bright yard, then off, then on again. Finally, a light came on. Moz recognized her father.

Suther Dann came forward reaching the car in easy strides. As he came, he loosened a blaster from its holster strapped to his side. Taking it out he inspected the charge and setting, then he stopped even with Borter and Helio.

"Something in the fields," he said quietly, in a whisper as if talking to himself, "killed two of my help. Tore them to pieces. Kees' wingmen. I hear."

For an instant, his eyes met those of Helio and Borter, "Get 'em in the air, gentlemen," he said in the soft, low voice they heard as he crossed the yard.

"Take blasters from the house if you need them. I know you boys carry your own. Bring 'em, if you want!"

49

Emmick

Emmick was not much to look at, not much as things go. He floated in stasis, center floor, enclosed in a clear globe, a thick gelatinous mass, no limbs at all.

Emmick controlled the vast floor at Parnel Space Port. Those he worked for; said he was the best floor man they'd ever had.

Masses of material goods and equipment come across the floor every day. It was all scheduled down to the last scrap, finding the right dock and the best shipment method, all overseen and arranged by Emmick, the only manager of any kind in the spaceport.

Above the planet a long carefully orchestrated line of space freighters waited in orbit. This he controlled too. There was nothing that did not come under his care.

The day itself was fairly ordinary. Shipments on schedule were made ready and checked. A big consignment for Canus was late and jammed the floor. Emmick's foremen hurried their workers after it until it was finally put in place. Scanners showed what was happening throughout the operation.

After the delivery for Canus was done and away, carried by robot-driven grav jacks, toward the chosen dock for shipment, he noticed the six tired-looking miners unload, from their land transport, a large, long black box. From the look of the transport and the haggard look of the miners, he judged it time to beef up security around the terminal. Security was placed on alert and the black box came his way.

Moz stopped in her tracks turning on her father. He had already headed for the landing pads. Clenching her fists, she hissed angrily, a deep frown gripped her face, her eyebrows knit. She stamped her foot and without looking, turned quickly, heading for the house armory.

Behind her, Parnak was hurrying to Dann' s side. Borter and Helio were making their way toward their quarters and readiness to join the hunt.

As the two pilots arrived at the pad, a hopper was just taking off kicking up a cloud of dust partially obscuring its own red and blue maneuvering lights. A single great eye of light reached out before it, casting a harsh beam between trees, onto the ground.

Parnak squeezed aboard a hopper with Dann and was gone. Moz pulled her hopper up, next to the pilot's. Helio made a way so she could fly in the center of the three. Borter came on the hopper's intercom.

"You can't come," He spoke just loudly enough to make himself heard on her headset above the hopper's din.

Helio said nothing, looking away.

She bawled at him! "I get paid to fly just like everybody else."

Borter pouted! "Your old man said to stay, and you get paid to follow orders - nothing else!"

She made a face, sticking out her tongue, and turned to the controls of her hopper. "You're going to miss all the fun. We're wingmen, you know?" Seeing no hope of changing her mind he readied for takeoff.

Borter eased his hopper into the air before Moz and Helio.

"Fine," he muttered.

Small, the hoppers were capable of quick turns and good speed. Borter and Helio had seen them take lots of punishment and stay in the air.

Above the orchard, they formed up on each other's red and blue lights. Switching on their bright forwards, their beams cut deeply into the Ganempshan night.

Moving forward, in closer formation, the front skids retracted gently. Larger skids at the rear were fixed in position.

When on the ground, forward skids gave the compact body of the crop duster the appearance of an insect ready to leap. At mid-fuselage, the disk sprayers angled back and a little down when in use. Released from their locked positions on either side of the hopper they produced an even more striking comparison to an insect.

Not the newest, ship-to-ship radios crackled with static, but were otherwise quiet. Scanners probed ahead in the dark. A hopper pilot watched his screen at night or when it was impossible to see. Often, big storms came in from the desert. Most times, they were filled with sand instead of rain.

The three sped across the rows of trees toward the beast's last known position. They kept up with other flights by radio. The attack had been at the farm's edge, near the Ords.

They pulled up close together as they flew, the standard practice. They could see the dim lights of one another's instrument panels. At times, there would be a sweep of darkness in the cockpit as a moving hand or arm worked one of the controls or another regulating the flight of the little ships.

The planet's single moon rose as they flew making visibility a little better. To Helio, it seemed a great red eye peering into the night and seeing all that went on below.

Many times, at night, when flying above the white clouds of some planet or other, with a strange moon or two staring down at him, he'd thought of Dillisome hanging far distant in space with its ice that at night resembled clouds, its single pale moon, and dying sun. At those times he missed his planet and wondered how things were there for his family. Often, he said he did not miss it and didn't want to go back to banishing any such thought as it entered his mind.

Reaching the halfway mark, Moz looked across at Borter's hopper though she could not see him. Suther Dann would be angry went he found out she'd disobeyed his orders. That is, if he found out!

Ganempsha in the darkness or the vast orchards of the farm at night had always intrigued her. They'd been her escape from the big house that at times seemed more prison than home. They'd lived there forever, it seemed. Since her mother died.

Dann had kept the place for her, and he'd tried to be both mother and father. Results were mixed. Moz, it seemed, turned out all right.

Dann's compulsion to overprotect her said, perhaps. He thought there was still some question of her growth having reached its full potential. She felt lucky to have learned to fly a hopper at all. The flyer who taught her had been fired.

Borter had come with Parnak, hadn't he, that time before? She smiled to herself. Her feelings had grown quickly for this man who'd come with this Parnak, a strange guest.

It was unusual that two men he was going to hire had not eaten with the rest of the help or had not gone directly to the bunkhouse. The three had dined with her father and herself and after she was practically wished out of the room, had remained late, talking far into the night, in low voices from which she could make nothing.

Mad Moz, the wingman, Borter could almost feel her eyes on him in this darkest of cockpit night. It was a talent of most Magneans, that, being able to tell when something was about to happen. It was what made them such good pilots. It was true enough.

Magnus had produced more than enough good pilots, their names read from the history of the galaxy like a roll call.

Parnak, it seemed, had written huge histories of Magnus and her flyers, Effects of *agnysl gjbar* on pilots, On gifts SB AU zfeg Cil Feu, and A History of the Galaxy.

Parnak had forced both Borter and Helio to read it. The work had achieved some fame as required reading at, of all places, the redoubtable Fleet Academy, where anybody who was anybody as a flyer was educated, meaning, of course, self – satisfied Magneans.

Moz was getting to be a problem for Borter. Oh, she was pretty enough, in her own sort of way. It wasn't only that loving Moz meant settling down. It did, or changing his life did. Magneans got old like everyone else.

As Suther Dann's son-in-law, he'd have it made. He just wasn't ready for that especially not for Mad Moz. Plenty of Magneans were farmers, it wasn't so bad. Where had she gotten that name?

50

Rand Sabbling

Other things were afoot on or near Ganempsha, a planet of the star system Laura Zed. Invisible in the first hint of twilight. The haze of Ganempsha's first sun lingered in the sky.

A small shuttle, in a great deal of trouble, entered the atmosphere. Its lateral stabilizers shot away, as had its radio and rear deflector. The craft's twin engines were stretched to their limit and beginning to fail; damage done.

Rand Sabbling, at the controls, used engines to keep the ship level in the air. His hands moved across the control console of the Kithronese shuttle. The great flexibility of the Marcellean armor he wore was as good as a pilot's bare hands, as good as Borter's or Helio's.

That was not going to save him unless he did something else fast. The shuttle, ungainly in distress was beginning to show signs of breaking up. Blasting away from the Kithronese warship, he'd been set upon by a wing of Modallas' fighters which had, then, damaged the craft. There was the briefest of vapor trails in the upper air as the shuttle's instruments finally winked out.

In turn, local fighters, Ganempshan, set upon the Modallians. It was too late for the ship, in any case, except that it preserved the pilot or, at least, forestalled for a time, his fate.

For the instant it took to reach his sandy destination, the Kithronese, having destroyed the Modallian interceptors, sent word the shuttle was down and where it was. There was little more they could do.

The fleet itself was too greatly damaged and disarrayed to offer assistance to other than to those closest to it. The Kithronese went home.

Sabbling angled his forward deflector and wrestled the controls for stability, hoping to hold on and make a safe landing on the planet rushing toward him. There were seconds, a minute, in which to pick a spot that was clear.

The shuttle leveled a bit.

He slowed the ship. He waited until only a few meters from the surface to break the sickening dive the craft had taken. Sabbling felt himself pulled forward by the breaking action. There wasn't really a choice of safe places to land.

He set aside the fuel in that thruster for a second attempt action when he wanted to kill his speed altogether on landing.

He swooped in on The Ords, a remote area near nothing.

Red sand reached for him as he leveled one last time. The deflector would hit first in front. Next, he shut off the automatic override so that it wouldn't switch off his engines, as it was supposed to. Sabbling would do that.

The shuttle descended onto red sand. He felt the deflector hit, tear away, and shake the whole craft. The last thought he remembered having as he crawled away – why was it so – hot?

The wreckage was on fire and so was he, safe in his armor. The sound of beating hooves, many, came nearer.

Modallas moved through space, nearer Laura Zed, more distant from Ganempsha. Within the turning cylindric shell, The Helmsman slowly paced the Con. The black freighter was on his mind. It had escaped him on Marcellus. Now, it troubled him at Laura Zed.

Moments before, one of his captains brought news that the freighter had been tracked to the planet. The captain stood waiting, a moment longer. The Helmsman considered his options.

"Captain." The Targan stepped toward The Helmsman, "Alert all cells on the planet, priority to resupply, until further notice!"

"Sir!" The Targan was ready to turn and carry out his orders, before he could The Helmsman went on.

"I want AF6."

"Yes, Sir!" The Targan looked at the masked creature in black armor whose face, he, like all others had never seen, who made his forest blood run cold.

That captain was quickly on his way. Even for a Targan, those who prided themselves on their fear of nothing were glad to be away from The Helmsman.

Never, not even when, as one, among the most primitive of those new from the forests, did he experience this feeling.

On the outskirts of Suther Dann's farm, hours before dawn, a small fleet of hoppers drew up near a most gruesome sight.

Borter and Helio stood together with Parnak and Suther Dann. Moz edged herself forward, squeezing between Borter and Helio for a look.

"It must have gotten very crowded here," he said. Dann turned to leave, "In fact," he said fighting a wave of nausea, "It's very crowded here, now!" Not far away he gave up his last meal to the Ords. A moment later, Moz followed. "Well," Parnak spoke up, "I have to be getting back to Parnel."

"Story to get out?" Borter smiled looking askance.

"Yes! Big – story!"

51

Chibba The Spy - The Battle In The Bar

The limousine bearing Chibba the Spy rounded the corner taking up much of the narrow street in Parnel. He knew already his two pilots were in the bar.

Few there knew of Kithron's destruction. Very few would care. Chibba had known shortly after it happened. There was little he didn't know.

The car came to a halt. A smallish man approached, who seemed unlikely to have ever seen such an automobile, much less have business with the hard looking occupant sitting in its back seat. An opaque window slid down with a muffled whir to one-quarter open.

Chibba leaned forward. "They are here. I think these flyers like to drink." The man smiled, his eyes straining to see into the dark car. He could only make out the cold, hunter's eyes staring out at him.

His wide limousine sat across from a dingy bar, parked, halfway between the corners of the street. He grunted.

His normal scowl on his face, he sized up the front door of the bar. It had no back door. A neon light of the window sign invited females of any species to enter, would have hurt his eyes had it not been for the opacity of the car's glass.

The forests of distant Marcellus were Chibba's, and the night, even in the city, even one so dingy as this seemed his as well. The window hissed closing and the spindly man stepped back as the limousine moved away from the curb and back into the rough cobblestone street. Much was left to be done. His orders had come directly from The Helmsman himself; the Ghost Pilot was to be destroyed at all costs before the invasion of Ganempsha. His dark-dressed men, his fighters, were there to see to it. The attack force was on its way.

There was no prior arrangement, not much of one anyway. The grim doorway of an abandoned building already held one of their skulking figures. The job agreed with Chibba. The long hours spent hiding, the plotting, the occasional, random violence – enough to make it all worthwhile.

He glanced briefly behind, caught at the light dust and trash in the street lifted up in the draft of his passing car.

The street was on the edge of the downtown area of Cross Anchor. Certainly less than splendid, it served because of its abandoned buildings and dim light, all good spots for ambush.

At last, he would know, who was this Ghost Pilot? This would please his master, as well. For some unexplained reason, this pilot and his tiny freighter were of great importance. Chibba, of course, knew of The Marcellean Heart.

The device could alter the very fabric of the galaxy itself. Its power was that of the Old Ones, the ancients of Marcellus, those who were no more.

This flyer must have something to do with it, he thought. Chibba would, then, know and act.

Mere speculation was less than efficient and in his business, dangerous. The network of informants and killers he supported would show results, his efforts would not be wasted. Chibba was shrewd. He knew this Ghost Pilot would come to him, he had only to wait.

They were there, the little man had told him and had been for hours. Inside, amid toiling dancers and loud music, Borter and Helio played cards. Before each was a drink and another card player, neither was Ganempshan. Nor had Borter or Helio seen them before.

"Death Quest," he announced, "for keepers," he added, making it for money, only a friendly game. Helio dealt with and called the game as was the dealer's privilege. Death Quest was outlawed on as many planets as had heard of it.

Ten cards went to each player, except the dealer who was allowed twelve designated throwing cards. All the rest were placed in the middle of the table as the draw. In some places on Dillisome, Death Quest was still played only for the life of the loser, but these were the most backward parts of that distant planet of ice. An uncle of Helio's had died in such a game, a card hurled into his skull as he lay down his losing hand. A rough-looking man kept an eye on the game from the bar.

No one had seen him before. His eyes glowed like those of a great jungle cat in the dim light as he shifted, glancing at the card game across the room.

Helio noticed him. Borter looked only at the hand he'd been dealt, but his partner knew better. He heard the snap on the pilot's holster making the blaster grip easily accessible.

The hair on the back of Borter's neck stood as he noticed the man at the bar. He gave it little thought. He had several draughts of a Ganempshan specialty, something called Moon Bag, and was finding it difficult to raise excitement about anything. Helio had a similar helping of the stuff and was enjoying himself immensely, it seemed.

Burlesquing a serious manner, Borter leaned over to him, between hands, smiling, pretending to concentrate, raking in the pot from the win.

He affected a most devil-may-care manner, not difficult at the time, and informed Helio in a whispery airily high – pitched, sing-song voice, aping disregard for his own situation,

"The man at the bar," Helio shifted, glancing aside toward the dark figure some twenty feet away while absently arranging a new hand of cards, nodding as he did so in a reply.

The Dillisome had noticed the man, also, "What do you say, we let this one get away?" He smiled insincerely back at Borter.

"Well, alright, if he leaves us alone."

He heard the discreet snap of Helio's holster guard as the blue man released it, "But, only if he leaves us alone – first!" He caught the fierce glint in the Targan's eyes as the man glared at them. Helio threw a credit chip to the center table, dealing himself into the pot, again examining his hand.

He had six pairs, his best hand all night. Borter raised and called throwing in three cards.

"Six Targans," muttered Helio. putting forward the hand. Faces all around the dingy table screwed up in frowns as they stared at him. The copilot stared back, then said, "– 'cuse me, I mean - six pair!" The others threw in their cards.

"Too good for me," said one. The other sighed heavily and pushed away from the table and agreed, "I fold." They left their money, scuffing their chairs back on the floor, making that low, wood scuffing–on–wood noise.

As soon as they were up, Borter felt a wet kiss on the side of his face that made him reach for the Reggian blaster already loosened in its holster.

"Moz! What are you doing here?"

". . . duh, it's getting a little crowded in here," said the co-pilot, loud enough to draw his attention.

"What?" Borter looked at him annoyed, through the alcohol haze that drifted through his brain, the gloom and blare of the place.

"Just earning the mad part of my name," she said pushing in as the warning hairs on Borter's neck bristled stiffly erect, in spite of everything else.

"Dad really did it this time," she giggled, "ordering me not to come here!" It was then that Borter saw what Helio meant.

Moz leaning over, her arms around Borter's neck, her naked back to the bar and the door, her head against his.

"Uh . . . Borter?"

He looked into her face, "It's getting a little crowded in here!" She looked hurt, feeling her attentions to be un-appreciated.

Her eyes dropped away as six big Targans came toward the table making no effort at all to hide their blasters as they did. The leader was about to speak and as he did, he placed his right hand lazily on the butt of his blaster, still holstered at his side. Helio saw the blasters, hung on their right sides. All Targan were right–handed, the co-pilot noted silently.

Borter, nonchalant to the end, smiled, looking again into her eyes, "Say, uh – kid! Did you come in here – alone?"

He turned his smile into a self-mocking, one-sided grin that said he wanted hope-against-hope there was a back way out. "No," she said flatly. "You're here – very much the same!"

The six impossible fellows, arrayed before them, were not having it – a joke, turned on them by some likely look-ing space strangers, that – a joke, they would all laugh about the next morning.

Maybe, they just wanted the table. "You guys want the table?" He asked, blankly, then looked, smiling pleasantly, at Helio for a nod, then, up into the six grim faces, "We were just leaving!"

The leader glared down, his eyes glaring in the low light, and rasped angrily, "Tell me what you know about a black freighter!"

Borter's attention went to Targan's hand which still rested on his well – used blaster. "How did you get here?" He demanded an answer.

Two of his Targans stepped forward heavily, drawing their blasters from beneath the forest green cloaks they all wore. The leader held them back reaching out, his left arm pressed against them.

"You better tell me," he grinned, leaning forward over the table. Borter and Helio had not been so close to a Targan since the battle on Modallas' Third Plain the year before.

He grinned, "Or, you can tell them," he looked around at his men, squeezing all the threat he could from his words!

"Well," Borter grinned, leaning back on his chair, trying to look at ease, "in answer, to you – my friend."

The Targan cocked his head as would a large mastiff confronting a serious bug at its feet. "We arrived two months ago, passengers on this tramp freighter. I think it might have been black. Nothing to it. We took down a couple of pieces of prime farmland out near The Ords! Fine land! Thinking of settling yourselves?"

The Targan growled.

"No? Well, we don't know anything about black starships. "We're just – theeeezzzzsgguyyss," Borter shrugged, nodding at his co-pilot.

Helio drew his blaster as they started forward. Borter found his own at that same instant. The Targan charge halted abruptly, they scattered, diving for cover.

"Borter?" Moz whispered vehemently between clenched teeth, "Assuming that we survive this and my father asks if I'm here – I don't want you to lie for me, ever! Understand?"

Borter nodded, "I understand!" They reached the floor, behind the overturned card table. Wood from the table near Dillisome's head burst into burning shards as a blaster recoiled across the room.

Another followed that and then another. Smoke filled the bar. It became hard to breathe. Borter fired. Exploded shards scattered half a room away. Borter could see nothing and didn't know if he'd hit anything. Targans did not give themselves away by crying out when wounded or dying. The gunfight continued.

It looked bad for them. The was nowhere to go, no other door than the one through which they'd entered the bar. There were the first six between them, not including the one who'd sat at the bar.

The leader of the Targans called out to his men to hold their fire, "Ghost Pilot? Ghost Pilot, surrender yourself and your friends can leave unharmed!"

Borter and Helio exchanged nervous glances. "I don't think Targans have an – unharmed." The co-pilot nodded. Damn, Parnak. He's got us into it this time," the pilot moaned to himself. They let the smoke clear a bit and then fired again in the direction of the voice.

Borter hunkered down on the floor with Moz as a fusillade of blaster fire ripped by, overhead. Helio was off to one side, safe, unseen for the moment amid the wreckage of overturned tables and chairs and spilled cards. Blaster in hand, he waited for a clear shot.

In front of him, something moved on the ceiling. It kept to the shadows, in its right hand a blaster. No friend, The Dillisome knew it, he'd seen Targans practically run straight down the cliffs on Marcellus. The blaster rose.

There was no sound, hardly any noticeable motion as it pointed toward Borter and Moz.

Helio lifted a face card bearing the likeness of a king, from among the spilled cards. Good enough, he spun it at the dark figure.

The next instant, a blaster clattered on the floor, and the Targan made for cover. Borter bolted up and fired a shot that reached him. He fell, a playing card stuck in his wrist. Borter glanced at his partner across the wreckage, "How do you do that?" He demanded!

Helio shrugged off Borter's query as another shot exploded a roof beam.

Fiery debris rained down. "Geez," Borter cried out. He swiftly spun off another blast at a coming Targan. Moz risked a quick shot at another, both missed. "How do we get out of here?" Helio pumped another shot toward the bar!

"How am I supposed to know?" Borter angrily shouted back, firing again. "Do I look like a builder? Should I make you a new door? Just tell me where you'd like it and I'll have it right up!" Borter stopped mid-sarcasm grasping the idea contained in the very words he used.

"Right there?" Helio pointed. He gestured at the rear wall of the bar just behind them.

"Yes? You don't have to yell," muttered Borter with renewed aplomb as he glanced back and forth between the Reggian blaster and the wall. He turned the power indicator up all the way to - Illegal.

It had never let him down from the moment he'd wrestled it away from the Reggian pirate to whom it belonged.

There's nothing like leaving a deadly weapon in the hands of something that wants to kill you, the pilot mused briefly.

Stone from the wall burst outward into the dark alley. The trio quickly followed. Our pilots had been asked to leave many of the galaxy's lowest drinking establishments, but, this was the first time they'd made their own door.

As they ran, they covered their escape, each turning to fire back into the dark bar. The Sand Rock stopped abruptly in the darkroom as the jukebox was hit. The Sand Rock, playing, scraped to an end. Borter counted that a good sign, in the dark or not.

Another cloaked figure stood facing into the bar from the hole which was just higher than his head. He moved out of their way, bidding them – *come.*

Borter stopped for an instant, half in wonder, half in dread. He'd seen this before and did not want to see it again. He knew the bearing of the figure, that stance, and the particular cut of the cowl and cloak, the blinking red dots on one shoulder. He beat a hasty path through the alley and the new piles of smoking debris there.

They ran. As he came even with Helio, he shouted breathlessly to the Dillisome. "Did you see that?"

Helio nodded. *Yes!*

"That was quick thinking, Borter," he gasped, keeping up the pace. "I guess that's why you're the Ghost Pilot."

Borter was breathing too hard to shout the correction. Moz, out front, called back, "C'mon, you guys! You run like old ladies!" Borter, Helio, and Moz ran through the shadows of Parnel's streets until they thought they were safe.

The three moved toward the space port and their hoppers. Their clothing stuck to them as they silently went on. It had been hot that day and humid and rain came shortly before darkness. Altogether, it felt awful.

"I thought you were the sarcastic one!"

"No. I'm cynical. You're the sarcastic one!" Borter nodded toward the breathless Moz. "I don't know what she is!"

They ran like old ladies. Cross Anchor's streets echoed their footsteps hollowly as they went along hand in hand feeling safer. A nervous Borter hazarded to glance behind. There was no pursuit. He did not know why.

His experience on Marcellus taught him not to take safety for granted just because he saw nothing. He paid attention to the warning hairs on the back of his Magnean neck, especially where Targan were concerned.

At times, dim lights of the street fell across Moz's face. Borter, looking, noted her beauty, again, perhaps, for the first time; perhaps not.

She was tall for a female, almost as tall as him and the curves of her body were athletic. She seemed strong. The warning hairs on his neck rested, limp.

Her face held him though. Her lips were a light red, and she smiled, showing straight white teeth. Looking in her eyes made him stammer and say foolish things when he could get words out.

Her hair was dark and full in what light they had. The Pilot noticed. Which then, with moisture offered by Cross Anchor that night, shone, reached her shoulders in length, and there it spread like a soft mantle.

She saved her questions about what they had seen, as they made their way down another alley, for a later time.

They made their escape. The hoppers lifted off into the night. Helio broke away, heading for Suther Dann's. Borter and Moz broke away, for a place in The Ords and each other. The place the pilots had hidden Soarer.

Moments before the eruption of violence inside the bar, Chibba's limo slid away from the curb across the street tires hissing on the rain wet stones, forward, as it picked up speed.

Targans, troopers from AF6, had come on schedule. They had gone to the bar and waited.

They were in charge of their own situation. He was no longer needed. As an important person, he left his further service to The Helmsman and Modallas. He chuckled to himself as he was driven away hearing news of Kithron's destruction. He'd like to have seen the maddeningly smug looks on the faces of those Kithronese as their end came.

Oddly, the management of the bar were no strangers to visitors from far planets going so far as to pride themselves on that fact, printing in bold letters on their cocktail napkins the words, THE GENISUS BAR – A PLACE IN SPACE.

They stopped short, for a second, hot. The figure that filled that newly Borter created *exit* to the alley, standing, tired, hot, draped in darkness was no mystery. He knew a Marcellean when he saw one.

For this effort, none needed a leader. It was purely biological. Whoever it was stood silent, the tiny red dots on his shoulder blinking into the murky depths of the bar. Since ancient times on far Marcellus, language for this had never been a barrier.

On his left hip, a blue light began to appear and grow. An eerie voice spoke out to them, all around. It said the word, the last word for them all. It spoke its own name with a reverberation that shook each down to his boots. An echo possessed by its being as it came from its scabbard – a Companion Blade – the last!

52

To Kithron Show Mercy

Borter rose stiffly, losing himself from Moz's embrace, and shook himself out as a sudden chill took him. They'd slept in an isolated part of the ruin having been led there by one of the clones and seen nothing more of Parnak or Helio, since the party. Arms reached skyward trying to capture meager warmth generated by the single, just risen sun, Moz, beside him, rose stiffly and stretched herself. Her small hands curled into fists that, as she flexed, seemed to shake at the sky. She yawned.

The pilot stared out far into the desert surrounding them. The horizon was an early morning blue in which he saw nothing but color. Above that, the sky clouded, first in a sort of dull grey haze, then brightening into billowing, fair-weather clouds that reminded him of Spring on Magnus and good flying. Moz looked around at him and smiled weakly, the early morning yet showing a little, even in her young face.

She'd never loved anyone as she did him. He was independent, with no single thing to hold him. She loved that. Borter smiled as he returned her gaze.

There was the smell of food in the air. Both turned toward it as if the odor triggered an auto-response. It could only have been breakfast.

"Food," Borter exclaimed.

He said it as if there could be found no more valuable thing in the galaxy. It was as if he discovered a whole mountain of trolleite, that singular substance that rendered anything it coated friction free.

"We'll have to leave the planet today, "He said with authority. "Ganempsha is no longer safe for any of us."

"You aren't even going to stay for the concert they're putting together?"

"How?" he said. "It will be too late, then!"

Moz looked at him curiously as if a Thee Starr concert would solve everything. "Thee Starr can't stop this. Everyone here will die," he said.

"Together?"

Chibba turned from the video screen and smiled coldly at Judd, commander of AF6.

"I have an operative at Suther Dann's farm capable of dealing with our problem." Chibba nodded curtly toward the screen, also eyeing Judd for his reaction.

"Aren't these the same off–worlders who shot their way out of that miserable establishment at Cross Anchor?" Judd asked without needing to know. "They've escaped your operatives once

already – "

53

Black Box – The Delivery

Except the rolling sands of the desert, there was nothing beneath. He circled one way, then the other. He zigzagged a course as crazy as the freighter's evade had been on the chase down. It was just as he was about to give up the search altogether that Slide popped up behind, got off a quick, telling burst, and sent the fighter plummeting straight into its end.

Quantum was impressed. Slide sending a damaged fighter back home, forgoing death. Then, the odds more even, he slowed, pulled up behind, damaging it so badly it fell into the desert and exploded.

Seemingly bored with combat, Slide, moments later, put The Hammer down in the desert – easily – then lowered the cargo ramp and delivered cargo, the black box, into the desert. Quantum looked on.

"Well, isn't this the address on it?" He gestured at the box querying her.

Quantum nodded.

"Borter would have done it better," she critiqued.

A hint of sarcasm crossed the commander's face as Chibba squirmed.

Chibba replied, "Yes," even more coldly as Judd looked up at him from his command console at the very center the attack force position.

A hint of sarcasm crossed the commander's face as Chibba squirmed.

Chibba had not gained the position he enjoyed by squirming at the remarks of others. He caught himself and went on. "The agent I have in mind is well suited to this purpose, even for a Targan."

The pair, were many kilometers distant from the ruins from which their remote spied on the red clones and their guests.

An evil smile came to his face, one to counter that of the commander. "Call in your men," Chibba told him quietly, smiling, "We will have no more need for them. My operative is already on the trail of this - Ghost Pilot!"

Judd shook his head from side to side in disbelief, chuckling.

"So, troopers from Modallas are no longer good enough for you?" His face wore a new smirk as he looked over at Chibba.

"They prefer these metal corridors of Modallas, now, to the forests of home," said Chibba. "And, as you know, my friend, we must have our Ghost Pilot brought before The Helmsman."

The glances between the two became more knowing, more conspiratorial as they went on. Both swept the head-quarters for casual eavesdroppers.

The place was empty to their cats' eyes. Speak as they now would meant a swift and sure death, if any overheard. The mood between the two became more cautious.

"The Helmsman borders madness in this questing after the pilot," claimed Chibba. "He's no more than a freighter pilot, a carrier of merchandise around the stars!"

"However, The Helmsman wants him or them," Judd corrected. "And, if he wants them, so do we! He's the connection to the Marcellean device. Could the freighter carry it? Finding out is a risk, but a risk worth taking if it leads us to our goal!"

"Maybe," Chibba accepted the other's reasoning, "but I do not think so. This is a blind chase," he spoke solemnly to Judd.

Judd paused, he meaningfully at Chibba, "These thousand years of struggle have been too long for him. The inevitable has come," Chibba spoke. He shook his head, not wanting to believe. "This little planet will yield nothing unless it is our own deaths."

Judd grunted. "Life is not so much that I would live it out beneath a madman. You are too good a leader yourself to be any different!"

Chibba spoke as if to himself, staring at the floor. "The Helmsman is mad. For that reason, we may have Modallas for our own. Keep your loyal troops ready. When we strike, it will be quick!"

"They are ready," Judd rose to his feet. He turned quickly and said nothing else as he strode toward the bunker door.

Borter sat near Helio among the gathered clones. Moz was near him, and Parnak was now a bit distant from another of the Kith Rees. Low chatter abounded. The early morning breakfast as the clones talked among themselves excitedly and nodded in Helio's direction. It had been a long night, and Borter was feeling it. They were older than him. Shouldn't they be more tired?

Breakfast was served from a common pot brought around behind everyone and served to each in turn from the left side as was considered polite in The Ords.

Borter hesitated. He recognized in the mixture several vegetables cruelly mashed into a kind of mush to be ladled out to each individual on a flat, hard bread served first, given by another clone from the right side. Like it or not, he took a helping, he smiled saying thanks to the Kith Ree of that moment, who was, of course, the one with the pot.

In fact, as hungry for outside contact as for food, at that moment, most of the clones had already taken a turn at conversation with Parnak before he'd even realized it. The total knowledge of the Clones was boring to the point of madness.

That was so when Borter and Moz arrived.

"We've all got to get off this planet soon," Borter spoke, raising his eyebrows once more to emphasize the obvious.

In an equally soft but insistent voice, he went on! "The Helmsman is here and we're tops on his hit list. We've done our job, let's go!"

Helio smiled tipping his head to one side playfully, looking tousled, boyish, shaking his head, "No," he said. "You go if you want. I have something to do here!"

That was all he said before he turned back to the delegation of smiling little men, all identical, all exactly Kith Ree.

Borter was about to say something but did not, knowing the answer he would get.

However, at the mention of Marcellus she'd whispered, "Do you follow The Heart?" She'd asked him that one time. It had not crossed her mind before.

To this, Borter grudgingly croaked out, "No," his throat gone dry. He became tense, not exactly sure if he should have answered. Moz seemed to look at him – differently after that. He liked her – very much!

Elsewhere, Parnak, surprised, as any, by the turn of events in the desert, trudged the red sand toward the cooler ruins.

Kees' wingmen had not been replaced in the time since their death in the deep orchard. Suther Dann had not wanted more of their kind on his farm. They'd annoyed him the moment he'd laid eyes on them and every time after that.

Kees was the last of them and when he was gone, there'd be no more.

Borter and his daughter had only just returned from The Wastes when they were off again to work. Wanting Moz to rest before she went up with Borter, he'd offered him the day off or at least enough time to rest.

It was not the norm on any of the farms during the growing seasons, a flyer did not expect, nor did he receive any pampering because of a late night out or all night, in the case at hand, even if Dann had okayed the trip. Moz refused and returned to her hopper, and Borter to his.

At least, the trip back from The Ords had been calm. The planet's second sun rose behind the first in the sky to greet them. Moz blared Sand Rock from her hopper.

Suther Dann waited, hand on hips, his best fatherly pose, at the landing pad, a very grim look on his face as they touched down.

His one consolation was that she flew wingman with Borter.

Later, a second bit of fortune crossed his mind as he watched them on their way back to the orchards. He'd never seen a better pilot. Kees had been sent as far from the young pair of flyers as the boundary of the farm would allow.

54

Ganempshian Skies

Kees landed his hopper alone in a remote section of the farm. The area had been dusted the day before and there was no one around to see him. Above, the sky was a clear, pale blue. Beyond, still a little way, stretched the formidable Ords.

His cold thoughts ran to all four adventurers from the farm if you included Moz as a partner with Borter. Helio and Parnak. Kees did.

As he went about the task at hand, he mulled the failed attempt on the flyers at the bar in Cross Anchor. His points had slipped with Chibba on that one. It was bad for Chibba with The Helmsman, too. This time, in the sky, there would be no intervention.

In the forests, they'd hungered for the destruction of everything Marcellean. That was a biological truth of the planet. Generations of his forbears had lived aboard Modallas. That born of the cylinder world was the conquest of the galaxy. He was not given to failure.

To the left strut of the little hopper, he attached a long, straight tube of grey metal. At the forward end, there was a cone of about six centimeters from base to point. The base itself was about four centimeters wider than the grey tube, which had a diameter of about ten centimeters. At the rear edge of the tube, attached by a six by six by four – box – of identical color, connected to the fuselage by a thick black cable. He would do the same for the right side.

Kees looked old as he went about his labors, more worn than old, but old, older than either Borter or Helio. His physical condition could be described as hard, his face leathery. His manner was all business, moving around the flyer with a sort of practiced fluid grace that would awe a dancer.

His hands were powerful, but they, too, were quick and supple-fingered in their movements. They were enough, not too big, not too small.

Thick, silver hair fell in a single lock across his grim forehead as he bent over his work. It appeared slightly like a pelt on his head, long, piled on top, and cut neatly around his ears.

Modallian instrumentation that had been installed that morning mottled the light in the more crowded cockpit. Information flooded the new computer that presided over it all. Kees' targets had been detected and tracked hours before. Time in life for them grew short. Time until interception was equal. There would be no repeat of the bar fight.

The beast was once again on Modallas itself. The dead being found everywhere. Rumors and stories, it was impossible to tell one from the other, flooded the air. The Helmsman had raged at Chibba though it was not his fault.

Chibba turned to Kees raging at him, though it was also not his fault.

The Targan knew fear well enough when he sensed it. This was fear – secondhand fear. The Helmsman's?

There was something he was afraid of, terrified of, this Marcellean T'Sog. His wingmen had died searching for it in the orchards. He knew what had killed them but said nothing.

There was little he could have done. His first task on Suther Dann's farm now was to eliminate the Ghost Pilot.

Borter and Moz worked their way across a vast orchard, for the moment, distant from Kees.

Finally, Kees drew himself straight up and stepped back to admire his work. This is one hopper he would not return to Suther Dann.

He'd never take the Ghost Pilot in his black ship that he knew. But, in an armed crop duster, it would be different. The grey rods and cones of the pulsars satisfied him, a grim smile reached his face.

They would make quick work of his targets. He would destroy them in one felled swoop.

He regretted only Moz's death. Kees wanted her for himself. She would have been formidable even against the women of the forests. Her wild ways might have seemed mad to those of her planet but not to him. It was a shame; she'd not live out the morning.

Modallas' tracking sensors were his. Borter had been found in the desert along with Dann's Moz. He would sweep the Ghost Pilot from the sky, easily, forever.

Kees climbed aboard, settled himself into the single seat. A screen came to life on the control console and the computer's crisp, dry voice, sounded in his ears speaking pure Modallian, a language now dearer to Kees and the other Targans calling Modallas home, than the guttural, grunting Knruul that was the tongue of the forest.

The savagery that existed there seemed distant, even to those who could claim no more than a few generations aboard the artificial world. Except for Kees' leathery exterior and his stoic manner, one seeing him in the orchard preparing for takeoff in the newly weaponized hopper would have found him quite civilized. That is, excepting knowledge of his mission.

The hopper's engine whined, leaving the ground and quickly was above the trees of Suther Dann's orchard. The computer began to track two hoppers flying abreast, working the orchards deep in the farm. It could be no others, Modallas confirmed.

Kees' went for all the altitude he could get. He would swoop in from behind on both. He would be swift, without mercy!

It had been midmorning, hours before when Borter and Moz lifted off their tiny flyers.

The sky was clear. Any clouds that had been there had long since burned off. Borter liked the clouds because they gave the sky a fairy tale effect. A clear sky held no secrets or surprises for a good flyer. As a child Borter enjoyed all the tales of sky born castles and lands of giants hiding treasure, in the clouds.

Moz flew as before on his right, banking with him as if they flew only one hopper. Borter pulled back on his stick and pushed his throttle to maximum, climbing to the limit of the craft's ability. The deep greens of the farm crept beneath, a view of the same rich carpet. Looking down, as one of Borter's fantasy giants would have seen it.

They chatted ship to ship, alone with their shared thoughts. Borter thought of settling down. The life of a flyer was difficult at best. Moz had not spoken it, but she thought of him, someday, running her father's orchards.

They talked of things, avoiding the current unpleasantness surrounding the planet. Modallas and The Helmsman did not matter in the plans they secretly made with each other in those moments.

They flew into a sunset as red as the desert itself. Borter would finish up his contract with Parnak. If Helio, his friend, could stay on the planet, so could he. And there was Moz.

Ganempsha's first sun rose higher in the sky, the second followed, twin orbs forever each in the other's grasp. The way it should be, Borter thought.

Returning from The Ord Ruins, he was willing to chance that one of the returnees was the Ghost Pilot. Two flyers would be one-third fewer problems.

Kees descended slowly, waiting for the best angle to take the two close-flying hoppers under fire. The pulsars could track through his onboard computer. If one flyer should happen to survive, he could kick in his afterburner and deal with it, the added boost compliments of Modallas. With it, he could far outrun a counterattack and even, should he have to reach sub orbit for rescue. Kees could sit back and watch his own turkey shoot.

The two flyers were quickly in the target window, and the twin pulsars opened fire with telling accuracy. One of the crop dusters exploded into flames, instantly trailing thick black smoke and debris down to the orchard. The second limped away, trailing smoke and flame, one side ravaged by the explosion of the other ship. It veered sharply back toward the open desert. Its attitude controls shot up and useless, causing it to veer right heavily, losing fuel.

The hopper spun down toward the red desert in burning shards. Kees followed at a respectful distance, waiting for the helpless flyer to ram into the ground and finish itself. It would not be much longer.

The flyer was in its death throes. Kees wondered what was on the pilot's mind.

He shot by, overhead, amazed at the strength built into the cockpit of the crop duster as it surrendered its skids, its engines and everything else from its outside, only the ball shaped pod itself was left.

As he overshot, the hopper came to a rolling stop just on the sandy plain.

Moving his hopper into a quick turn, Kees planned to come back and destroy the remains of the downed craft and its pilot. A figure stumbled, then fell onto the sand from the pod. Borter lay unmoving.

Hardly fifty meters above the plain, Kees began his strafing run, meaning to kill him. Nearing his victim, he pressed the trigger rigged to his control stick. The pulsars fired, smashing powerful energy into the sand, driving toward the pilot.

There was a quick motion on the sand. Kees was not sure that he'd seen anything as the first round of blaster fire smacked into the windshield, throwing glass into his lap.

Kees closed his eyes and veered away, overshooting his target.

Shoving the throttle forward roughly, trying for and getting attack altitude, turning toward the ground at a steeper angle than before. The pilot ran lamely toward the dunes. Quickly bracing a blaster on the raised crook of one arm, he fired at the oncoming Kees. The half – chance shot, destroyed his instruments, before he knew it.

The hopper spun away, Kees grappling with shattered controls. The craft, helpless, climbed spaceward.

His fingers numb, the Reggian blaster dangled loosely, in hand, at his side. He let it stay there.

He felt more tired than he'd been in his whole life, heavy beyond sleep, battered but alive. Borter looked on amazed as Kees' ship rocketed away, trailing the faintest wisps of smoke. He agreed with the little voice in his head that he was hard to kill. Nothing said the same for Moz!

Injuries, though small, gathered on him, forcing him down. He sank to his knees and then lay flat on the sand. A roar emerged in his ears, a roar that turned into the sound of Sredir hooves, bearing down on him hard, said Sandriders. He lost consciousness.

55

Sandriders

There was a crash of thunder in Borter's ears. He rose awkwardly to his feet some distance from the wreckage of his hopper. It lay crushed, its windscreen broken, electronics torn, burned.

He staggered a few more steps from it in case it should explode and fell to the ground, dazed, stupored, and sick in the pit of his stomach. He saw them coming across the Ord sands toward him. Sandriders.

His sore mind shook as badly as his ears thundered; he viewed them as rag-tag and miserable. These mounts were big, their hooves broad, ideal for the fast sands of The Wastes. The riders, terrible looking, worn from the desert, uniforms so long in disrepair they were hardly recognizable as clothing. Each carried a lance, upright, at rest.

The column rode double file as they reached him. They dismounted as he tried his feet once more. His blaster lay on the ground, out of reach, had he needed it.

There seemed to be no officers among them as they dismounted and came over. Someone walked up, leaned over, picked up his blaster, and slapped it into his holster. "Here. We can't have our Ghost Pilot going around like that!" The trooper smiled.

A crusty sergeant stepped up, ahead of the rest. The man, this sergeant, looked grubbier than the others, by far and walked as if he hadn't been off his mount in a week. His walk was that of an old man, spry or otherwise, coming as if he had springs on his heels or, relieved of his despair, at his feet, never again touching the ground.

He smelled bad, too, Borter thought, worse than any of the others and most certainly worse than the animals they rode. He rumbled as he looked into Borter's eyes.

"I've seen worse falls from the back of Sredirs!" Sredirs, as Sandriders called their mounts. "Don't be such a baby. Stand up straight!" He got a slap on the back.

Borter grimaced. He hated blowhards. He hated the military, even one as ragged and comical as this one appeared to be, making money bringing downed flyers back to the farms.

"What are you supposed to be – somebody's mother?" He murmured back.

"Somebody's mother?" The sergeant's face reddened beneath a week's stubble. He smiled through ugly brown teeth, the butt of a really cheap and misused cigar unceremoniously shoved between his uppers and lowers.

"Well, we got a smart one," his breath flooded Borter's nostrils. Borter had no question in his mind what the man had eaten for lunch that day and that it was exactly the same thing eaten by his Sredir. Smoke from the cigar followed, although it was not a relief.

Borter mounted behind a corporal, or the man he took to be a corporal from his ragged chevrons. This rider, too, smelled bad and looked bad. The small column turned itself around in the dust, Borter holding on for dear life, his stomach reeled with effort.

It struck him suddenly that Moz's flyer was nowhere to be seen. Then, he remembered what had happened to it and her.

Kees' hopper had lurched away under his fire, but it, he thought, had stayed airborne. At least it didn't crash right away. He looked to his side and saw his blaster there. The dusty column moved farther out into The Ords.

The desert mounts rode smoothly. Borter had expected worse. They were covered with long, shaggy hair of matted tendrils as long as his forearm from head to hoof, front to back. Borter had seen nothing like them.

Travel by Sredir was more tedious than by hopper, especially in this desolate place. The column moved again two by two. Borter protested, at first, pointing out that Suther Dann's farm was in the other direction. "Aren't we going the wrong way?" He shouted.

"We're meeting the Captain," the grizzled sergeant laughed, jeering him, and was joined in doing so by others. It was a disgusting performance as the sergeant ended the exchange, propelling an angry, wet stream of brown, the desert weed he chewed, deep into a nearby patch of scrub brush. They continued into The Ords.

"We have to show you to the Captain first. Then, we can get you back to Suther Dann's." He smiled a greasy smile. "Won't take long!"

His back and legs hurt miserably. He longed for his pilot's chair aboard Soarer, even for the cramped, hard seat of a hopper. As for the desert itself, he'd rather have had the closeness of buildings if only of the grittier space ports he knew across the galaxy. It was as if The Wastes had opened up and swallowed him.

There were not more than twenty in the little band that seemed smaller the farther they went. The Ords were like space, vast, desolate, Borter mused.

Space was not as imposing as the sandflats they crossed. The sergeant spat more of his brown juice, staining the whiskers of his chin. His uniform also bore old evidence of the practice as he dribbled there as well.

This was strange discipline for soldiery. The old sergeant never had to turn and check his men. He knew they would be there. They held together, long practiced, in the heat.

Borter became miserable. There was a halt, and the sergeant grumbled, ordering him to dismount and had water poured over him.

"Nothing's too good for one of our guests," the man spat, laughing at his own joke. Borter turned away and became very ill. He was wretched into the sand.

In a while, they went on. It was almost dusk of Ganempsha's second sun before their encampment was in sight.

The little column came to a halt in front of the Captain. Behind him waved the Sandrider pennant, held by another poorly kempt trooper. Others waited behind.

It was the only bit of ornamentation to be seen anywhere in the dusty valley. It was multicolored, bright blue, green, white, and a particular yellow found only on that planet, called Ganempshan yellow. It was little more than a rag to him. Neither did the pilot find out the significance of the individual colors. Helio was the sub-culture special-ist, not him.

The place, indeed, reminded Borter of Dillisome. However, unlike Dillisome's populated areas, this place merely served. It had no name.

The Captain, on the other hand, surprised the sergeant by greeting Borter like a long-lost friend, shaking his hand vigorously and clapping him on the shoulder.

"So, this is the Ghost Pilot we've heard so much about," the sergeant heard him say – "from our good friend Suther Dann?" The Captain wore a long saber at his side. His Sredir bore him on a better-looking saddle. In all, he was clean-looking – by comparison to the other Sandriders.

Borter smiled, though his head still ached as he remem-bered Moz's death at Kees' hands. Praise always embar-rassed him.

Yes, Suther Dann had been told of her death, and her body already returned to him. Another patrol had taken care of that. Indeed, her hopper's wreckage had come down several kilometers from Borter's. Kees had not been found. They suspected him of having made a safe landing beyond their reach. It had not yet settled on Borter, still too numb from his own close call to feel anything for a while. The pilot hadn't wanted to be the one to tell him of her death.

Had he heard about the Ancient One? The Captain brightened. Apparently, this sergeant had his own notions of security. No one had said anything to him. The pilot was always last to know.

There had been another crash, a Kithronese shuttle. Aboard, they'd found an ancient one in full battle armor, injured, but alive, Borter nodded. Painfully, saying he'd witnessed the battle near Kithron.

The Captain, then, went on, babbling with great excitement like a man long denied and alone, suddenly thrust into the spotlight.

Borter forgot the pain in his head and shuddered. Marcelleans, he thought, damn! The man babbled on.

The Ancient left, gone a day or two before, and his injuries quickly healed. A beast had come for him, one — from the legends. He said.

"Been trying to get in touch with Suther Dann all day," The Captain mentioned in an embarrassed aside to the pilot. "Connections are down, nothing coming through."

He smiled. Borter decided, to himself, the man's connection was always down. The pilot smiled back as if understanding.

"We can drop you off. I have to go into Cross Anchor for a few things, supplies, you know?"

Hours later, The Sandriders were at Dann's door.

An hour after, Borter moved Soarer out of its hiding place in Suther Dann's orchards and skyward.

"Sorry to hear about the loss of your daughter, sir," The Captain mumbled solemnly. "We must be going." Both nodded politely in farewell. The Captain and his Sandriders were off to Cross Anchor, a smaller suburb of Parnel.

56

Rebellion I

At his command, all traffic from the planet stopped, and ships attempting to enter or leave were destroyed. Orders had gone out as Modallas had taken orbit. At the same instant, his fighters had taken positions around the planet, though still high above the atmosphere, ready to stop any escape.

His AF6 arrived, to no opposition in The Ords. A ring of his escort vessels blockaded the planet.

If his suspicions were correct, once captured, this Ghost Pilot would lead him to The Heart.

His blue man, his copilot, did not interest The Helmsman. Somehow, Helio never quite captured his attention the way the pilot did. At least he would have a new chance to destroy him before he faded once again into the galaxy's backwater.

Rebellion. Behind the Magnean was The Heart. He didn't know how, or even care for that matter. At Marcellus, it was not the Marcelleans who held him up. It was the Marcellean Heart, a device built by the oldest technology in the galaxy. He would have that single object of power for himself.

They sought an even more obscure planet where they might begin again in peace.

It was too good to hope for. All indicators pointed here to this planet.

AF6 alone would be more than enough to subdue this insignificant place. There were no planetary defenses or any great space fleets to battle here. They would destroy anything standing in their way. It would be swift, fierce, and over.

Glimpses of the planet below came between shutters, opening and closing overhead, as Modallas turned in rotation.

All went well. Movements were coordinated and carried out with practiced ease. His Targans responded as they had been taught.

They were no longer the forest-born hordes who thrust themselves into battle in any fashion to be slaughtered. The Helmsman, long ago, used their natural behavior, their biological priorities, for his own ends. He would put them up against any in the galaxy, any Kithronese, if any still lived, or even the warriors of old Marcellus. Through a viewer on the Con, The Helmsman watched as his plan tightened around the undefended planet.

There had been trouble finding the leaders of Ganempsha.

The leadership there seemed to be a loose coalition of farmers, growers, and agriculturalists, as they called themselves. No single individual in charge or any political body is to be found.

In the wastes, The Ord Desert were a number of clones who seemed special to the planet philosophically. His agents returned perplexed, shaking their heads, bewildered. They could understand nothing said to them. It was then that they discovered, as they put it, a youth cult following, it seemed, the near worship of a particular kind of music, originated on the planet in recent years.

His Targan heard of it and had heard it. It signified nothing and reported it marginally as lacking significance.

The Helmsman decided to use this movement to air his demands on the planet. There was a brief non-violent resistance to the idea, it was as short lived as those who suggested it. After several summary and quick executions, that media, solely dedicated to the broadcast of Sand Rock, became a Modallian entity. The Helmsman, himself, made a demand for the surrender of Soarer and the Ghost Pilot.

57

Helio in the Desert

Parnak was elsewhere beneath the surface. One of the clones was showing him around, but why down there, exactly, was unknown.

Helio didn't think much about it, just then The Ords were most peaceful. The sky was clear, like spring on any of a dozen planets known to him.

The morning had a coolness all its own. The red clones stayed nearby. They liked him. Their ruins in this barren desert stretched to the horizon. They were old, older than ancient. Beside them the building blocks of a great civilization that were tumbled down. All this had happened long before any of them were born.

Columns reached out, splayed like broken fingers into The Ords. He'd seen nothing like it anywhere. The double suns took the white of the stone and made it painful to the eye. There were no clouds, but farther away, deeper in the desert, there was the sound of thunder. Helio turned to the clone nearest him and asked what it was.

The clone was called Kith Ree, as they all were.

The day before he'd come there, finding out, not only did they all look alike, but they were also, all, exactly alike, down to their name and genes. It did not matter who or, rather, which of them was beside him, to see one was to see all.

"Sandriders?" Helio asked with a growing interest. The clone raised an eyebrow and looked into Dillisome's face with an easy, bemused expression.

Strangers did not easily understand the truths of the ancient world, specifically the reason for the tour beneath the surface.

"It happened quite a long time ago, friend Helio."

On Dillisome, children were brought up on stories because there was not much else to do. He asked his Kith Ree to go on.

"It happened a long time ago."

"You've already said that." It was also a habit among the children of Dillisome not to let the storyteller become boring or repeat himself. However, the clone did not seem to mind.

"Tell me," said Helio.

"It is most difficult," said the clone, "It is the Knowledge of Ror. Off-worlders, that is, non-clones. With it, not beyond it, nor before it, all else is exclusion!"

The clone that Kith Ree eyed him as they moved farther away from the others was an unusual act in itself. "To be is not to know. To know is nothing."

"The knowledge of Ror," said Kith Ree, "begins, I think; therefore, I am nothing!" He paused and, seeing nothing in Helio's eyes, went on.

"To Be is not to know."

There was still nothing in Helio's eyes, no expression whatsoever – something like a slight haze.

"Yes," Helio replied solemnly, "Tell me about the Sandriders!"

58

Kith Rees Story

"At one time, we were the keepers of a great trust placed here, where it was created."

"Civilization, save one single individual, was destroyed in a disaster of our own making; from that survivor, all were made identical, one after the other."

Tears rose in the old clone's eyes. His pathetic few, long whiskers blew in the desert wind. Helio said nothing as he looked into the strange old face, the only face of all the survivors of that race.

"We do not see things about to happen in our own world."

Kith Ree sobbed lacking any control. There was the sound of more sobbing from the near ruins as the others wept the ancient shame.

"The ancient power, theirs," he nodded toward the thunder made by the Sandriders in the far desert. His brow wrinkled in great concern.

"Helio, my friend," he said, meaning our friend. You are our forgiveness, our sign that the evil greater than we did to ourselves will find defeat here.

59

Jibba and Chibba

Judd paced and watched as Chibba sat, confined. There was a definite silence in the room. Moments before, word came that rebellion had broken out aboard the cylinder world. Judd was silent; measuring options left him. Chibba the Spy, also, was silent, but for different reasons. There was little else he could do aside from wait.

"You are nervous, Chibba. Do you worry about our great leader? The Helmsman can look after himself," the Commander belittled him.

Reports were coming in. They were incomplete at best and vague at worst. Judd, as any good commander would, bid his time and waited, making his patience a weapon. He did not trust Chibba. He never had.

The Ords incursion was too convenient, too easy. AF6 comprised most of The Helmsman's personal guard. They were considered an elite among other Targan. Their present situation served the purpose of others besides the commander of the cylinder world. He was most curious about Chibba's involvement.

The red cliffs, one of the only landmarks in The Ords, remained visible behind them in the desert.

The camp buttoned up as the winds coursed a path from the far desert. This was the main base of operations on Ganempsha in the total military sense. Judd's sentries stood their posts. All was well. All was silent save the ever-present howl of the wind from the sand flats. It was like a presence, sometimes not. To Judd, it felt like the time he'd waited, troops, standing formation, waiting hours, for his appearance. Finally, The Helmsman arrived, reviewed them briefly, and was gone.

On the orbiting demi-world, a battle raged. In the Control Center, those loyal to Modallas waited and worked. It, the fighting, was growing street by street, building after building. There was little any could do about it. They, like their master, remained at their posts.

Bolts of pulsar energy crisscrossed the far sky. Elements of his own air cover strafed and bombed buildings and streets on two of the three plains. It was nothing seen on Modallas before.

A Targan flyer was hit by rocket fire and cartwheeled, trailing smoke to the ground where it impacted, too far in the distance to be heard. Only the White City appeared calm. It was yet a place of solitude and peace; no one went there, and in it, there was nothing alive.

All power stations were secure, he was told. There had been some light fighting at one of them. That had been put down by his troops, crushed by those who obeyed his commands.

This restlessness, as it was called, had been growing steadily for a long time. Could he have brought them too far from the forests? It was not working as well as he thought it should. That was academic.

This was the time for fighting, to reclaim that which was his and Modallian from those who no longer followed truly. The cleaning of the Modallian house was to begin.

Judd smiled at Chibba's uneasy manner. Chibba was heavy, too fat for a Targan, this man had grown soft spying, manipulating the fate of others. None of that required a hard body. Judd wondered how long the chair would hold his weight.

The laugh was grim. Targans, those closer to the forests, laughed that way, in a manner tinged with death, especially the death of others. Word on Chibba's fate was to come within the hour. There were those with more subtle machinations than Chibba had dreamed ever.

Judd let the entertainment go on. It was a rare treat. He wondered whether or not he'd be allowed to tell Chibba of The Helmsman's suspicions toward him, to chide him about his lack of awareness, at the nearness of death.

Judd's eyes narrowed in anticipation. His smile turned to a snarl. All things being equal, he'd bet his money on the softer-trained Targan aboard Modallas.

He did not look at Judd. He didn't need to. That he was called to the command center on such short notice was an indication of what he would see there if he did chance a look.

He would have already been dead, had there been any evidence against him, moldering somewhere, unburied, forgotten, except by those who tempted similar fate, plotting against the only power in their universe, The Helmsman.

Judd's gaze had already settled heavily on him, leaving a lingering, uncomfortable feeling that he did not like and couldn't shake.

He'd been called in early and made to stay late. Trickery, in this instance, would not do. Both were a - ways from the forests of which they were creatures, Judd the Commander and himself.

Now, one of them was about to find out just how far he'd come or merely how close both stood to a sad ending.

Chibba The Spy mulled the chance dealt cards in his current hand, his fate, again and again. He, his life, to the Forest Spirit, that wraith he'd never known, and the cards he'd dealt himself were, yet, good enough.

One generation away from the forests, his parents were barely verbal. Judd had pulled himself up by keen animal cunning to his present status in the Modallian army.

There was no other way of putting it. The trail of corpses to his present position was long. His AF6 had ravaged the Inner Galaxy without mercy. Nothing stood before them.

This would take a bit more care than he'd anticipated. Chibba's kind of Targan had grown in millennia of training aboard Modallas to look down on those new from the forests as if they were nothing. That day, it might have been Judd who was more surprised.

He'd not covered his tracks so well, Chibba thought. It would take more than a routine harassment by a jealous attack group commander, even one as revered as Judd, to unnerve him further.

However, Judd did not regret the act he played for Chibba. Even these detestable soft Targans could be dangerous. Long ago, he'd learned never to underestimate an enemy. The door slammed as Judd left him.

60

Rebellion II

Above, on the orbiting demi-world, a battle raged. Within the Control, those who controlled Modallas fought the battle, it was growing street by street, building by building and there was little success.

They, like Judd and like their master, remained at posts and remained calm.

Modallas was open to attack by weaker forces. There was damage. Now, to maintain total security, he must see to repair.

Modallas, his sanctum, had been violated by more than the beast.

The planet below and the Ghost Pilot himself must take a backseat to that repair. Without Modallas there was nothing.

His authority would once again be complete. He turned the Con and his control grip over to the Targan lieutenant and left the center to pursue the remainder of the rebels.

Perhaps, he thought, he had raised them too far from life in the forests. Perhaps it was not working as well as he thought it should. That was academic. Now was the time for fighting, for reclaiming that which was his and Modallian from those who no longer followed him.

The cleaning of his house had begun. He decided this was so. If this was not a bad time, it was a good time.

Judd smiled at Chibba's manner. Chibba was heavy, too fat for a Targan, the man had grown soft spying, manipulating the fates of others. None of that required a hard body. Perhaps that shortened one's life. The laugh was grim. Targans, those closer to the forests, laughed that way, in a manner tinged with death, especially the death of others. Word on Chibba's fate was expected within the hour. He suspected nothing. There were those with more subtle machinations than Chibba The Spy ever dreamed.

Judd let the entertainment go on. It was a rare treat. He wondered whether or not he'd be allowed to tell Chibba of The Helmsman's suspicions toward him, to chide him about his lack of awareness, to death. More than likely, the knowledge that The Helmsman himself was directly supervising the investigation would be enough to shake him. Judd's eyes narrowed in anticipation. The smile on his face had turned into a snarl.

In return, Chibba had not liked Judd, ever. All things being equal, he'd bet his money on the softer trained Targans aboard Modallas. He did not look at Judd, he didn't need to. The call to the command center, on such short notice, was indication enough of why he was wanted there.

Had there been any evidence against him, he would have already been dead, moldering somewhere, unburied, forgotten except by those who tempted fate, plotting against the only power that was their universe, The Helmsman.

Judd's gaze had already settled heavily on him leaving a lingering, uncomfortable feeling that he did not like and couldn't shake. He added up the cards in hand again and again. He'd been called early and to stay in the game had to raise the stakes staying long, a bluff would not do. He prayed to the Forest Spirit, that wraith of the forest, he'd never known, this hand he dealt himself was good enough.

They were a distance from the forests of which they were creatures, both of them, Judd the Commander and Chibba the Spy. Too far, now for one of them. There was no easy answer.

Sometimes, he let himself believe that you just had to wait it out. Chibba would place his hopes on that. The Helmsman kept different rules.

Judd was one generation away from the forests. His parents were barely verbal. He had pulled himself by animal cunning to his present status in the Modallian military. There was no other way of putting it. The trail of corpses to his present position was long.

His AF6 had ravaged the Inner Galaxy without mercy. Nothing stood before them. This effort would take a bit more care than he'd anticipated.

Chibba's kind of Targan had grown in the millennia of training aboard Modallas to look as if they themselves had no roots on the planet.

It would take more than routine harassment by a jealous commander, even one as redoubtable as Judd, to unnerve him further. A hard–looking officer had pulled him in, depriving him of his blaster.

He wished he had it back for just a second. However, Judd did not regret the sergeant's routine action. Even these detestably soft Targans could be dangerous. Long ago, he'd learned never to underestimate an enemy.

Finally, he was moved to another room, a small one, to be sure, with blank white walls. He was no longer kept in Judd's sight.

Detained, it would only be until the rebellion on Modallas was ended one way or another, going either way, then, his release was possible. This thought gave him a little ease. The hours there, in the little room, were long and there was no switch to dim the lights so he could sleep.

There was little left for Chibba to do. Unless things changed dramatically, it was inevitable he would die at Judd's hands.

Had he not been taken by surprise at that hour of the day, he could have made some winning, personal plea; at least, he could have made an attempt at escape.

Confined alone in a small white room in which there was a single, uncomfortable chair and a single guarded door. There, in the door, was a smaller portal at which a guard's face would appear at brief intervals as it snapped open. There was little else to do but pace. He was, indeed, assumed guilty never to be proved innocent.

He was no longer being held in Judd's own sight. He was merely being detained as a questionable person. That was unlikely. He wondered which of his plots had been discovered. There was nothing he could do, separated from his own operatives. It was possible that one of his agents might reach him, even there. There was, it seemed, a form of loyalty among them. Isolation was his worst enemy.

61

Judd and Chibba

It was to The Helmsman that his fast reaction forces were taking such a beating. This was unexpected. Fighting raged in the bigger areas on the urban plains. He had not thought the rebels among his Targan to be so well prepared. He wished for the option to recall his best attack force from the planet, but there was no way and no time.

There was much on his mind, the Marcellean beast had appeared again, the resistance on the planet, passive, but resistance, nonetheless. Worse, the rebellion that was now open among his most faithful, on Modallas itself.

The galaxy seemed far from his grasp; truthfully, it had never seemed more distant. The destruction of Kithron should have stopped all resistance, but it did not.

Lowly Ganempsha was proving not difficult, disturbing. A few displays to the public, executions and takeover of their piddling, small media outlets should have done it. The last straw had been, despite his orders, a thing, a Sand Rock festival, in the deserts beneath his feet. He would not have it. That, unfortunately, would have to wait until later.

At last, it began to die down. The rebellion had been crushed. Only a few scattered areas held out, and his loyal forces tightened their control. Things would return to normal before long. Other matters would soon receive his attention. Those on the planet below would be dealt with and the Ghost Pilot, too. For the moment, he'd forgotten that one.

He stood at the helm of a changed Modallas, one transformed in the white heat of battle, more so than the temporary invasion of Marcelleans, but of open rebellion against him. It did not yet seem possible.

He would never look upon his Targan or take them for granted again. He'd been forced to call air strikes against his own cities within Modallas to stage raids against elites who defied him, retaliation.

The Control Center, his control center, looked as polished as always to his eyes. He could not name it. Something was different.

There were other things to look to, things that demanded his attention. Modallas had been wounded in more than pride.

The rebels must be flushed out to the last. That was even of greater importance than stopping the Marcellean beast – loyal personnel.

Now, to maintain security, he quickly looked to their repair. The planet below and the Ghost Pilot himself took a backseat to that priority. Without Modallas, there was nothing. That came and went among his Targan at will, even aboard Modallas. More than that beast had violated his sanctum.

The cylinder world was open to attack by weaker forces. Several key gun turrets were destroyed with the loss of

Those on Ganempsha were those who did not know how to revolt. Soon, those left aboard Modallas would not have that knowledge either. His authority would once again be complete. He turned the Con and his control grip over to the lieutenant and left the center to pursue the remainder of those rebels. He touched the control activating communication with Judd, on the planet.

62

Rebellion III

Above, a battle raged. Within the Control Center, those who controlled Modallas fought the battle. It was growing street by street, building by building, and there was little success yet that any of them could mark. They, like Judd and like their master, remained at posts and remained calm.

Bolts of laser energy crossed the sky in the distance. Element of his own air cover bombed and strafed buildings on two of the three Modallian plains. It was nothing seen on Modallas before.

A Targan flyer hit by ground fire spun downward, trailing smoke to the ground where it impacted silently, too far in the distance to be heard.

There were other things to look at, things that demanded his attention. Modallas had been wounded in more than her pride.

Modallas, his sanctum, had been violated by more than the beast. Modallas was open to attack by weaker forces. There was damage. Now, to maintain total security, he must see to repair.

The planet below and the Ghost Pilot himself must take a backseat to that repair. Without Modallas there was nothing.

His authority would once again be complete. He turned the Con and his control grip over to the Targan lieutenant and left the center to pursue the remainder of the rebels.

This restlessness, as it was called sometimes, had been growing steadily. He had raised them too far from life in the forests. Again, it was not working as well as he thought it should. That was academic. Now was the time for fighting, for reclaiming that which was his and Modallian from those who no longer followed him.

The cleaning of his house had begun. If he decided this was so, this was not a bad time, but a good time.

Judd smiled at Chibba's manner. Chibba was heavy, too fat for a Targan, the man had grown soft spying, manipulating the fates of others. None of that required a hard body. That shortened one's life. The laugh was grim. Targans, those closer to the forests, laughed that way, in a manner tinged with death, especially the death of others. Word on Chibba's fate was expected within the hour. He suspected nothing. There were those with more subtle machinations than Chibba the Spy ever dreamed.

It was a rare treat. He wondered whether or not he'd be allowed Judd to let the entertainment tell Chibba of The Helmsman's suspicions toward him, to chide him about his lack of awareness, to death. More than likely, the knowledge that The Helmsman himself was directly supervising the investigation would be enough to shake him.

Judd's eyes narrowed in anticipation. The smile on his face had turned into a snarl.

In return, Chibba had not liked Judd, ever. All things being equal he'd bet his money on the softer trained Targans aboard Modallas. He did not look at Judd, he didn't need to. The call to the command center, on such short notice, was indication enough of why he was wanted there.

Had there been any evidence against him, he would have already been dead, moldering somewhere, unburied, forgotten except by those who tempted fate, plotting against the only power that was their universe, The Helmsman.

Judd's gaze had already settled heavily on him, leaving a lingering, uncomfortable feeling that he did not like and couldn't shake. He added up the cards in hand again and again. He'd been called early, and to stay in the game had to raise the stakes, staying long, a bluff would not do. He prayed to the Forest Spirit, that wraith of the forest he'd never known; this hand he dealt himself was good enough.

They were a distance from the forests of which they were creatures, both of them, Judd the Commander and Chibba the Spy. Too far, now for one of them. There was no easy answer.

Sometimes, he let himself believe that you just had to wait it out. Chibba would place his hopes on that.

Detained, it would only be until the rebellion on Modallas was ended one way or another, going either way, then, his release was possible. This thought gave him a little ease. The hours there, in the little room, were long, and there was no switch to dim the lights so he could sleep.

Had he not been taken by surprise at that hour of the day, he could have made some winning, personal plea; at least, he could have made an attempt at escape.

Confined alone in a small white room in which there was a single, uncomfortable chair and a single guarded door. There, in the door, was a smaller portal at which a guard's face would appear at brief intervals as it snapped open. There was little else to do but pace. He was, indeed, assumed guilty never to be proved innocent.

He was no longer being held in Judd's own sight. He was merely being detained as a questionable person. That was unlikely. He wondered which of his plots had been discovered. There was nothing he could do, separated from his own operatives. It was possible that one of his agents might reach him, even there. There was, it seemed, a form of loyalty among them. Isolation was his worst enemy.

There was little left for Chibba to do. Of course, he was rightly accused, and unless things changed, he would die at Judd's hands.

At least, he could have made an attempt at escape. He'd been confined by himself in a small white room in which there was one uncomfortable chair and one guarded door. There, in the door, was a smaller portal at which a guard's face would appear at brief intervals.

Isolation was his worst enemy. There was nothing he could do. There, separated from his own operatives, henchmen, he wondered which of his plots had been discovered. Merely being detained as a questionable person, it might be possible one of his operatives could reach him

– even there. There was, it seemed, a form of loyalty among them.

If he were to be detained merely, it would only be until the rebellion on Modallas ended one way only, then, his release was guaranteed. This thought gave little ease. The hours there, in the little room, were long, and he could not sleep.

With a heavily armed elite guard, he approached the central square of Urban Plain 2. In one hand, he held a heavy blaster. There was to be no mistake among the Targan what that was, or who wore it.

The attack advanced. There were no prisoners. He stormed the final enclave of rebels at the head of his troops. He handled it - as well as any Marcellean, who, after all, still considered it their weapon.

The last fighting was hand to hand from floor to floor in a bombed-out building. In a series of moves that would have won approval from his arch-enemy, Soal, The Helmsman captured the rebellion leader, wiping out his guard in doing so. As the building burned, he tore from the man, the names of those involved in the rebellion.

As the man died. The Helmsman spoke by direct link with the planet below. His order was terse and succinct. From both its origin and tone, the Targan receiving it knew it was to be delivered and carried out immediately; in Commander Judd's hands, it read simply, "Execute Chibba the Spy!"

That was all of it.

Chibba's agents reported to their new boss. They were, in turn, ordered back into the field. One operative, Kees, was en route to Cross Anchor by way of The Ord's edge.

He flew the same hopper he'd used to attack Borter and kill Mad Moz; Judd knew Kees' mission and was dissatisfied with the smug reply that had announced its completion.

Judd was in direct contact with Kees. He was known to have been Chibba's best, and he claimed to have killed The Ghost Pilot.

The Helmsman was unconvinced of the Ghost Pilot's death. The Helmsman must be made certain. Nothing less than Borter's head on a platter would suffice him. However, he would, at last, accept Kees'.

It was out of curiosity more than a regard for any military chain of command or protocol that he spoke to the man personally. The Ghost Pilot was a mania. Kees was bright and caught the message quickly.

The Helmsman had followed him across the galaxy, that commander of the feared AF6. Never had The Helmsman been so distracted than at that moment, now was the only time he had. Judd wanted to know why?

"I want confirmation – " Judd's voice exploded in his ears, "not vague claims!"

"Sir, to find the body, as you wish, would involve a long search and may involve the people of The Ords, the Sandriders." Kees would question several himself.

They, were no more than the poorest ragged derelicts of Cross Anchor. They hung around the food pantry and empty back lots. They knew nothing, just babbled, even under the most persuasive tortures available – nothing. Their intentions in any matter never been fully known.

"I suspect that there is more to them than meets the eye. I urge caution. From other contacts, there were legends of them, something about an ancient power like nothing else in the galaxy, and of their other planetary connections to other legends involving them with a dark starship, its pilot, and the red clones in the desert!"

"I don't want legends," Judd thundered loudly enough to cause his Targans in his Command Center to cringe. I want proof of his death. Show me a body. Show me anything concrete. I want the Ghost Pilot!"

"Yes, sir," Kees replied.

63

Borter and Kees

Something, large and very black blocked his rear view. It had not shown up on his sensors and now it pulled up, just above his head. Its wingspan blocked the suns. Suddenly, as suddenly as it had come upon him, it lowered. There was a loud clang. The controls nearly slipped from his hands.

Instantly, he lost twenty or thirty meters in altitude. It pushed him down and then backed away, off to one side, where he could get a good look at it.

Borter swept off just far enough and tilted his near wing down low enough for Kees to get a good look at who manned the cockpit. He noted that Kees was impressed, visibly.

"Sir," Kees shouted into his microphone, "Sir, I think I've found him!"

Borter used Soarer's greater bulk to bash Kees' hopper lower in the sky and then back away again to enjoy his turkey shoot. Long before, he'd decided to play it out as long as he could. He played with Kees for a while – until it became boring; the Targan could not escape, even if he'd landed in the vast orchards. Borter made up his mind to follow him anywhere and, if necessary, hunt him down in his own forests. Moz's killer would pay, and those, as well, who sent him.

His Marcellean armament sprung from the lowered wing pods. He took his time and greater pleasure in shooting away the antennae and sensor gear from the hopper. Next, the landing gear was sheared off.

A rare moment, Borter laughed. Like any good Magnean, he was flying Kees right out of the sky. Kees squirmed.

Modallian fighters came from above and others from the rear.

He nudged Kees again, spilling him down.

The hopper dropped toward the desert floor; a chance not better than he'd offered Borter himself not long before. To Moz, he gave no chance at all and meant to give this Ghost Pilot less.

Borter took the time to watch as Kees was impacted. His fuel pod exploded in a display that was impressive even in the light of Ganempsha's double suns. As that happened, he hit Soarer's throttle and raced into the sky. The computer images on his screen were getting close. There were four altogether.

He had never done this without Helio. It made little difference. They came for him. He wheeled Soarer first one way, then another; he wove and dodged like a mad butterfly.

Targans were fierce but didn't fly as well as they thought they did. He leaped forward and then fell back until he got behind one. It spiraled in easily, smoke trailing.

Two more spun in, then, the fourth. It did not seem at all difficult. Nothing to it. Thus satisfied, Moz had been avenged, he laughed at the notion that The Ghost Pilot had been the one to do it. He imagined the thoughts going through the dense little minds that had sent them in the first place.

64

Sandriders

In the course of things, there came a time for another part of the legend to take its place on the tablet of things passing. Happening in the hours that the Sand Rock concert began in the desert, a band of the city's children gathered to taunt the Sandriders, a fair representation of whom could be found wandering Cross Anchor any time of day or night in forlorn groups of two or three.

The old Sargent walked in one such sad trio. He was unshaved and ragged, as were all, as usual. Today, rocks were thrown at them. The fear in the air was a real thing among the children doing the stoning.

Young and loud, brought up on the planetary legend, part of which said they would be protected always by Sandriders. Now, with AF6 in The Ords, they were afraid and needed to take it out on someone, someone who could not strike back. He pretended anger and glared at them. The children laughed and came back, jeering and throwing more stones.

One caught him in the temple hard enough to drive him to his knees and cause the stub of his unlit cigar to drop from his mouth. The other two rushed to him. Revenge against these children was unthinkable. It was over quickly, for the moment.

It was then something happened. All three stopped at once, looking toward the sky, though it seemed to come from all around. Others went about their business, hearing nothing. It came from The Ords.

The three came to their feet. It seemed an echo at first, barely sounding through the streets. Then, it was the thunder of massive hooves swiftly coming closer, a call to arms. There was turmoil. Everyone ran except the Sandriders. Sredirs came into view at the edge of Cross Anchor end of the street. In their saddle loops rested long power lances. Newly saddled and bridled, Sredirs were almost never seen in the streets of Cross Anchor. Soon, there were more, led by a few Sandriders in proud new uniforms. It was time.

There were new uniforms for all. Others, Sandriders, still in their rags, ran up to them. The old sergeant tore away his rags.

Within moments he was on a Sredir's broad back, and the cigar butt also reestablished in his snarling face. His chevrons were emblazoned on the sleeves of the new jacket. He shouted, and chaos became order.

They formed by twos behind him, ready for a return to the desert. They were many now and the children who moments before hurled stones at them stood back, afraid, now in awe, silent, agape.

The desert mounts were larger than they'd ever imagined them, and the Sandriders themselves were as magnificent as they had ever been described.

Again, the call sounded, there was no mistake, they all heard it. At another order unintelligible snarl from the sergeant they were off, riding toward the Ords. The children left behind would now have something to tell their grandchildren before they put them safely to bed in years to come.

65

To Kithron, Show Mercy II

Modallas plodded a nominally close orbit to Kithron. There, The Helmsman released the control grip of the gigantic artificial giant to an automatic pilot. He turned from the command console at which he'd stood continuously since leaving the scene of battle only days before, on the edge of system Laura Zed.

His control center was silent. Except for the occasional going to and from, shuffled feet, of his Targans at stations around him. Sensor screens bathed everything in dull lights and brought out the normally deep lines and hardship worn on the hard-looking faces of the forest men he'd brought to his cause.

Beneath them, rolling peacefully, lay Kithron, the jewel of the Inner galaxy. That world below them was not at peace as one might have supposed from the slow-moving clouds that crossed its surface both night and day or from the vast seas that lapped against shorelines. Kithron, instead, was a smear of bristling guns. They were not the defeated people one might have expected.

True enough, The Helmsman had not destroyed the fleet at Laura Zed and also the forces of Modallas had suffered losses at the same time, but had not pursued their enemy as had Modallas and destroyed them. The

Kithronese fleet had been too disorganized to mount a fair counterattack and The Helmsman had controlled his with an iron fist – an iron fist, so it was said, that had never failed.

Targans were the huge battle guns that were part of Modallas' armor. Ready to launch was an air force rivaling that of any planet in the galaxy, though truth be known. It was surpassed by a single, lonely star-freighter, still hidden on Ganempsha.

Kithron beneath his armored feet. The Helmsman stalked back to his quarters to rest and to wait. The days at his station had matured him he steered Modallas across the void between galaxies. That had been infinitely longer. In that vastness he had been there, been there for Modallas and his masters, it, whose land it had been, then, as now.

The White City on The Third Plain, his thoughts turned back toward those first days of his image service, but he could not remember them. All were blurred and run – together.

Overall, he had a dull feeling about it, his years at the helm and all the destruction his duties had brought. All he had done was his duty. That's all there was, ever, and he supposed, all that ever would be.

They dealt with the outside through impersonal androids. That population, also, was responsible for all the heavy work on the planet - all work for that matter.

It should be explained that the androids are of foreign design and that they are made to look and act like the natives of Finians themselves. They could mix among the Finians as they liked.

66

A Tale of Two Freighters – The Princess Odeon

They sat. Borter, Helio, and Parnak in the disused back room of some disused building. Before each was the remnant of breakfast. They sat, staring blankly at each other across a round table.

It had begun a day or two before. Soarer had gotten work through Freighter Amalgamated. A cargo of androids was assigned from planet Finian. Borter had, of course, been there. All had been there. They needed the money and Parnak could no longer pay.

Parnak's money had been shut off by the turbulence brought to the galaxy by Modallas and The Helmsman. Borter's freight forwarder had signed them on for a trip off-planet. They went.

For Finian itself, or of it, there was no story. Though it deserved the obscurity it had, it was not quite what could be called unimportant. The Galactic Atlas told where it was and listed its major exports. It listed mass, orbit and other physical qualities. There was little said about its people. In fact, none of them had ever been known to leave the planet. They were considered an odd lot. It remained a shipping hub if nothing else.

In fact, being a bit crusty about that sort of thing, that's exactly what the Atlas said about them in bold print, and why not expect much?

There was one, only, space port on this whole planet and off-worlders, were expected, even required, to stay androids and none would know the difference.

Many thought, those who thought about such things, that they did make use of those who came to their planet directly, though it had never been proved, rather than the androids. Could it have been the planetary natives, not the androids, who left the planet? Who knew.

Finian was a great laboratory for the study of all galactic life forms; others suggested that if the first part were so, then the second was merely entertainment. Some coupled a mixture of the two with a need for anonymity. Still, it remained that everyone came to Sinobia to take or leave something. They were rich; if they did not need the money, what was the take – back?

All of them wore blasters. All four/three, including the reluctant Parnak. It was early in the morning on Sinobia, where they sat. They had been there all-night waiting, playing cards, their habit when bored and that of most galactic travelers, when waiting. Blasters for all, the usual subtle touch.

Remains of the poor breakfast rested on the table before them and the remnants of the disposable container that carried it, as well.

The android that delivered it had been watched carefully as he'd left his truck and rang the bell at the service entrance.

Borter and Helio had drawn their blasters at the first sound from the door. Parnak had been selected by elimination, or so it seemed, really by the insistent nods of the others, to answer the bell.

Was it as simple as it had seemed? Parnak paid for and received the food with money from Borter. The android went away quietly. It seemed a feast to them after so long on the reconstituted food of their galactic travels. There was nothing else aboard the freighter in the way of real food.

Borter thought Parnak was such an insensitive boor that the quality of food did not matter. Really, he thought it amazing that Helio, who he'd thought sensitive to the point of genius, found toleration of Borter possible.

Each, at that particular, quiet and very strange moment, was lost in the thick of his own thought, brought on, in its turn, by boredom and fatigue.

Waiting at the Odeon, big as it was, became a prison for them, freight runs aboard Soarer aside, for several days or for weeks at a time. It was at least a place to hole up. Outside there were those who searched for them.

In other days and now, sometimes, the Princess Odeon was a popular theater entertaining off – worlders exclusively on their layovers at Parnel. Its most recent days were those of disuse. Friends of Parnak opened it for them. The journalist seemed a galactic charitable institution.

Everywhere, Borter and Helio shuttled him, someone, always somebody, waiting, who knew the great Parnak.

Right now, the – great – Parnak sat with the not-so-greats, waiting.

Two days across and back. It was at the end of the first day going they'd reached Finian orbit. There, large freight containers had been attached to Soarer's tube. There were three, all large enough for a man to walk inside and down a narrow pathway left between the packaged androids. Soarer's outer hull bore hatches to each. This was the standard method of transporting freight in the galaxy. Soarer's tube was left to her crew.

Against the rigors of space, the containerized sealed and pressurized cargo were docked in orbit to be delivered at the point of destination the same way.

It was an easy run for good money, and they'd seen no reason to turn it down. Finian and Sinobia were outside the Modallian sphere of influence for the present.

Heading out toward Parnel from Sinobia, one of the androids freed itself from its packaging. The container hatch opened to Soarer's tube, and the android let itself in. Parnak, Borter, and Helio watched as it stumbled into things, even the simplest things that were common surroundings of Soarer's tube. Parnak cautioned them, androids fresh out of their packing cylinders needed time to become fully operational. "Leave it alone." Word came from Soarer's chief pilot.

The android, unaware of its own name, answered everyone else's. Parnak suggested silence as the best cure. Helio, meantime, went into the cargo container and checked the parts list from the shipping cylinder. The name given on it was Quantum. He returned through the hatch to the ship's more spacious tube, then, to the cockpit where Borter lounged in the captain's chair.

He'd turned himself from the controls to watch the android in the tube. The blue man jerked a thumb toward the confused figure in the tube and said her name softly to Soarer's passenger and pilot at once, Quantum.

Quantum's head swiveled toward the sound of her name. Repeating it to herself, as if having heard it again, that it was nearly forgotten after so long a time.

Consciousness for the artificial being seemed to be an indistinguishable shape at the end of a long, grey tunnel with only a tiny light at the end. Another few seconds, and she seemed oriented.

Life seemed to ease within, and, not for the first time, the flyers noticed the femininity of the form and the new grace that took its movements. She wore no clothing.

The scene in the tube was no longer so entertaining. It was awkward. The two pilots glanced at each other as if confirming in some masculine solution the evidence of their eyes. Quantum noticed the attention and moved toward a darker part of the tube, but noticing Parnak, already there, shied away.

Parnak motioned for them to turn around in the cockpit which they did. The tube of the small freighter in space was no place to get on someone else's nerves. In a way that was for one of his physiology friendly, Parnak smiled. Quantum did not respond immediately, instead she stared at the floor, looking for something to do with her hands.

At last, she sat and looked toward Parnak as he spoke quietly to her. As he would explain later, androids were a lot like natural humanoids except that they were built fully grown and matured emotionally to what they were in a short time.

Quantum looked toward the cockpit and found Borter looking back. There seemed to be a moment of electricity between them, at least for the android. Helio had busied himself with the ship and had not turned away from that task in some time. However, Parnak observed as was his habit. Quantum smiled at Borter, then seemed to blush.

Parnak smiled to himself. He was totally bemused by what he'd seen. Borter looked at him, startled and confused, having felt something stir within himself.

Quantum sat smiling calmly, quietly, her gaze settled on the Magnean. She seemed content.

Parnak rose, nodded politely in her direction, and walked to the cockpit and Borter.

"What's with the android, Parnak?"

Parnak snickered. "She is not merely an android!" He loved having the upper hand on the pilot. It was always such fun making him a fool.

"She," he said grandly as if introducing the belle of the ball, bowing toward Borter formally, at the same time, making a sweeping gesture toward Quantum, his arm outstretched, his hand flat, it gracefully stopped at that area of the tube in which Quantum sat.

Time left getting to the planet was unexpectedly pleasant as Quantum became more and more animated. Helio relinquished his seat in the cockpit. She learned the controls of Soarer. Borter, of course, was her tutor. Parnak was a little less amused by this turn of events. Borter was surprising sometimes in the most curious ways.

Parnak claimed she would progress rapidly. She was beautiful to look at and would have done anything asked of her. Such was the reality of her imprint. It would, of course, modify as she went on, but this was the intended first step and very important in Android development, though not intended for the pilot who transported them as cargo. Quantum was a child by any standard. Borter would not let her touch the controls, however.

By the time Soarer returned to Sinobia, Quantum had progressed far, even to Parnak's expectation. She and Borter had become very close, in a daughter-parent sort of way.

Helio looked on but said nothing. Anything that would save Borter from the loss of Julia and their inability to rescue her from Modallas was a godsend. Borter perceived Quantum now as a young woman, a bit young but interesting, nonetheless. Androids were born with fully mature bodies. It took some time, after they were mentally awakened from the packing cylinders, they began to mature as adults.

As required of all incoming androids, she was sent to a registration center.

Then, politely, unceremoniously, she would be sent back to him from the receiving center in Parnel.

At the center, new androids were carefully unpacked and sent directly into process, the specifications of which were particularly Carnelian. Most often, they were imprinted to a senior android, that is, if the new android was a socialized model. Others of lower caliber were merely imprinted. These most often were menial workers where individuality was not a valued quality.

Quantum was not such an android. Her intelligence rating matched her physical rating. When Parnak wandered into the cargo container one night late aboard

Soarer, he was quite surprised to note her designation as a superior. He wondered at it; her manner was that completely of the girl next door.

He wondered how much of her development had been included in her pre-awakening package and how much was influenced by Borter and her accidental awakening. They were still in orbit at the cargo docks when she was returned.

Quantum did not seem unhappy. She'd been more than happy to explain how she'd come to awaken in the cargo container mid-flight. The process androids in the center at Parnel had been very understanding and had just sent her back to Borter.

This was true enough. Quantum had imprinted with Borter, and it would be sometime before she would, of her own accord, even consider leaving him for more than a short period. Thus, she belonged to him.

Quantum choked back tears, the first ever in her brief life. The receiving shippers made it plain, though gently so, that she would not be used among them. Her implanted knowledge told her only that she should return to The Hammer and Tulso Slide.

As she made her way through the narrow streets of Cross Anchor, more of that implanted knowledge awakened, but no more than was due as her maker intended. It was true, she enjoyed a youth in full flower. Her beautiful form swung playfully through the busy streets like the child she was.

There was little in her mind save a sorrow that her primary purpose had been scrubbed. There was no thought of Targans, Modallas, or the turmoil that swept the galaxy.

Many, including the Targans, who trailed her on the journey back to The Hammer.

The Helmsman was the same as the race of androids to the masters of Cross Anchor.

Were they not Targans of the planet Marcellus? They were the best of that race from the vast forests covering the planet and were, in fact, well-trained.

The streets were choked with off-worlders and working androids. The Targans did not stand out particularly. They wore loose trousers of faded khaki and loose shirts. Their black night cloaks were kept elsewhere, safe. At their side, each wore a powerful blaster of Modallian design. There were two of them. Quantum did not notice.

As she wound her way through the narrower streets of her implanted knowledge awakened, but no more than her maker intended. It was true, she enjoyed the full flower of young womanhood, her firm, roundly curved form swung attractively though the busy streets like the young girl she was.

The way back to the spaceport was instinctive. She wiped her face with the back of her hand and sniffled loudly, walking on. There was little in her mind save a sorrow that her primary purpose had been scrubbed.

There wasn't knowledge of Targans, Modallas, or the turmoil that swept the galaxy. Many watched her progress in her journey to Soarer with appreciation.

The Targan first impression had been one of amazement, one could say astonishment, at the perfection of the androids who worked the city. Aboard Modallas, it was they who did that kind of work, but in the streets, they saw these perfect beings carrying out mundane tasks, instead of themselves.

A sort of chord sounded in their minds as they realized they, to The Helmsman, were the same as the race of androids, to the masters of Finian, where these, not Targans, were masters of Marcellus. They were the best of that race, which battled the Marcellean warriors. They, from the vast forests covering the planet, were highly trained and, in some cases, many, in fact, well educated. However, they were still Targan, forest creatures, forest men, only half savage or half civilized.

They did not think of it too long. There was the mission, this female android led them to the Ghost Pilot, the one who had eluded their master for so long. It would be worth it to them to go to the trouble of either capturing or killing that one.

67

Quantum II

Quantum hurried back. Tulso Slide waited for her somewhere in the crowd, near the stage, he said. The show would begin soon, later than he predicted.

She felt a pre – show excitement many felt at concerts. Starr had quickly become a favorite; they'd never met and never would. It was something in his distancing – a singularly aloof quality that did it, some thought.

Slide, also, had been a different man than Borter. She loved him in a different way.

Her attraction to Slide surpassed that to the pilot, swiftly. Helio had been nice, a sort of friend. Parnak? Parnak she could not explain.

It was a rapid maturation process built into androids. She could not help loving Slide any more than she could explain her sudden disposition to the pilot.

The crowd became a multitude, huge. Swelling to the Ord's very edge, they formed a crescent before a stage of gigantic speakers and vid-phone enhancers.

Not far ahead, Tulso shaded himself from the fading Ganempshan suns. His work done, for the moment; he went to Quantum.

She'd assisted, flying co-pilot. Slide was both pleased and amazed at how quickly, how far, she had come along.

The flights in and out had been simple affairs. He'd not run them in his own Silver Hammer, but in the available farm-haulers. There were several other pilots in service, all had been stranded, so to speak, by The Helmsman's blockade. There was constant chatter that the Ghost Pilot had been traced to Ganempsha. That did not excite him.

Someone on the stage barked numbers, checking the speaker system. It was requisite, expected, something without which it wouldn't have been a concert. There was a shattering electrical squawk punctuated by an amplified bump and a brief squeal of feedback. Everyone moaned, everyone cringed. A thumbs up from the stage manager said all was well with the sound system.

Quantum was far more interesting. The Helmsman did not interest him more than he'd impeded the honest earning of a living, or a little more, on the planet.

The festival was taking shape. He'd ferried twenty or thirty musicians to the stage area himself. Most of them are known acts from other parts of the galaxy.

Starr had promoted the whole show on his own, and the draw instant. It had been easy. He was the best draw in the galaxy.

Returning, she began to realize just how big the crowd was. The throng stretched kilometers out from the stage. Pacing up to a worried Tulso Slide, she could only guess how long she'd been gone.

He breathed a sigh of relief that she was back, the same feeling all new lovers shared when parted too long from one another, even under less-than-unusual circumstances. She would not have understood had he been angry.

They came, rich and poor. There, the neat, the hairy and those who were shaved and those who refused to wash. This, all and all, was an amazing audience.

The concert was beginning and was only a little late. Who cared? It was expected to go all night. Longer, who knew? No one cared, not even the Modallian occupiers and their master.

They seemed less menacing and very distant. Few there had ever seen a Modallian, a Targan, or would have known it if they had. Danger, far distant to them, equaled receiving the report of an unknown star having gone nova, how could it affect them? They were far away in The Wastes.

Everyone heard the orders to stay away, but few did. It did not seem to matter to any of them. All they knew was peace on the planet for the most part, and those from the surrounding galaxy wanted to know it.

The Helmsman used them to, as he put it, "pacify local resistance. Pacification, in the current campaign, had decimated several planets in the Inner Galaxy. These were his punishers, powerful ones at that.

Midafternoon had not yet come. The music began.

Armored carriers and artillery of the AFD settled down in the distance drawing up in a circle, a few kilometers, from the actual crowd. They waited.

Tulso Slide and Quantum lay down, side by side, comfortably wrapped against the coming night.

Bands had performed since late afternoon.

The music was painfully loud, irreverent and laden with images. Each band had its own admirers. They floated on the sound, each, in their own, small, circles.

Different, each unique. They built to a musical peak trying to excite the greatest part of the multitude. In this, none were the victor, until it came time for Thee Starr. No one else read moods, social shifts and sentiment so well. His presence on stage was like no other. It - was an experience, a true event.

68

To Kithron, Show Mercy III

For one hour, there was silence behind the door closing the chamber; four guards watched. Behind it was The Helmsman.

They, for that hour, hear nothing until he emerged from the pitch darkness of the chamber.

In the narrow corridor that led them to their master's quarters, there was a wide, clear portal extending several meters. Kept spotless, it afforded the walker, idle in the corridor, a superb view of Modallas, the best, in fact, there was.

The Helmsman's chamber was on the trailing end of Modallas' great, tubular bulk, above everything making the vast complex work. Vast, above that, control, of power and the management of energy.

Beyond, reaching into the air space of the turning cylinder, was Control where The Helmsman commanded and coordinated everything that was the cylinder world.

Each far corner of that object, created by beings' complex, is truly powerful enough to be known as a world unto itself. This astounded Borter. Modallas had clouds, a fact when first observed by Helio.

Borter had been busy at the time escaping Modallian fighters to be very impressed.

Parnak, with them later, explained the clouds hung weightless in the zero-gee center of the cylinder that could be compelled to give up their moisture, when desired, onto the three large tracts of land clinging to the inner surface of the cylinder as rain.

Within this place, on the land mass known as The Third Plain, their adventure with Lord Soal ended, the valiant leader standing his ground as his forces withdrew, under orders, to the invasion fleet and escape.

From the big window, one could look up to see the Third Plain and the distant White City that rested there.

At equal distances on either side of The Third Plain, two other land masses appeared to the eye, one descending from the clouds, one ascending to them in the curious interior revolution of Modallas.

Resembling gardens only a little less than did The Third Plain, these, also, were not the home of Modallians but The Helmsman's Targans, those gleaned from the forests of Marcellus, as the best, for The Helmsman's purposes. These included the fields, bases on which forces were trained for battle across the galaxy.

Beyond, far down the tube, a gigantic airlock served as a star port. The size of it dwarfed all but the largest Kithronese battle platforms. Beside it, large, staging platforms for single seat fighters dotted the outer hull.

At places along the outside surface, nestled between the constantly opening and closing shutters, a transparent sky swung open and closed with absolute precision, not unlike passing ranks of soldiers saluting the dark space outside.

69

A Battle of Titans

It was Kithron's battle, the entire Inner Galaxy at stake. Her fleet of dreadnoughts, her heavy battle platforms, accompanying cruisers, gunships, and carriers near the star system Laura Zed were arrayed throughout the system in a billion-mile formation. Agents of Kithron's intelligence service received rumors and scraps of information on enemy movement. Nothing appeared.

Space did not seem big enough for those who crewed those ships. They had heard much of this enemy. Nerves wore thin, and plans were made and remade.

The routine wore on. Gunners drilled their firing regimen and fighter-scouts patrolled far ahead of the fleet. Commanders maneuvered their ships in mock-battles and rang klaxons in practice - boredom set in.

Nothing had been seen, though his agents had from time to time been discovered. From them, not much had been learned; they refused to be taken alive. Ferocious battlers took more than one would-be captor to their oblivion. All of these things, fact, and rumor, traveled with the fleet.

The Kithronese heavy battle platform Giantro was the flagship. Around its bulk, half a dozen protective destroyers hovered. Both to and from it, a constant stream of shuttles came and went to all parts of the fleet. Aboard, a crew of twenty thousand serviced its six-kilometer hull.

Giantro was one of the most ancient ships of the fleet. Its history of service to Kithron read like a history of the Inner Galaxy. She had risen from defeat so many times that one only had to mention the name Giantro, and the stories would pour out all night.

70

Alien Bar – Nightlife

The way back to the spaceport was easy. One could say astonished at the perfection of those androids who worked the city. The Targan first impression of androids had been one of amazement. Aboard Modallas, it was they who did that kind of work, but in these streets, they saw these perfect beings carrying out ordinary tasks instead of themselves. A sort of chord sounded in their minds as they realized they, to The Helmsman, were the same as the race of androids to the masters of Cross Anchor.

Were they not Targans of the planet Marcellus? They were the best of that race from the vast forests covering the planet and were, in fact, well-trained.

71

To Kithron Show Mercy – The Helmsman

These resembled gardens only a little less than did The Third Plain, but these, also, were not the home of Modallians, but The Helmsman's Targans, those gleaned from the forests of Marcellus, as the best, for The Helmsman's Modallian purposes. These contained the fields, bases on which The Helmsman's forces were trained for battle across the galaxy. Beyond, far down the tube, was a gigantic airlock that served Modallas as a star port. The size of it dwarfed all but the largest Kithronese battle platforms. Beside this were several large staging platforms for Stiletto fighters on the outer hull serving the fast battle fighters, now the main fighters of Modallas and its fleet.

Turning greater in-sync with the cylinder of Modallas were the extended farming pods that fed all life on the artificial world and at places along the outside surface.

Nestled between constantly opening and closing shutters protecting the interior. A transparent sky, it swung open and shut, in turns, in absolute precision, like ranks of saluting soldiers.

72

Alien Bar – Nightlife I

After dark, the two fled the old theater for a safer place. Parnak knew that Targans gave up only when dead, even those possessed of Modallian training. The night was their realm, silence and secrecy. The Journalist's connections abroad on the planet and the galaxy itself were many.

One of Parnak's friends, one who owed him a favor, was to meet them later on. This friend was a long way off.

The shadows took them willingly. Quantum taking to the dark with great ease. Parnak steered her through the city streets with equal cleverness. A dismal rain had fallen, leaving a vaporous dinginess across the night itself. The streetlights showed a pale, drenched yellow from the lights above and from the night places they passed, glowing out into the sticky street hollows of those beacons.

They kept the silence of the night between them, letting others they passed make noise for them. They'd picked up no Targan tails, of this Parnak was quite certain. His powerful antennae warned him of nothing big. Even Parnak, with his long, thin legs, could not walk all the way across the city in a single night.

There were those, of course, who would be inhospitable because they catered to those of a world whose atmospheres were dangerous or merely unbreathable or both. He meant to cut a path through them toward the spaceport or until the contact met them. He did not even consider the possibility of running into un-friendlies along the way.

Parnak's shod feet began to ache; he hated wearing shoes, but it reduced the attention to his mechanically jointed feet.

Otherwise, the flexible exoshell made a very smooth, dark appearance to one who looked at him as if he were anything out of the ordinary. In fact, Parnak's home planet, Jillian, was very far from the Inner Galaxy and himself, a very rare individual.

He carried a small blaster in his pocket. He did not usually carry a weapon. However, his experience with Targans was long and he had not survived it by taking chances with them. The weapon would be of use at close range only, then, if he could get it into his hands quickly better that he use his powerful hands and body. His insectoid strength was great. Over the years he had been a war correspondent, he'd learned many ways to kill using only his hands.

The galactic squeeze for money had sent Soarer off into orbital space on a long delivery route, a mission that Parnak envied in these moments in the back of his mind.

The Helmsman retook his place at the Con. He turned Modallas toward Ganempsha and that one thing yet standing between him and these heroes of Marcellus.

He'd reinforced his agents on the planet days before in his search for the freighter, already blockading near space.

Now, Modallas would join the hunt. The cylinder world leaves the orbit of Laura Zed, to arrive before any support ships at Ganempsha, those taken from the conquered worlds of the Inner Galaxy.

Damaged goods, as long as they were androids, were not returned to the manufacturer for repair or reconditioning. Androids were considered a life form. In early models, more robots than androids, even though the stages when they qualified as androids, that is, artificial life forms, were sent back for repair. Now, if one misprinted as Quantum had, they were allowed to make their own way in the galaxy.

Later, on the planet, as they walked around Parnel, Quantum had, Borter thought she had, the perfect humanoid form he'd ever seen. Her short, straight blond hair waved in the gentle Finian breezes. Her blue eyes shone brightly in the planet's sunlight. Her face always smiled, it seemed, always.

An hour later saw them at the door of another club, the fifth such club. The manager, this time, was waiting for The Great Parnak. The streets, too, had become livelier. Cars raced in all directions; the hiss of tires on slick asphalt and the fading whine of their turbo engines droned far into the night.

In spite of himself, Parnak became a little drunk from the free drinks his reputation earned him. However, his physical strength and force of will held him in good stead. There was a succession of places, a club catering to inhab-

itants of water planets, for instance, where they were allowed to walk through a glass tunnel as patrons viewed
them from all sides.

Interest was great in Parnak and his lovely companion
everywhere. The bar's patrons floated all around them,
some merely dangling long tentacles, some Parnak
thought, looking hungry, if not downright predatory.

Parnak was glad to leave as was Quantum, though neither said so. They were more than halfway and doing well
not to have met Targans.

Parnak's plan was working better than he'd hoped.
He'd decided he was ready for a fight if one came his way.
This was all quite brave of him. Secretly, he was just as
glad none did. There was enough combat already in the
galaxy and he did not wish to add to it.

The hand drifted slowly out of the mist or seemed to.
Parnak stopped short, and Quantum ran into his back;
he'd come to a halt so quickly. The vapors of the club's
doorway were different from those in the streets. The hand
drifted back, money shoved into it by the insectoid, with
one of his business cards.

A few seconds later, the hand reappeared, this time
waving them inside. With one arm carefully around
Quantum, he went in.

In dim light, the hall they entered was nothing special
and showed the signs of both age and frequent use. The
hand's owner was a humanoid something noted by Parnak
when the hand came out of the mist and stopped them at
the door.

This humanoid, this man, was thick-set but moved
gracefully. His head was completely hairless and almost

square-looking. Clothing was light and simple, beige in color, baggy trousers, a large shirt, baggy as well. Parnak noted both items were cut from some coarse material, covering him from neck to ankles. His feet were bare.

With the same gesture he'd made at the door, the man turned and motioned for them to wait where they were. This time, Parnak and Quantum stopped together. Before he turned and walked farther down the corridor, Parnak caught a second glimpse of the man's face.

There had been a familiar tattooed marking above the eyes and between them as well that denoted a particular social rank, that of warrior from the planet Omega. To meet one was certainly a rarity and to find him working as doorman at a Parnel night spot was nothing short of amazing. The warrior cult of Omega was one of his pet interests, after those of Marcellus.

A flash of deep indigo came to him as the man walked away in the corridor lights. The mark itself ended in a fork shape, the upper widened on the forehead to the edges of the eyes and the lower one, smaller, just draping itself over the bridge of his nose, to either side.

The Omegan returned quickly, his motions leisurely and unconcerned. Behind him came another humanoid, this one more squat looking, rounder, less blank and better clothed for the evening. As they reached Parnak and Quantum the doorman stepped aside and the second man came forward, his hand reaching out to clasp Parnak's in a gesture of old friendship.

The two exchanged greetings as Quantum and the Omegan watched. The friendly hand reached out for Quantum's hand, which she gave happily enough after

Parnak's example. Without a word, the Omegan returned to his post. The smaller man smiled broadly and gazed up into Parnak's face with twinkling eyes. He motioned them forward.

The red mist permeated the place. They'd moved down the hall to the main room. There, the music they'd heard since entering boomed in their ears. It was Sand Rock, a variety that saturated the airwaves of the galaxy. Sand Rock originated from the planet they walked on, the distant Ganempsha. The current, single, greatest exponent of that form, Thee Starr, then on stage.

That end of the club was alive with writhing dancers, mostly humanoid. The air was quite heavy with other things than were normally in the red mist, some of them illegal, if Parnak's senses were right. The stout little man smiled broadly all the time they crossed the dance floor toward some secluded tables near an exit. They had come far, and it was late. An android appeared to take their order, which he did with a minimum of warmth and with a marked indifference to Quantum. One android knows another, decided Parnak. It was sometimes difficult to get one android to serve another. Prejudices were everywhere. It was time for a rest.

However, as thick as prejudices could be, at times, there were easily as many friends of Parnak. In the past five places, there had always been someone who knew him.

At any rate, these Parnel islands of light were theirs to walk across as far as the spaceport.

They'd hardly sat before Quantum was up again dancing to the Sand Rock. Thee Starr fronted a vid of his own band whose aggregate name escaped him for the dozenth time. The video itself was a recording, a video minus one. That one, was filled by Thee Starr.

More revelers entered the club. All seemed unruffled by their passage beneath the gaze of the Omegan. Parnak breathed a little easier as he noted no Targan among them. They were tall, good-looking people, male and female humanoids, off-worlders, without a doubt, Targans in neither dress nor demeanor.

Parnak wrangled with Starr's management the entire time he'd been on planet, for an interview, without success.

Quantum moved easily before him. He thought she danced as well as anyone. She looked, in fact, so attractive to him that he almost forgot they were on the run. She nearly dragged him onto the floor.

Parnak didn't dance, but had no choice with Quantum. He wondered for what purpose she had originally been designed.

At length, they sat. On the table they found drinks waiting for them, compliments of management. They'd been served by the same, frigid appearing android. Parnak nodded his thanks to the short, broad man who'd brought them in after the Omegan doorman.

Parnak squinted in the half-light toward the vanishing bandstand. The holograph reduced itself to a fading, multicolored speck, stage center, and what had been the band he had seen swirled away into the speck. Now, there was something more happening. Musical equipment was being brought on stage.

Quantum sat by him. More drinks came. Parnak was about to say he hadn't ordered any when it struck him there were three instead of two. He turned, looking over his shoulder, and as he quickly turned again, any smile on his face was gone. The insectoid buzzed beneath his breath. Quantum noticed and was about to ask when he answered anyway. "When he speaks," he spoke through his translator, "the gods listen!"

"Who?"

Parnak jerked a thumb, indicating a person arriving behind him.

"Tulso Slide!" he droned.

"Hello," Slide said agreeably enough, nodding toward Quantum. "Parnak. It's been a long time – what, a few hours?"

Slide leaned across the table and picked up his drink. He smiled at them both, taking a long sip.

Tulso Slide was a freighter pilot like Borter or Helio. Parnak thought of him as something of a fraud, especially when he opened his mouth. The man was a good enough pilot, though not as good as Borter. He called his freighter The Hammer and led their same nomadic freight carrier's life across the galaxy.

"So, how are things on Jinzikan, Parnak?"

"That's Jinzikan - Tulso. Things are fine."

He was tall and lank, Parnak had seen his like before, one place or another. His eyes shone out dimly in the half light of the bar. The insectoid found it hard to trust those eyes.

Slide laughed easily, affably. He jerked a thumb at the now active bandstand. The band, they're flying with me. *I'm Starr's roadie!* I thought you knew. Thee Starr, ever hear of him?" The flyer arched an eyebrow and made a challenging face. Parnak nodded.

"Oh, everyone has," Quantum said, smiling broadly! Tulso smiled back at her, one other lost in her good looks.

"I thought we were flying with you – "

"You are," Slide smiled.

"He's warming up for a new tour. Thee started in places like this, you know?" That's why he's here – to remind himself of his roots."

"I know," Parnak said. "He's playing that concert out in The Ords!"

Tulso Slide and Quantum stared into each other's eyes dreamily, at least for the moment. Quantum, then, looked beyond the flyer to the stage.

Parnak to Quantum, "Do you know what a special person you're traveling with?" He said to her.

He was silent for another second. He smiled once more, then, going on, he said," It seems Mr. Starr got a glimpse of Borter this morning and was quite impressed. He wants Soarer. Borter and Helio will be available, won't they?"

Parnak didn't need to reply. Slide knew the answer. Like Borter, like all Magneans, he was intelligent. "It seems I've been paid in full; the only stipulation is that we come with you to the spaceport and see Starr board Soarer. "

"If not Borter, then Helio." I think we can get Borter to listen to reason – well?" He paused. The question perplexed Parnak as well. However, he found all Magneans painfully alike.

It would not be enough to travel among the entourage. Quantum and Parnak would have to be hidden among equipment cases on the way to the spaceport. About to complain, Parnak remembered the hunting Targans who were still on their trail.

"Already taken care of," Slide smiled. "They're on their way to meet us."

He stayed at the table with them for another half hour, dancing off and on when the music played, with the quite agreeable Quantum. Parnak glowered alone into the next round of drinks, again, free via management.

They returned to the table as Starr took the stage. Actually, just before he was supposed to appear, Slide had these things timed to perfection. He had the interview for Parnak.

Quantum seemed flushed and slightly out of breath. Slide, himself, merely sweated, a trait among humanoids. Slide was running Borter a close second in one more category.

Parnak could hardly restrain himself from recoil and disgust as the flyer settled down.

At least, thought the journalist, he smiled, a pleasantry among humanoids, something Parnak learned to do in place of rubbing antennae, which Borter did not do.

Parnak thought about their situation. He was playing a losing game.

Targans could close in on him at any time, Quantum, too. They could depend on no one around for help. It would not be long before they showed up. He scanned everywhere with all of his senses for that familiar, that feline, supple grace of the forest-bred killers. Nothing.

The small blaster he carried was a backup weapon of Borter's. The larger, more deadly, pirate blaster carried by the pilot himself, always. He was never without it. At this point, Parnak could see why.

He listened, also, for the quiet, the silence really, that accompanied Targan into any room anywhere, an aura pervaded the air around them.

It was one of those things that made it worthwhile having antennae among humanoids. Parnak could feel them if they were anywhere near.

The pilot had always claimed to be able to sense them with the fine hairs on the back of his neck. He said they stood up if there was danger of any kind around. Parnak, himself, put little faith in any of Borter's abilities. He was a good enough flyer. If you got where you were going, that was good enough.

"The Hammer is next door. Ready and waiting."

Sand Rock was nothing new to the galaxy, it had been around as long as he could remember. He knew more about it than Thee Starr himself. What he knew also had little to do with it, with anything. Thee Starr looked a little ordinary in Parnak's view.

Much of it was wind-swept desert, patrolled by an ancient calvary. There were only the usual planetary legends about them, they were merely curious, possibly worth a literary mention, if they figured in some regard, to Sand Rock and Thee Starr's story.

The planet had its lusher aspects, as well, there were towns and farms, vast ones. On Ganempsha there was only one town large enough to be called a city. That was

Parnel and it held that city status because it was the only space port on the planet.

Parnak's mind turned over like a file of the planet, there were the obscure, red Sargon clones in the Ganempshan desert, The Ords they were called or simply, The Wastes, and a cult, large for that, known as The Children of The Heart. The clones might make an interesting story.

Sand Rock was it though. People of the galaxy were wild about it. The sound had been handed down from generation to generation on all planets by their young people.

It was loud, at times unmusical, but always theater, one could never completely be rid of it. The voice of disobedience, of disregard and lack of concern for other tradition, Parnak would have paid to banish it from the air waves.

Thee Starr was only the latest exponent of the genre. After him, another would come to sweep away public imagination, just as there had been before him.

He felt the excitement in the air as Starr took the stage. There was nothing else like it, as they said, like holo-vid. He waved to the faithful who attended, those who had to be there, and those fortunate enough to have been invited.

Sand Rock blared for the pleasure of all, Parnak watched the stage with interest. Starr and his band danced back and forth to their own sounds. Starr, before playing VID, wailed indecipherable lyrics to his barroom audience.

Intensity surpassed volume, riveting those who were before them more. Parnak's sensitive antennae found nothing in the air but sound and alcohol, no pharmaceutical diversions.

The scene blurred before the great journalist's eyes. He was having too much to drink. Tulso Slide looked at him across the table, saying nothing, his smile holding all he meant to say. Slide, moments before, returned to the table with a broad grin on his face as he did, first at the natural innocence of the cult, then, more cynically, more sarcastically at Parnak.

A Magnean like Borter, both excellent flyers. And, though he did not like to admit it. He'd be safe with Slide almost anywhere. It was, the almost anywhere part of his thinking that bothered him.

73

Alien Bar - Nightlife II

Thee Starr stared back at Borter with hopeful eyes. He smiled like the hopeful boy he was. He looked more innocent to Borter than he had in his holovids. The pilot looked first at Starr, then at Parnak knowing he was beaten. Whenever, he'd not wanted to go somewhere, Parnak pulled the client contract on him. This was the first time he'd done so without paying.

Helio came down the ramp, wiping his hands, and announced that the Centralizer did, indeed, need an overhaul. Thee Starr shook his hand as Parnak introduced him. Helio, at the same time, smiled his rarely-seen smile at Starr, saying he'd been a fan for a long time. Parnak was pleased. Helio was never difficult. Borter glared at him.

He strode up the ramp past Helio and Starr toward the Centralizer. Along the way, he opened a storage cabinet, searching in the dim light for the overhaul kit. Finding it, he shut off the light, slammed the cabinet door, and left.

An angry hour later, the repair was still undone. Helio inspected it carefully before he allowed Borter to power it up. He said, "No."

Parnak did not like the idea of going to Modallas to rescue Julia, as Helio explained to him. He liked it less as

Borter joined the discussion. Borter eyed him darkly saving comment for later. Soarer's tube was dimly lit as it was most of the time. They talked there for a few minutes. The conversation, in quiet earnest, Borter doing the most talking.

There were a lot of ships carrying freight in the galaxy, he explained. Soarer was just another one, just like all the others. If The Helmsman was suspicious of one, he had to be suspicious of them all. That would be a big job even for him. When Parnak reminded him that he also had a lot of Targans working for him, Borter shrugged, saying that Targans were only Targans. Parnak, however, was correct. If Borter's plan worked easily, and there was some reason to believe that it might, they still had to find Julia, free her, and get out alive.

Parnak agreed in principle to rescue Julia. She was Lord Soal's daughter, and it was the least he could do for his old boss. There would be a need for more than the three of them to take part, and Borter had no right to endanger the lives of others.

74

So Much For The Walkers Of The Rimm –The Rescue Of Julia

They were away from Parnel and Ganempsha within an hour. Sensors behind read only Tulso Slide's Silver Hammer following them. From the spaceport there had been no sign of Targan pursuit. Parnak explained what had happened to them the day and night before. Borter said he would be ready. Sub-orbit was clear.

Starr was aboard Soarer talking to Parnak. They were going to drop Starr off at Ganempsha and make their way back toward Modallas and Julia; Starr refused, saying he would go along. Borter did not understand and, shaking his head had gone to the cockpit and powered up his. In – orbit, Borter picked up his freight containers; big boxes, longer than wide, were attached to Soarer's hull. Helio made sure the hatches from Soarer to them worked properly. He replaced the bolts that attached them to the hull with explosive bolts in case they were forced to dump them quickly. The system was in place, and dim lights glowed in the darkness, warning of danger in the tube.

Thee Starr sat quietly talking to Parnak without much animation. Every minute or two he would look toward the cockpit at Borter's shape as he worked the controls. He'd sent Slide along to Ganempsha with the band and equipment. Starr was very interested in Soarer, Borter, and Helio.

75

So Much For The Walkers Of The Rimm

Far distant, Soarer quit the plane, Parnak and Helio. He'd forced Kees to his death on a hill at the edge of The Ords. He'd done something better of a job with the Targan killer than the Targan had done with him. Once again, it was open space. First, he'd keep his promise, and he'd journey into the galactic Rimm in search of a Walker to deal with The Helmsman and Modallas. His problems with things of both Marcellus and Modallas were at an end.

There was a curiously weak pursuit. He was not interested in a fight. He threw in enough of the little freighter's extra muscle to get away. They faded from his sensors altogether, with slight notice from the planet, of Parnak, of Helio, of The Helmsman. He'd see them again and that miserable tin can, Modallas, in the company of a Walker.

Borter set his course for the planet known only as Lordus, the shadowy stronghold of the Walkers. Lordus meant death cubes and Walkers hurling them. They were the single force remaining in the galaxy that could face The Helmsman and come away with whole skins.

Covered in mystery, there were seventy Walkers, one for each death cube in existence. They did not rouse to aid just anyone. Your trouble had to be very bad and very big.

Borter did wonder if there could be a line at their door and, if so, how long would it be?

Lordus was days away at top speed. He checked the internal readings of his ship. Everything looked good. There would be no need for any changes in course until he reached the planet. Two days, and he'd be back.

This was the first time he'd split from Helio or been released from Parnak's contract. Hadn't the Dillisome split from him? He hadn't asked either of them. They'd merely disagreed. This chase of his might work if he could happen across a Walker or find a way to put in a call for one.

Wondering about it did not help. His friends could be dead when he returned, very dead. If he were fortunate enough to return with a Walker, would there still be a planet called Ganempsha? Could Ganempsha hold out?

Indeed, he knew what had happened to Kithron, a very powerful place. The galaxy, without the planet, was something of an empty concept. The Kithronese and their sophistication would be missed. It would be as if the galaxy's internal clock turned back a thousand years and as if the best speed available to star pilots was sub-light.

His engines were at maximum. Soarer was a blur. There was not a vessel in the galaxy that could match her. At that velocity, he cut back the miniature powerhouses and hurtled on toward his goal, coasting.

Rubbing fatigue from his eyes, he settled back, meaning to sleep. Already, it was proving to be a dull flight. Too much time to himself, The Ghost Pilot, indeed!

He was uncomfortable. Space, save for the near stars, was dark. Soarer was silent, and nothing seemed to move.

He turned and looked back into the empty tube. Parnak's things were gone, removed before takeoff. Parnak, at least, had hope of a future whether or not anyone else shared it. He had to smile thinking of the insectoid. Borter was sad, somewhere in his conscience, to have left him back there, on that rock.

There had been twice Helio had saved his life or both his life and Parnak's. To Borter, it was coincidental that Parnak had been there to benefit from Helio's attempts. That Helio would save Parnak without Borter's neck having been involved was out of the question, a concept Borter's ego was quick to understand.

Had it been one or the other of them and saved only one, Borter would readily have wished Parnak a pleasant journey into whatever afterlife was available to insectoids. Personally, Borter knew of none.

There was the first time Helio saved him. Borter arrived there barely past his youth to, as he said, hunt Waugreb. They were large four-legged beasts of the snowy, frozen wastes of Dillisome. Borter had made the kill, though he insisted on doing it alone. The Dillisome, young himself, obliged and moved away, taking the only turbo sled. The creature was disturbed as it rooted beneath deep snow and charged Borter.

He killed it but was nearly killed by it in the bargain. From a kilometer away, Helio came running. Borter had been brash, too foolish, he said, using a primitive compound bow as he had, and after switching to arrows tipped with exploding heads, still not enough. He forced the agreeable Helio to a distance so far away that any backup shot by blaster would have merely been an irritation to the monster's thick hide.

Unknown to him, at that time, the impressionable Helio had decided that this crazy Magnean needed a keeper, and that is what he became.

Borter mended in the family home. They cared for him, shaking their heads at him in disbelief. Many had killed Waugreb, and many came to their planet to do just that. However, none had ever considered the beast a real means of committing suicide.

Most Recent, the event for which Borter owed Helio his continued existence was from the year before, from within Modallas itself.

The Last stand on one of the great pyramids that comprised the city on the forbidden Third Plain came to be. Borter was there, in the fighting, with Parnak and Soal's Red. Soal unfurled his red flag ordering all other Marcelleans to retreat, to leave Modallas. Helio, aboard Soarer, picked the two up with the rest of their fleet and got out. Soal, 5D hurled themselves at the coming Targan horde.

Lord Soal, to the pilot's dismay, named Soarer his flagship for the invasion. The Heart of Marcellus spoke to Helio there.

Borter fancied danger, rather inversely from Parnak. He disliked authority, something the insectoid took as most ordinary, by instinct. That was the difference between them, the Magnean theorized privately. That was the reason the Magneans, early on, took to the skies and space itself and why the socially regimented insects of Parnak's species, at least, tunneled deep below the surface.

76

Helio In The Desert II

Dawn, a strange time in any desert, but particularly then, at that time, in The Ords. Parnak noticed the stirring first, then Helio woke. They looked at each other for a moment, both wondering if the other had an answer. They went outside.

Ganempsha's suns had yet to break the horizon.

The desert was windy that morning, windy. It added to the feeling that something was about to happen. Helio rubbed the sleep from his eyes, standing near Parnak as the clones filed by quietly in twos and threes. They did not turn to look at either of their guests and did not talk among themselves. The only things heard were the wind and the shuffling of their feet as they moved by toward the edge of the ruins.

Clouds formed, speeding on the wind toward the horizon. Was it about to rain? Helio looked to the sky. It was The Ords, and it never rained there.

The whole of The Wastes seemed changed and alien. Parnak watched the clones as his instincts developed during the years of his service, compelling him to. In his time, he'd seen many odd things, alien, strange, weird.

There was little else, nothing. They walked the ruin's edge behind the clones and watched them. It was what the clones did, silently, moving very little, as clouds swept by. Very much like a vigil, Parnak noted. Helio looked at him sadly as if he'd already sensed what was about to happen.

77

Sandriders

Families, still in bed clothes, late sleepers, leaning from windows and balconies at the parade headed toward The Ords.

Awakened by the noise, children ran to their windows.

Small boys who'd thrown rocks the day before stood silent, stood empty handed, mouths hung open, agape, as the riders left the city, two by two, in familiar column.

They Sandriders moved out. New uniforms, mounted, plumed shakos, power lances in hand, at rest, pointed skyward, they rode toward the Ords. Hooves of the Sredirs thundered in the old town streets. They were called. They alone.

Stopped at once, brought to silence. It seemed to come from all around. It was an echo at first, eerily sounding through the streets, then it was the thunder of massive hooves swiftly coming closer. It was time.

The children, the stone throwers, would now have something to tell their grandchildren before they put them safely to bed in the years to come.

The Helmsman watched his screens as The Ghost Pilot easily outdistanced his fighter pursuit at the outer reaches of the planetary atmosphere. Borter pushed Soarer into Star Drive and disappeared from his scanners.

This one in all the galaxy was his enemy. His long duel with the Marcelleans and their minions across the galaxy paled in comparison to the level at which he wanted – not hated, this simple pilot. It was just this kind of action that angered him. The man seemed to run away from a fight, until, at length, he is cornered, then he fights and fights well. He was not cornered this time and he knew it.

"Commander Judd . . ."

78

The Charge Of The Sandriders

Here and there, the awakened children of Parnel leaned from their street side windows. The hooves of the Sredirs woke them.

The sight of renewed Sandriders left them agog.

Plumed shakos crowned new uniforms, sleeves, and pants decorated with red piping. They rode into the Ords, legends to those who looked on after them.

They crested the dune; backs as straight as the lances they held upright and ready. They waited.

Far across the sands, Thee Starr and The Children of The Heart began their music. It was mid-morning as the backup bands performed in *least – to – most – famous* order.

The Helmsman noted their movement. High above, he gave orders that moved his force toward the concert.

If this was the old legend, he was not convinced.

Spittle covered, the sergeant went from rider to rider, inspecting his men. The captain waited at one side for word the review had ended. Except for the sergeant's penchant for that brown desert weed, his men were unblemished.

Briefly, near the end of the single rank stopped pulling back on his Sredir's reins. The man did a doubletake stopping in front of one of his men. There might have been something wrong, but there was not.

He glared at the man, leaning forward as if making a challenge. Low growling escaped his mouth. He turned back to duty.

The captain rode forward to the center of his command, a color guard close behind. The sergeant met the small band. All stopped dead center and moved a short way before the single rank. They waited, colors waving a bit in a new gust of wind.

He nodded. All moved forward. The hooves of Sredirs were heard in the Ords once again.

Turning to his sergeant, the captain gave an order. "Sergeant, take them to the sky," he said, in nearly a whisper at half voice.

The line of Sandriders moved. A little way forward, they rose into the sky.

"Sir, I have movement toward the attack force."

"I have it," The Helmsman announced.

The concert went on.

A second blip appeared on Modallas' screens. The Helmsman nodded half to himself and to those around him. Unnoticed by others, the hand that guided Modallas cross-galaxy quivered.

"I have to–" he uttered the words behind his battle mask.

Turning, releasing the cylinder world's steering grip, he stalked to the transportation tube and the planet below.

As the flash of light cleared, Borter's vision returned. He peered up from his screen to see Rand Sabbling in Helio's seat.

From the bulkhead, where 5D's undulating, half–checkered presence jammed itself, a wet tongue reached his face.

"Sorry to drop in this way," Sabbling joked. "But you can't go."

"Wha–!" The pilot stammered, pushing back at 5D. "Who–?"

5D insisted. "He likes you!" Sabbling pushed the big animal away.

"Thanks!" Borter managed to speak. "What's going on?"

"Ah – understatement! Amusing! Where shall I begin? Ghost Pilot – it's all right if I call you that?"

"No – who are you?"

"I am Rand Sabbling." He smiled amiably. 5D's slippery, checked tongue licked his whole face.

"I am B-B-Borter," Soarer's pilot stammered.

Sabbling chuckled. "I know. You are the one who has been sleeping with my wife–"

Sabbling's eyebrows raised in mock surprise, "My wife speaks well of you. Soal's daughter – my wife? I believe you've been sleeping with her."

"Uh – aren't you – dead?"

"Not that I know of!"

The pilot took a long breath.

"Well, yes. Sort of." Sabbling went on. "She viewed your flyby in Modallas. You really threw them off. The

whole place shook. I was, then, able to rescue her – with
5D, here –” Sabbling, smiling, nodded toward the beast,
still at the bulkhead, his face shifting, drooping a bit, into
the cockpit. “It was an excellent *ruse*.” The Marcellean
smiled.

“But,” the pilot gasped. “that’s when you were dead,
right?”

“Uh—maybe not!” Sabbling smiled. “Can we get on?”
He laughed, and Borter nodded.

Sabbling went on, “We have to change course. The
Walkers aren’t coming.”

“How do you know that?”

“They said so!” Sabbling nodded assurance. “Now, can
we change course? You are expected back on the planet.”

“Wait a minute – aren’t you dead?”

“Well, in a way,” Sabbling smirked. His troops were
already moving on to the desert concert. We have to
hurry!”

5D panted. His tepid, moist breath went into Borter’s
face.

“Julia was much impressed by your gallantry. 5D, and
I thank you for the ruse.”

“A *ruse?*” The pilot inquired dryly.

“Your diversion. You didn’t think that would work –
did you?” Sabbling went on, “Come, now, the course
change – back to the planet! If you’re not going to do it
for me, do it for Julia! It’s already late.” Sabbling paused,
“You didn’t know, did you?”

“Nobody tells me anything. I’m always the last to find
out everything!” The pilot grumbled.

Rand Sabbling urged him on waving, like an admonishing schoolteacher. "Back to The Ords!"

The planet rushed up at them. Borter tuned in his seat. 5D filled the hatch to the tube. He put words to the moment, "No escape!" He muttered. In Helio's chair Marcellean smiled back at him.

An energy blast shook the freighter. "Close," the Marcellean grinned. "Nothing major. Your directional sensor is out."

Borter glanced at his controls. The Marcellean pointed to a spot near the edge of the Ords. Take your direction there!"

"I suppose I have no choice – "Borter grumbled, attempting to brush 5D' s massive tongue away from his face.

Borter drove toward the spot in The Ords. "Can you get him to stop licking my face?"

"He likes you!"

"By the way. You have a passenger out there. We'll be picking him up soon."

"That means we'll have to land."

Sabbling shook his head, not. "That's all right. He nodded toward 5D, "We'll take care of everything. Look. Right over there," He pointed, smiling.

The throng of clones shaped up below, just where Sabbling pointed. They drafted themselves into a great red arrow pointing for him, the way, his path. At their head stood Helio waving.

An instant later, Rand Sabbling and 5D were gone from the cockpit and bulkhead entry, and beside him in the co-pilot's seat was Helio. "Get as close to the cliffs as you can," Helio pointed to the upcoming cascade of stones ahead, "And turn hard to your left."

"Yeah. You know," Borter responded, half smiling, "this is sort of fun!"

Thinking there was nothing to be done, he thought it was too late. He would arrive later that day in The Ords beneath the hot afternoon of the planet's twin suns to a place full of decaying bodies—too late.

Not imagining what Soal might have said, he imagined the words of Old Face. He wondered what good, then, would all that high-caliber Marcellean technology packed into Soarer do. It was the Techno Dwarf who, on the Marcellean overlord's word, the flyer's wreck was recovered.

He'd got rid of the arcade bells and whistles Old Face had installed – as a joke. Borter sat in the cockpit, looking out into nothing more than empty space toward the spot where Ganempsha hung. Now, that he wanted to, he could not help at all.

Borter did not care that he'd made a grave error in deserting his friends and a helpless plane. His return to Ganempsha and his speed proved his regret.

He feared for both Helio and Parnak. He expected them to be among the dead when he did return. This displeased him; he didn't have so many friends that he could afford just to let them die at Targan's hands.

Facts could be manufactured, but not reality.

79

The Charge of The Sandriders II

That night they heard, a disturbance – a call. Even those in the streets and alleys of Cross Anchor heard it. There had been no sound, not even a breeze, or breath of air, a call, nonetheless.

They were nearly one hundred, drawn up in a single rank, waiting for dawn. The leading edge of Ganempsha's trailing sun was just beginning to rise above the horizon.

They were far from the place where Thee Starr was still performing his concert and far from AF6.

The Targan force, like them, waited. It had been a chilly night in The Ords.

Those without shelter would have felt it.

Their regimental colors had not moved forward. Lances, powered, were held upright, at rest. Sredirs wore well – kept saddles and bridles.

Before them, the old sergeant and their captain waited. The Captain dismounted at a field desk. Sredirs waited, patient, in the morning air. Occasionally, one snorted loudly, or another pawed the ground with a massive hoof.

They came from nowhere they came from everywhere. Their sergeant waited patiently next to the Captain.

The sergeant spattered his brown liquid on the ground. Beside him, a trooper held the regimental colors. In front, the Captain sat stiffly at his field desk. The radio's dome before him began to glow, a message coming in.

As they'd gone, for a brief moment, there was a lazy thunder in the little city's streets. Just a brief chaos and then the sound of Sredirs heading out toward The Ords.

A fine spectacle, their ancient weapons and their ancient mounts ready to confront a superior number of current soldiery.

The Captain mounted his Sredir and moved from place to place before the meager formation speaking to them.

They knew, every one of them, what he was going to say. They knew all of his speeches from memory, but they would listen once more.

"What cliffs? There weren't any cliffs in the Atlas," Borter complained.

"I don't know. Could be, there's a page missing – it happens! Just look for them!"

The once-ragged company gathered in a line straight across the blowing sand. The old sergeant roared abuse at his favorites. At his officer's signal, he stopped, joining the lead behind their colors.

This was the day, he told them. The sergeant spat again. A drool of brown spittle dangled from his chin. The Captain pretended not to notice.

The sergeant spit, grossly this time, more than before and this time more than the he could bear. Riding forward slowly to a place beside the sergeant.

"Sergeant Major," he said, his face stiff, looking straight ahead, his voice low, "That's disgusting!"

The sergeant smiled, exposing brown teeth, "Thank you, sir!" He nodded cordially, smiling his gritty smile.

The Captain smiled despite himself, but only a little, and glanced into the old sergeant's eyes, "The men are well turned-out, Sergeant. Ride behind me as I review them!"

"Yes, sir," the sergeant took the order, smiling once more.

The thunder of the Sandriders reached the ears of his Targans on the planet. It sounded like thunder and was taken for nothing more.

The sound of the concert nearly drowned it out anyway. They glanced at the clear sky, then, it was back to business. They did their jobs calmly, with professional assurance. It wasn't going to rain.

They toured the single line. The Captain stopped before a man here and there asking a question or two, making a comment or a congratulation, or offering encouragement where he thought it might be needed. Finally, the captain and the sergeant trailing moved to the front of the formation.

Lances, still, held ready as the line awaited the signal to move forward.

Sensors reported their presence. Word reached The Helmsman that instant.

This ancient calvary was far too slow to present any danger to his plans. The order to move forward came.

Distance alone would not be enough. The Sredirs, proudly came on. Thunder rattled the cylinder world.

Whiskers pressed back by the wind, the old sergeant was giddy, like a child, viewing holiday gifts.

They moved forward at a trot and across all of Modallas' screens. They even caused moderate interest among those in the headquarters of the coming attack force.

The dark thunder cell led them; in it, they came, invisible from the ground.

AF6's sensors read them. There was a round of disparaging remarks at the expense of this ancient calvary. They'd not have to worry about stopping them. The desert would take care of that if they kept up their pace much longer, said one officer. Another offered they had gotten started by accident and couldn't stop.

That they'd run out of the desert before they found something willing to stop them was another. Judd's Targans laughed. They would merely step aside as they went by – if they got near.

Still far in the distance, the captain turned, "Sergeant," he said, "take them to the sky!" He rode forward, saber in hand, raising it.

The Sergeant, through browned teeth, growled something at his troopers, lifting his own lance upward. He followed their captain. They, as well, rode into The Ord's sky and battled to the dark protection of the thunder cell.

The Children of The Heart turned their eyes toward the desert. Thee Starr hovered above the crowd singing, watching; his sidemen backed him, close behind. Sandrock reached out, its sound loud, like a rumble of thunder, like that, coming in the distance. It was the Sand Rider's time. They were not to be denied.

Nearer, The Ords trembled. The line of Sandriders broke from the dark cell. They descended a line, Sredirs still at a half gallop easily toward the distant Modallean guns down.

Nothing stopped them. They descended a broad line, Sredirs still, only, at a half gallop.

Modallas' weapons raged at them. This was their penalty, payment for a promise, something forgot, an owed something, a bargain made long before, too long ago for memory. They could do little more than stand and wait.

He suspected but didn't know; none of them knew; it was too late that day for Modallas and all efforts Modallean.

Earlier, "Is this under warranty?" Borter, at Parnel, demanded, calling back into the cargo tube.

"Warranty? You have my word, sir!" Old Face answered politely.

"I want something – more than that!" Borter knew a written guarantee was not forthcoming. Old Face's word was good enough. Borter just wanted someone to shout at.

Old Face turned and stormed down the ramp – "This is the last time I make a house call," he shouted. Parnel awaited!

The converter was fixed, at least. A moment later, The Magnean plotted his course to the Rimm and its Walkers.

The thunderhead opened.

The Captain turned, "Charge!" He gave the single word in a hoarse whisper, his eyes tearing.

Lowering his saber toward AF6 yet far below. He led them from the thunderous, dark cell.

The sergeant turned to them, growling through his gritted, stained teeth.

The Sandriders charged.

Sredirs snorted pressing forward. Sandriders' lances leveled, all coursing down toward The Ords, its red sands and blowing dust, they broke the dark cloud. The Sandriders charged. The weather cell, huge and very dark, roiled around them. They moved closer toward the ground, wheeling around in the sky.

Ascending, that slim line, followed the regimental colors, a sad, tattered display of wind-blown rags – of a certain old gallantry. From below, Thee Starr's Sandrock emerged, an unseen carpet for forgotten heroes, old protectors of a forgotten place or thing long past.

At Last, they swept forward, steeply, nearly straight down as they burst from the cloud speeding on.

The Sand Rockers gaped, awed, at the coming legend. The Targans of AF6 didn't grasp what came for them, but very soon, **they would.**

The music reached up, pushing them along, a carpet of sound.

Deep thunder ranged all 'round, across The Ords from one side to the other as The Sandriders and their mounts rushed their enemy. Shock waves reached out before them.

The Ords shook as they came.

Heavy guns of the attack force leaned over at them. From the Sandrock concert site The Children of The Heart watched.

The weapons of AF6 spoke out, Targans gazed up disbelieving. They began to know what came as the rumble drew nearer. This thin line from the protectors of a forgotten agency, came on.

Modallas' weapons raged uselessly. But, they could do little more than wait. This was the payment due for a promise, any memory, something forgot, something owed. A pledge made long before, too long ago for memory.

The Sand Rockers, at the concert, The Children of The Heart, gasped, awed, as they looked up at the oncoming legend.

From that first harrowing angle they dropped from the sky, level, to take the ground.

Leading the great noise, finding himself, his sidemen behind him, Thee Starr and company backed them with Sand Rock. Targans began to suspect what came for them.

Pouring from huge concert speakers. Thee Starr and company hovered on a stage of grav-disks above the crowd as the thin line passed by, placing themselves between them and AF6. Starr's voice echoed through The Ords.

They slammed into the wall of Modallas' weapons. Rubble heaped as the armored force was reduced and destroyed. Then, more rubble, more smoke, and more flame. Nothing stopped them.

The method was antique and obsolete, but it was theirs. They defeated the heavy weapons of AF6 – nothing would stop them.

Across from the empty copilot's seat, Borter spoke to himself. He breathed out heavily, his sigh an echo of the despair felt within. There was a trickle of light as he leaned back.

The space flashed. The shape of a Marcellean in battle armor took its place quickly. D5 nuzzled the side of his face. Borter tried to push the beast away, but the Marcellean spoke. "It's hopeless – he likes you."

Rand Sabbling laughed. "I am," he nodded politely, still dead and here to help!

Sabbling pointed to the place, a distant place, in The Ords. Borter looked briefly and saw nothing. Checking the ship's sensors revealed nothing. "You mean in Modallas? My sensors – are not –"

"I know," Sabbling confirmed broadly, smiling. Your sensors will be working—in a moment. This will help!" He drew the Snow Beggar's ion blade and pushed it into the console slot that had been so mysterious.

As promised, the proper light went on, and the ship's sensors worked again.

"There! Just beyond the dunes."

Borter refined his course. He saw nothing.

"Get in as low as you can," Sabbling urged.

"As low –" Borter noted, his ship was nearly in the sand, etching that ragged edge of The Ords, "as I can?"

Sabbling smiled again, "Well, as low as you can without getting us killed!"

Soarer came in lower as ordered. Borter swept the dune's ridge. Close.

Just beyond, something there came into view. A red arrow revealed itself, pointing toward cliffs, far distant, that marked the ragged edge of The Ords, the sand's end. The arrow seemed to ruffle, to move. At its tip – stood someone blue.

Soarer came in lower.

"Sure. What do you care? You're already dead—" Borter murmured.

5D returned again, in a flash of light, licking the pilot's face. He took Sabbling away, the Marcellean having done his job.

Soarer came on. 5D flashed away another time.

The faces of many, many red clones, looked skyward. Their leader, who was blue, not red, looked up, pointing, as well.

"Stop that," the pilot growled. He blinked at a 5D flash.

Another passenger, his vision coming back, found was planted in the co-pilot's chair. He recognized Helio. He muttered. "One out, one in! – what can I say?"

5D drooled at his shoulder, leaning once again through the bulkhead.

The Dillisome, as surprised as Borter, examined his clothing. In place of a clone's red robe, he wore a flyer's casual garb. I'm getting tired of that," he muttered.

"Nope. What makes you think I'm dead?" Helio asked, raising an eyebrow.

It, in fact, was his own – clothing.

'Not you – Sabbling!"

The pilot gazed at him.

"I'll let you know later - if we have a later." They traveled on toward the cliffs. "I like what you've done with the place!" Smiling from the copilot's seat, his place, Helio sat, his old self.

"It's," Borter shrugged, "been a long day!"

Helio gestured toward the windshield.

"That way, that column of smoke over there!"

"Got it."

Distant fire reached for them, aching for them, as they came down a little more, then more.

"Sir," a Modallas tech advised the new mark below their orbit. They are in the air, moving toward the attack force!"

Lances set, speeding toward the Modallians before them, cheered on from a distance by Sandrock and the Children of The Heart. The rolling tattoo of hooves reached the Modallian line with them as they reached the Modallian lines. Sand Rock blared.

The Helmsman turned and walked out. On the ground, gun turrets raged at their new targets.

"The other mark:" The next warning came to him—he did not stop or turn, going directly to the transporter. It blinked, and he was gone. " The freighter had returned."

"I –" The Helmsman spoke words barely above a whisper, tensely, to himself. He reached the transporter.

Sand Rock rivaled the sound of destruction in volume.

Leaving only destruction. Smashed war machinery, burned, wrecked, only a moment before firing at them, was ranged everywhere, nothing left. Just reaching the front lines, a moment later, Modallas' master found himself at the center of his biggest guns.

The thunder was all around. The Helmsman of Modallas watched grimly as the legend materialized around him.

In their turn, the Targans gave their all. The Sandriders left their armor shattered and went on. Finally, there was nothing left.

Noise and the receding backsides of Sredirs and their riders were all that could be seen or heard. He pushed through the burning mass. His dark armor cheated their formidable lances into a final victory. Destruction lay everywhere, smoking debris of battle still raging on the field elsewhere. His Targan troopers were gone.

Only that one was left in the wreckage. As they were away, another second player announced himself; the predicted red streak appeared on the far cliffs.

As quickly as they had come, Sandriders, their work done, climbed back to the sky and were gone – . Agog still, the Sand Rockers looked on after them.

Epilogue

"It's legend time! You have your target!"

"We have a target. Do we have a weapon?"

Nearby, Borter glanced at the scene. "Uh – " Helio tugged at his sleeve, pointing out of the cockpit, "Don't forget the cliffs!"

The Magnean turned, lowering Soarer's shields. "Right! – Close – Too low!"

Soarer neared the great plume of smoke. "Nothing left," Borter said.

"What happened to Legend Time?" Helio asked.

"I think that went with Sabbling!" Borter said.

"You mean the Marcellean from the bar? He was here?"

"Yeah."

Just like the old man himself, Old Face's engines complained of their inertial load as Soarer turned toward the battlefield, but they served. Only The Helmsman was between Soarer and the concert beyond.

Helio mused, looking at the blade in the console.

"Sabbling left it?"

"I wonder where he got a blade like that?"

Soarer was suddenly quieter as Borter made the turn, shields below, on full. In the distance, the Sand Rockers looked on. Thee Starr framed the moment in sound.

Borter angled into the turn, sliding sideways, nose down, toward the sands of The Ords, nearly flat on the cliffs.

The Children of The Heart, again, over-awed, looked up at their legend.

Picking up a circuit board from the deck, Helio announced, "I think this is where our navigation went!"

"Remind me to thank Old Face –"

Pulling himself from beneath a pile of rubble, he had little time to grasp his settings, in the debris of a battle already lost, surrounded by wreckage and flames.

Modallian armor lay in shattered bits scattered all around, from burning vehicles, their fuel, and explosives spread out on the sand.

The toll is taken among the Targan. The Sandriders missed nothing.

"Sir. That mark – coming at you from the cliffs!" The familiar voice of Modallas Control rang in his ears. The Helmsman reached into the debris, pulling something out, a thing – hot, but not destroyed, something that would let him make a fight of it.

Pulsar fire slapped the air around Soarer, tearing at the shields, the freighter descended into The Wastes. Something, someone, in all that wreckage was still alive and angry.

Helio gestured toward the windshield.

'Well, let's get on – that way, that column of smoke over there!"

"Got it."

"That was kind of close!" Helio noted as he settled into his old job.

Borter shrugged. "He's out there!"

"You're part of the legend is out there, at least," Helio looked into his console viewer.

"Look!" Borter urged. "Your, uh - adventure with the shields has turned the cliffs red – as foretold. We're heroes – us – we're legend."

The pilot turned the freighter away from the glowing cliff face.

"I'm not sure I want to be getting used to that sort of thing," Helio muttered in half a voice.

The Magnean flew almost sideways as he turned in a sharp bank to align himself with The Helmsman. Soarer flattened out, seeming to drift to one side, just far enough, and came on.

Helio glanced at his restored instruments. "I have a contact a few seconds ahead," he said evenly.

He got up a little in his seat, peering out the cockpit windshield.

"Nothing visual," he said matter–of–factly.

Pulsar fire reached out for them. Soarer rocked only a little with the blasts.

Weapons, lowered from wing pods, returned fire.

"It looks like we took a hit," he said looking at his screens. A thin stream of smoke trailed from one of Soarer's engines. "Not too bad."

Thee Starr watched from a distance. Continuing to pour forth, his Sandrock gave voice to the story unfolding in the near distance.

They watched, they sang Thee Starr's song, and they danced on The Ords' sands.

A pulse cannon, aiming it at the coming freighter, he fired shot after shot. Soarer's own guns fired back.

The ground erupted beneath him, around him and he was gone. As he went, he glimpsed Old Face's graffiti on Soarer's hull – I 'Heart' Sandrock.

Passing over the concert site, the graffiti drew bigger cheers, even than Thee Starr himself.

I Heart SandRock! As the words came up on his screen, Borter muttered again, "Remind me to speak to Old Face about that!"

"The shield or the graffiti?"

"Both!"

Soarer's pilots urged the little ship further into the sky, as both wanted a bigger piece of The Helmsman and his cylinder world. Ghost Pilot, the legend, disappeared upward toward the darkness of space, spinning off a victory roll, a last salute to those on the planet, a thin curl of contrail trailed one engine.

"Gallantry?" Helio whispered to him as if there were others who might hear, "What have we come to, Borter?" He smiled – just in time.

9 781966 565017